NEW BEGINNINGS

An Amish Romance

Seekers
Book One

Linda Byler

New York, New York

The characters and events in this book are the creation of the author, and any resemblance to actual persons or events is coincidental.

NEW BEGINNINGS

Good Books books may be purchased in bulk at special discounts for sales promotion, corporate gifts, fund-raising, or educational purposes. Special editions can also be created to specifications. For details, contact the Special Sales Department, Good Books, 307 West 36th Street, 11th Floor, New York, NY 10018 or info@skyhorsepublishing.com.

Good Books is an imprint of Skyhorse Publishing, Inc.®, a Delaware corporation.

Visit our website at www.goodbooks.com.

10 9 8 7 6 5 4 3 2 1

Library of Congress Cataloging-in-Publication Data is available on file.

Print ISBN: 978-1-964219-00-4
eBook ISBN: 978-1-964219-23-3

Cover design by Godfredson Design

Printed in the United States of America

"Displaying a bland, even an eerie, disregard for what appeared to be the facts of the situation, he fell back on an old habit of looking ahead to the next defeat."

—Loudon Wainwright III

Chapter 1

Amos was born the second child in a family of five, including his parents. From his first memories, an air of defeat had him in its questioning grip.

Some stray gene of his father, or his mother, had not been kind as far as physical beauty was concerned. He was large. Large and pudgy, his head solidly on his shoulders with the seeming absence of a neck. His eyes were small and too close together, his nose like a misshapen potato. His small mouth appeared to be no more than an odd pucker slashed into round red cheeks, and his thick dry hair was the color of dirt.

He had an older sister and one younger, both of whom were just as lovely to look at as Amos was unattractive. The two girls were often the object of loving looks from their adoring mother's sparkling eyes, whereas Amos more often felt her impatience and dissatisfaction.

Raised in a decrepit town on the far outskirts of an Old Order Amish community in Pennsylvania, he attended a one-room schoolhouse a mile and a half away. He rode his scooter with slow, careful precision, then bent his large face over his workbook. Tears often formed in the corners of his eyes, which he would wipe away with a dirt-encrusted fingernail, sniff, then shift his ungainly body to root in the pocket of his black broadfall trousers for his handkerchief.

"Alright, Amos. How far have we come?"

The presence of a figure beside him, the voice of his teacher appearing like a heavy cloud of doom over his head, and he leaned back, a hand going to his suspenders, worried with frayed edges as he stayed silent.

"Amos, no. That isn't correct. You're reading the numbers backward."

He expected the accompanying expulsion of breath—it was what his failure to succeed did to his mother as well. He figured it was something he was born with, the ability to induce this troubled expression.

So he sat, his head bent, his fingers working at the ruined edges of elastic.

"What are we going to do with you?" the teacher said quietly, as if to herself.

He would need special attention, more time, of which she had none to spare, with fifteen pupils from first to fourth grade.

He recognized the fact he was some sort of burden, a heavy object the teacher could barely lift.

He sat up straighter, sucked in his stomach, as if to lighten his weight, then looked around to see if anyone noticed this maneuver. He was accosted by the sight of glaring classmates, their eyes accusing as he heard the quiet inner voice telling him he was unfit, dumb, should be flunked again, the way he was the previous year.

"Rachel?"

A soft figure stood by his desk, so he slid over and the seventh-grade girl sidled in beside him.

Amos's life, so far, was made up of a house, a barn, parents and two sisters, a yard and garden, the changing of seasons, school, church, a horse and buggy, an occasional ride in a vehicle to buy groceries at Walmart or Rueben Zook's bulk food store. There were Christmas and Easter, with large groups of relatives, which he dreaded.

Raymond and Lydia Beiler had moved to Rochester, Pennsylvania, only three years before. They had found Lancaster County too crowded, too fast-paced, and it was much too hard to keep up with the aspirations of the neighbors, whose businesses flourished, whose homes were added on to, driveways blacktopped, fancy patios put on and where the best grills and outdoor furniture appeared like magic.

Raymond was not envious, never harbored a jealous thought or wished misfortune on his neighbors, but merely needed a less expensive place to live. So he pulled up stakes and moved to the fledgling community of Rochester, in the northern part of the state, where depleted coal mines created bleak landscapes and inexpensive land.

Raymond never imagined himself creating his own business. He was content to ride his old navy blue scooter to the chair shop where he had been employed most of his life, scooter back home on the wide shoulder of the Old Philadelphia Pike, pay his mortgage and his exorbitant amount of real estate taxes, provide food and family necessities, and go to church. He never minded abiding by the bishop's rules and never questioned whether it was fair or unfair. Mostly, he lived his life as a happy man.

His wife, Lydia, however, was not quite suited to flourish in the glow of her husband's contentment. She found it hard to rearrange the cheap patio chairs around the plastic pots of flowers on her front porch, and often cast a longing gaze at the heavy cement urns with cascading ferns on her neighbors' porches. She made do with her husband's paycheck, with his conservative budgeting, but the cost of groceries always sent her stomach plummeting. Things wore out, became shoddy and threadbare, and she tried not to care too much. But it was hard to give up all the pleasant things in life that she longed for.

Last Sunday, church services were held at Mervin Kauffman's, in the perfect stone-fronted shop with floor heat, the interior of which was nicer than Lydia's actual house. Lydia had gone inside the main house to the bathroom and stood in awe of the ceramic tile and glass doors, a potted fig tree, and a luxurious rug and towels, not to mention the huge mirror creating unkind versions of herself.

She looked obese, red-cheeked. Her covering was crooked, her hair matted on one side, her cape fell oddly over one shoulder.

She wet her hands below the faucet, the gold-handled spigot almost too pretty to touch, wet the one thin roll of hair along the side of her head and re-rolled it, opening the gold bobby pin with her teeth.

She turned and left the beauty of the small room, stepped out to find Linda Esh, a slim woman her own age. They exchanged smiles and she made her way to the kitchen, which she'd heard had been recently renovated. She found herself staring at all-white cabinets, granite countertops, brown hardwood floors, the healthiest houseplants she had ever seen. A great stab of envy completely ruined her day.

Nostrils distended slightly, her heartbeat accelerated, she turned to Linda and hissed, "*Dess iss* not even *chide*" ("This isn't even proper"). She didn't care if it sounded mean and spiteful, it was out of the *ordnung* (Amish rules) and it wasn't fair.

Linda only gave a vague acknowledgement of having heard, and Lydia felt condemned, cut loose from the safety of another person's agreement, that shoring up of her own strongholds. She sniffed as she scuttled quickly through the bitter January air to seat herself on the bench beside Becca Stoltzfus, turn to Lavina, and fix the bow tied haphazardly beneath her chin.

Her eyes went to the row of boys, searching for Amos, who was easily spied, his size keeping him apart, an oddity. He was just so big and overweight, his too-thick hair like a lampshade, his face like punched bread dough. She made a mental note to supply him with a small plastic comb to put in his vest pocket, with careful instructions to comb his hair before he went in with the boys. At least that would help a little.

She felt common, never quite able to squelch the desire to be noticed, to be someone deserving of praise and honor. She was often disheartened by the blissful bubble of contentment her husband occupied, sailing through life without the need to better himself. It didn't bother him a bit, sitting in that gorgeous shop with all the latest solar-driven gadgets while they themselves couldn't even host services like most of the others in the district.

And so, with his wife's badgering in his ears, his kindly disposition and compliance to her words, they sold their small property for a good profit in spite of disapproval from both families, who thought a hundred miles was just too far away.

What about Amos's schooling? He had a very good tutor here in Lancaster County, who was more than competent to help that poor child along with his arithmetic.

And Amos grew the sprout of knowledge in his young brain that there was something wrong with him. He couldn't quite keep up with his grade, he'd heard his mother say to a neighbor lady who arched her eyebrows and said it certainly couldn't be because of his size, now could it, and they'd both chuckled.

The chuckle stayed with him the whole way through school. Most of his life, in fact. He knew he didn't quite measure up, and that his mother found it amusing.

There was Cathy, the sister and favored daughter, who was brilliant, an accomplished artist who was allowed to help decorate the blackboard with colored chalk at Christmas. She was the recipient of many colorful dresses, more than one pair of sneakers for school, and a lime green lunch box with the Nike swoosh in black, a fortunate find at a yard sale. Amos had wanted it so badly his stomach ached, but he knew it would go to Cathy. He mentioned it to her, but she waved him away, shrugged, and said he was too little to take care of such a nice lunchbox. Look at his suspenders, she said—the way he picked at them, it was a wonder his pants didn't fall down. They probably would if he weren't so fat.

He guessed maybe he was fat, but his pants weren't too tight, and his three school shirts buttoned okay. He bowed his head to check on his buttons, just to make sure, then went into the kitchen to see if his mother would allow him a snack. A few pretzels would help his hunger, which he hadn't noticed till his sister told him he was fat.

"Mam, I'm hungry. Is there anything to eat?" he asked, pulling out a chair, filling the seat with his short bulk, fiddling with his suspenders.

She was folding clothes, eyeing the thin terrycloth of the blue towel she'd purchased at Dollar General, comparing it to some of the towels in other women's bathrooms, even here in Rochester. The feeling created a certain irritation. Raymond had found a decent job on a construction crew, but it still irked her that he wasn't motivated to push himself to make more money for the family. He had the skills to start his own business, but just didn't seem to feel the drive to do so.

"No, Amos," she snapped, folding the towel in half, then in thirds and throwing it on the pile of discolored, aging ones. "Wait till supper."

"But I'm hungry."

"What did I just say?"

She couldn't tell him the sight of his pudgy body only increased the irritation she felt at the threadbare towels, so she turned her back and grabbed another one. When she looked again, she saw him walk away, his shoulders slumped in defeat, his trousers stuck horrendously between two shifting buttocks.

"Amos, fix *die hussa*!" she yelled after him.

In answer, he lifted one heavy leg and plucked at his backside, before going out on the porch and flopping on a chair with his legs stuck out in front of him like sausages.

THEY LIVED ON the outskirts of the aging town, which had been a booming center of businesses and homes in the sixties when coal was a lucrative endeavor, miners and heavy equipment operators getting good paychecks and providing well for their families. Fifty years later, there were ravaged hillsides, strip-mined and destroyed, patches of scrub and small trees undaunted by harsh conditions.

Old houses stood side by side like elderly couples, window trims loosened, paint peeling, shingles on roofs held by crumbling rusted nails and good fortune. The railings on most porches looked like a mouthful of missing teeth, the ones remaining bent and twisted by a merciless sun blistering the paint, wet snows rotting them away year after year. Sidewalks heaved with frost and tree roots, weeds sprouting like missed shaving spots on an old man's face.

A few houses had stayed in the family, younger generations staying to work at Walmart or the CVS drugstore. There was the propane company at the edge of town, where Route 15 merged with 347, and various heating and cooling businesses and electricians.

Then the Amish began to move in, buying up the aging properties, briskly renovating, restoring, or slapping up buildings in no time, as the locals remarked.

They'd been met with welcoming smiles, for the most part, but there were those who only knew the dark stories they saw in the news and thought all Amish avoided taxes and doctors and abused their children and animals. Thus, sometimes they were met with unkind, suspicious glares. But as the years went by, the Amish were accepted, and even made friends.

Raymond and Lydia's property was actually in the borough of Rochester, an old wooden-siding house on the south side of town, set on a hillside, flanked by a car wash a hundred yards to the east, and a crumbling brick building that used to be a hide and tannery years ago on the left.

They had over two acres, plenty of pine, oak, and maple trees, a small barn, and with money left over from their property in Lancaster, they could afford a new shop and garage combination. Lydia felt proud to be able to host church services for the first time in her life.

They had made a frolic (work party) for the community, on a Saturday in November, and put new white siding on the house, painted the metal shutters a new coat of black, put on a new roof, and felt as if they were blessed to lie in this stately house on the side of the hill, with the winding drive and the new shop built halfway to the barn. Lydia was delighted with the result, her need for beauty more than fulfilled, finally realizing they had a rightful place of honor in the Rochester community. She would do her best to make it the home she had always dreamed of.

When the three children were all in school and she realized another child had not been conceived, she put an ad in the local paper looking for housecleaning jobs, and soon began receiving messages on her phone.

Raymond's face fell when she told him what she'd done, his wife's discontent like a pinprick in his bubble of happiness.

"It's okay, Lydia, but it makes me sad you think you have to do this. Aren't my wages enough? I thought Lester paid me well."

"Raymond, I'm sorry, but have you tried buying groceries lately?"

He admitted he had not.

"And there are other things I want. Things most other women have."

"Like what?" He glanced at her from the mirror in the laundry room, where he washed his hands and combed his hair.

"Stuff. Nice flowerpots, wooden rocking chairs for the front porch. Maybe some new towels. Rugs, curtains. Stuff like that."

"I see," he said mildly.

"And the teacher sent a note home from school. Amos can't keep up, which means he'll flunk again or else we have to pay a tutor."

"Can't you help him?"

Raymond turned from the mirror, his hair combed, hands and face washed, and Lydia felt the old love for her husband welling up inside. He was a good man, in spite of being content to a fault, to her way of thinking.

"I could, except I know I don't have patience with him. He's so slow-witted, so clumsy with his lessons, and it gets to be frustrating."

Lydia turned to the stove, stirred the gravy, before catching sight of Amos coming out of the pantry, a chocolate chip cookie being inserted into his small mouth.

"Amos!" Her voice shrill, penetrating, she berated her son, the irritation directed at his small eyes and tight shirt, his coarse, thick hair and slow wits.

"Put it away. Put that cookie away right now."

"But I already bit into it."

"Put it away."

Raymond reached out a hand. "Here. Put it beside your plate, then you can eat it later, for dessert."

He felt a certain need to protect, a pity for his overweight son, but knew he could not go against his wife's wishes. What was the old saying?

"Children go wrong when parents aren't in agreement." It seemed best to let Lydia deal with him, harsh as she might be at times. He felt best if he didn't make a ripple on the smooth surface of his well-being, and so decided his main role was to keep the peace.

He watched Amos slide the cookie beside his plate, then take his place on the bench, grunting as one leg went up and over.

"How was school?"

"Good." He averted his eyes, blinked.

"Could you do your arithmetic?"

Amos nodded, then said quietly, "Not all of it."

"Did you bring it home?"

"No."

"Amos, did I hear you say you didn't finish your arithmetic?" His mother's loud voice made him feel the need to hide, to withdraw. He avoided her eyes, knowing they'd only intensify his feeling of shame, the ever-increasing knowledge he wasn't worth much, not nearly as much as Cathy or Lavina.

By the time he was halfway through school, he weighed as much as most of the upper grade boys, or more. Nicknames were hurled, some to be humorous, some out of spite, but every one like a dagger. Piggly, Lardbucket, Roly Poly, and so on, the children sometimes cruel and taunting as they will often be. He laughed with them to make it seem like he didn't care, picked at frayed suspenders, and chewed at too-short fingernails.

The air turned cold in October; a blast of frigid air pushed prematurely down across Canada and into the New England states, bringing snow and pellets of ice to shred the flamboyant hues of a Vermont autumn. In northern Pennsylvania, it caught a horde of Amish school children on their scooters, fluorescent vests blinding in the sun, the light jackets and sweaters letting the sudden cold air through like a sieve.

Bending their heads, tensing muscles, they placed the right foot down, the left one proper on the scooter, and pushed as fast as possible, the competition causing them to forget Amos who lagged behind. He smashed his torn straw hat on his mop of brown hair and put all his strength into pushing, but still the other children quickly disappeared out of sight. He gave up, slowed, and walked up the hill, his face streaming, the color elevated to a deep purplish hue, his breath coming in embarrassing bursts, his shoulders rounded in what had become his usual posture of defeat.

He walked slowly, to catch his breath, stepped off the shoulder of the road to allow a car to pass. The wind roared through the treetops, ripping colorful leaves, bending dry brown grass in its wake. A plastic bag skittered across the road before getting hung up on a milkweed plant.

A car stopped on the opposite side of the road and the driver leaned out of the window. Amos was slow to respond, the sight of the milkweed plant taking his mind to an article he'd read in *National Geographic.*

"Hello there, son."

The stranger was middle-aged, with a normal face, short hair, and a clean bill cap. A friendly face, a rather nice smile.

Amos stopped his scooter, lifted his hat before settling it back. He said nothing, afraid of saying the improper thing.

"Your buddies are way up the road. You want me to take you to catch up with them?"

His mother told him never to talk to strangers, so he thought he should say no, although it was tempting.

He shook his head.

"Come on. Get in. You'll be late."

Amos stood like a stump, and shook his head. "No."

"I won't hurt you—I'm not a stranger. I own the car wash beside your house. I'm actually your neighbor."

"What would I do with my scooter?" he asked.

"Put it in the trunk."

Slowly, his mind recalled stories he'd heard about unsafe men prowling around and decided to be resolute with his decision.

"I'll walk."

"A'right. Catch you around."

Amos nodded, settled his hat back on his head, and pushed off.

The wind in his face almost took his breath way, and by the time he reached the schoolyard he was soaked in perspiration, the bell ringing out its deep cast iron clang.

Cathy glared at him. "Where were you?"

"Behind you. It was windy."

She snorted with distaste. "You're sweating. Go wash your face before you come in."

He did as he was told, then slid into his desk, his bangs dripping water. He shifted his weight, grasped the wrinkled handkerchief, and swiped at the droplets of water before turning to smile at his classmate, Bennie. Eli Beiler's Bennie, a tall, thin child with a smattering of freckles, snaggle-toothed, and curly haired, the only person in his life who did not call him names.

Bennie did not smile back, but when Amos looked a bit longer, he lifted one eyebrow and the corners of his mouth twitched, which was a smile, really, and Amos was overjoyed inside, as if a flower had opened to the warmth of the sun. He did not know yet that he was starved for love, shriveled up inside for lack of it. All he knew was the slightest acceptance sent out a shower of elation, as if his mother allowed him all the chocolate chip cookies he could eat.

But at recess, Bennie wrinkled his nose when he came close, saying, "You stink."

Amos blinked, tugged at his suspenders.

"Why do I?" he asked, truly wanting to know.

"Go ask your mother."

"I will," Amos said agreeably.

And he did, which was like opening a can of writhing, disgusting worms.

"What? Who told you? Well, you're so heavy, you sweat twice what others do, so you'll have to start using antiperspirant. Most kids don't need it until they're older, but I guess we'll have to buy you some." She sighed, and Amos felt like apologizing, but he wasn't even sure what for. For being himself, he guessed.

He felt like a bucket of lard every morning when he applied the deodorant. He knew he was disgusting, and hid the plastic container in his dresser drawer beneath his boxer shorts. If it kept him from having a bad smell, he would use it, and he felt a quick, unreasonable appreciation of his mother. She was a bit hard in her opinion of him, but she was, after all, his mother, and he loved her. He cared about her, he really did. She worked hard to provide things like deodorant and school pens—she had even gotten him colorful gel pens—and nice erasers in the form of bucking broncos or grizzly bears.

And although his life was bearable, he felt the increasing slide into a solitary existence, his weak father taking to the combative views of his wife, saying nothing when her words bit into Amos, ripping and tearing at his vulnerable self-worth.

In eighth grade he sprouted big pimples with yellow centers, which added to the ridicule, the girls offering pins from their aprons, the boys chanting in unison to pop the pimples. He slunk away, went to the boys' privy, and stayed dry-eyed, but hurt terribly inside, a clawing, inflamed wound that never closed. Sometimes he felt in awe of the cruelty of human nature, the flaming arrows of conceived and hurled accusations. Often, he simply stood against the board fence with one heel propped on the lower rung, squinted at the sun, and felt as big as a dinosaur. A monster with horrible growths on his face, a putrid smell emanating from him like smoke from a chimney.

He watched the girls flitting from base to base, their dresses like attractive flowers, and tried to imagine himself to be tall, thin, without pimples, before reality sent him headlong in to the tunnel of despair.

He developed a love of jigsaw puzzles, sitting for hours contemplating pieces snapped into others. He sat hunched in his folding chair by the woodstove, the puzzle forming on the card table, humming low under his breath, hymns and tunes he made up in his head, the longing he felt in the depth of his spirit.

His mother urged him to exercise, bought him weights with her housecleaning money. His father asked him to get a job, earn some money. Cathy told him he was lazy, a Mama baby, sitting in the house by the fire like an old lady.

"Get a life," she said.

And gradually, he learned to hate, an emotion he could physically feel. It was real, clear, and bright, and crowded out the deflating sense of self-loathing he couldn't otherwise seem to escape.

CHAPTER 2

EIGHTH GRADE PASSED IN A BLUR OF DISAPPOINTMENT. HE GOT through the Christmas program, a head taller and a hundred pounds heavier than any of the other children, his shock of stiff, heavy hair giving him the appearance of an angry grizzly.

And he really was angry. He was embittered, often filled with rage, lashing out silently at the immense circle of unfairness surrounding him. He'd been overweight since birth, which wasn't his fault. He was born three weeks overdue and gigantic, already a clumsy walrus. He'd heard his mother's account of his birth, the size of him, the pain he had caused. Laughing, he'd heard her tell her friends no, she had no idea where he got the size or the dyslexia. He'd looked up the word, and thus learned that he had a disability, which wasn't his fault either. Just another injustice. He graduated from parochial school with a C average and did not have to attend vocational class at all, having flunked a grade, and very nearly another one.

How often had he cried silently, his stomach knotted as he desperately retained tears, his workbook lying open, the problems insurmountable? Defeat was the mechanism by which he moved through life, his sister Cathy ashamed of the fact he was her brother.

Sometimes, Lavina was nice when they weren't in school. She would kneel on a folding chair, lean on her elbows, and peer through her heavy glasses as she searched for pieces of his puzzle. Sometimes they would even high-five, their hands slapping together like true buddies, and the smile in his heart stayed for weeks.

Lavina did not think him loathsome the way Cathy did. By the time he was fifteen, his face resembled a plowed field, furrowed and crosshatched with acne. He begged his mother for help, but she told him it was from all the toxins built up in his system from overeating. She gave him literature about the sin of gluttony.

He felt his father's pitying gaze, his mother's shame. And now he was stuck in Rochester, finished with his parochial education and nowhere to go.

"Get a job," they said. "Go out and get a job."

Ashamed to face the world, he asked his father to get him a job at the company he worked for, but his father said there was no way he'd get hired at his size. Too bulky, ungainly.

He was turned away at the hardware store. They said they prioritized candidates who had a high school diploma or GED. The local feed mill wasn't hiring, but said to check back in six months. He asked Abner Lantze about a job at his woodworking shop but was told he'd need some experience first.

Amos washed his face with peroxide water, with vinegar, castile soap. He finally convinced his mom to buy an over-the-counter remedy for acne, saying it might help him get a job, but it didn't make any difference.

Sixteen was like a rite of passage into the world of friends and social gatherings. It was when you got your own horse and buggy and decked it out to impress the girls. But Amos had no desire to be thrust into more painful situations, so when his mother began to complain about the price of a new buggy, and him without a job, he told her firmly, in his new, low man's voice, that it wasn't a problem, he had no intention of running around with the youth. Not now, not ever.

Thus began his mother's whining tirade about the importance of joining the youth. What else was he going to do with his time? If he didn't run around, he'd have to do something, and often this would lead to running with the town boys, in which case he'd be led into every vice in the book. "The works of the devil," she said.

His father's rumbling voice came from the chair. "Get a job, Amos. Get a job. If you work, the rest will follow."

One night, in a frenzy of wretchedness, he left the house and walked alone toward town, with no plan and no goal. He walked aimlessly past the propane gas company, the Shell station, past a row of houses gamely supporting each other, like a line of friends. The air was warm and the scent of the winding creek came from the right side of Route 15. He drew the tips of his fingers across the ridges of his cheeks, brushed the hair away from his forehead to allow the sweet night air to circulate along the surface of his inflamed face. He felt at his lowest point with nowhere to turn—not to his parents, certainly not his sisters. Bennie had been the closest thing to a real friend he would ever have, but he had gone to join all the social gatherings of the youth without him, without extending as much as an invitation.

He heard the sound of pulsing music coming from behind a high board fence, followed by a warm, spicy, garlicky odor. There was laughter, the low rippling of a man, followed by the high-pitched shriek of a girl. The pleasures of life on a warm summer evening seemed as far from him as the planets spinning in outer space, unattainable by every wild leap of the imagination.

His fingertips explored the deep fissures of his face, and he knew he was monstrous. Even in church, where everyone was at their Sunday best, there were quick glances, almost frightened expressions, before features were folded into a neutral expression. He always lumbered in with his head bent, his gaze to the floor, and was seated on the bench a head taller and so much wider, dwarfing the boys beside him.

He never felt a part of the Amish church, never felt a sense of belonging. He shivered with fear at the thought of hell, sin's consequences, but didn't really grasp Jesus's place in it all. His parents never read their Bible, at least they didn't when he was around. They never prayed together, either, and his mother never taught them the German children's prayer his classmates talked about.

If he prayed, it was generally short and meaningless, though he sometimes begged for his sins to be forgiven from time to time to avoid provoking the big, white-clad Ruler on his throne in the sky.

It was all so distant, so wrapped in mystery. He imagined his parents did read their Bible occasionally, else it wouldn't be sitting there on the small table by their recliners. He saw his father reading the daily paper and *Game News*, the *Busy Beaver* and *Reader's Digest*. His mother's *Good Housekeeping* and *Better Homes & Gardens* were glossy subscriptions she received in the mail every month, a respite from the plain world in which she lived.

With the ongoing work of housecleaning "*fa Englishy liet*" ("for English people"), she grew even more discontented with the furniture in her own house, the pictures and vases and baskets. The beauty she encountered at well-to-do homes did not go unnoticed, but created a restless need to acquire things. Things that spoke to her of class and beauty, of setting her apart from—or at least keeping up with—her contemporaries.

She was often tired, harried to the point of snapping at Raymond or the children, and potato soup with grilled cheese sandwiches were served once a week, sometimes twice.

Slowly, nice things were placed here and there. A pillow, a plaid throw, a basket of strange greenery. There were new rugs and fresh paint, a new set of dishes in the cabinets. Mealtimes were infused with discussions of dollars, how much was a fair wage, how much cleaning was expected of her when she felt she already went above and beyond basic requirements.

And Raymond, always supportive, would nod his head, smile, speak gentle words of caring, saying she worked too hard.

THAT SPRING Amos was approached by the owner of the bulk food store, asking if he'd consider helping him load and unload trucks, then help out building the new warehouse. Rueben was a fair man, endowed with Christian love, and often felt pity for the ungainly Amos in church.

Rueben scuffed at loose gravel, watched Amos's face, and waited for an answer. When it came, he could hardly believe his ears.

"I would take the job, but I'm not fit."

"Who told you that?"

"No one. I'm big, but not that strong."

"Well, Amos, a good way to get strong is to start lifting fifty-pound bags of flour and sugar."

A hand to his face, Amos said he'd have to stay in the back where no one could see him, with his face the way it was.

Rueben shrugged. "Don't worry about it."

He went to his first day of work with his mother's approval and his father's best wishes. He carried a new blue-and-white Rubbermaid lunchbox packed with his favorite sandwiches, his fear of being a failure churning in his stomach.

He was given the job of rearranging, cleaning, and organizing the back area, catching mice, watching for cockroaches, washing windows, and sweeping the accumulation of dust and dirt every week. Four girls worked out front in the actual store, and Rueben's wife was often helping as well.

The third day, while sweeping, he accidentally kicked a fifty-pound bag of sugar, creating a small rip in the side, the fine white granules seeping through the paper in a thin stream, settling on the floor in small pyramids. Sweat broke out on his upper lip, his armpits tingling with fear and defeat. Rueben would fire him. His mind raced for a solution. His eyes darted around the room, searching for tape, anything to repair the bag. A mouse darted along the wall, and his heart plummeted, knowing any sugar that seeped into the floor cracks would only attract more mice.

He had to find tape. Had to go through that door and ask for it. He swallowed, found the hidden reserve of willpower to push it open.

Four pairs of eyes accosted him, then turned away.

"Uh, is there . . . does anyone know where I . . . uh . . . I need tape."

Clumsy, couldn't get the right words out, he thought.

One of them, he had no idea who she was, asked if he slit a bag, and he nodded, miserable.

"It happens. Here, I'll go with you. We'll load them upside down on the lift and bag the sugar right away. Or was it flour?"

She smiled at him, and he turned away.

Three fifty-pound bags were loaded easily enough, and she said he was strong, that he made it look effortless. He didn't know what to say, so he said nothing.

Alone at lunchtime, he washed his hands, arranged a few bags of flour into seating space, and opened his lunch. He looked around, afraid of being seen. If someone spied him, they'd tell the remaining workers how gross he was, sitting on those flour bags. He stuffed the first sandwich in his mouth as fast as possible, then quickly grabbed the second. He was ready to take the first bite when the door was flung open and a girlish voice called back, "I'll get it."

At the sight of him, she recoiled, lifted both hands, and said, "Oh, you scared me. I didn't know anyone was back here."

She came closer, peered at his face.

"Boy, do you ever have a case of acne. You know what? I bet your mother doesn't believe in antibiotics, right?"

Too miserable to open his mouth, he shrugged, willing her to go away, his eyes rooted to the toe of his huge brown work shoes.

"Can't you talk?"

He nodded, felt the anger well up inside.

"Well, your face is bad. Really bad. It's infected. You need to see a doctor. You know you can get clear skin, don't you?"

He shook his head.

"I'm Katie. Katie Fisher. My dad is a brother to Rueben, so I'm his niece. Who are you?"

For a few seconds he considered telling her it was none of her business and to bug off, leave him alone. He had no idea what she looked like, except for the appearance of a black pair of sneakers.

He lifted his face so that his gaze might have been level with her knees, but shifted his focus on the stack of Honeycomb cereal behind her.

"I'm Amos Beiler. Raymond Beiler's Amos."

"Nice to meet you, Amos."

"Mm hmm." He could not get out the proper words, the way everything bunched up in his throat and wouldn't go up or down.

"Which group of youth do you belong to?"

"I don't, uh . . . go."

"You mean you don't run around?"

"No."

"Why?"

He shrugged, felt the cloying defeat like a second skin.

"Probably your face, right?"

"I guess."

Her name was being called in strident tones, so she wiggled her fingers in his direction, said, "See ya."

He watched her go, but later could only remember a blue dress with a black bib apron, the white covering on her head.

He lifted his sandwich and began to eat.

To APPROACH HIS mother about seeing a doctor was more than he could manage on his own. She was strong in all of her opinions, but especially where medical doctors were concerned. He knew she wouldn't even discuss it. Doctors were worse than useless in her mind. Heaven forbid if she herself needed to be hospitalized someday.

Amos spoke to his father instead, stumbling over his wish to seek treatment for his face. For long moments, his father said nothing, then slowly shook his head.

"Amos, I would love to see your face cleared up. But your mother . . ." He looked into Amos's eyes.

"Aren't you supposed to be the head of the house, Dat?"

From anyone else, this question might have sounded like a challenge, but Amos was innocently asking the question he'd always wondered about, why the household was run by his mother. There was not a trace of disrespect in his voice—only a quiet desperation that made his father pause and think.

"I am, I suppose. But I married a strong woman, and everything goes much smoother if I allow her . . . well, she doesn't lead exactly, but I think you know what I'm talking about."

Amos nodded.

"You see, I do love your mother. A lot. She is the light of my life. And I know she feels the same about me. That's more than many men can say. She's a good manager, so does it really matter if she goes ahead with decisions? Not for me, no it doesn't. But look. I'll see if I can get her to agree about seeing a doctor."

As he pushed past Amos, he patted his shoulder, sort of a gentle squeeze, a slight touch of affection that stayed with Amos for days. His father had actually touched him with real kindness, real caring. There was a spring in his step as he left the barn.

His mother was cooking supper when he let himself in, her wide hips covering most of the stove front. But a warm, spicy scent wafted from steaming kettles, the rich smell of frying meat. Cathy was setting the table, Lavina was putting ice in water glasses, and Amos felt a wave of contentment, if only for a fleeting moment.

"Amos, how did it go?" she asked, turning but keeping a hand on the wooden spoon, stirring with swift efficiency.

"Okay."

How could he tell her about his clumsiness, the leaking bag of sugar, his own failure to perform the easiest task?

"Do they like you?"

"I guess."

She was satisfied, even a little pleased. Amos had finally acquired a paying occupation, which meant she had done a good job raising her son. If he learned to work, made his own way in the world, the rest would follow seamlessly. Some homely forgotten girl would be happy to accept his overtures, and in due time he would be married with a home of his own, present her with grandchildren, and become an upstanding Amish husband and father. He was far too dull to be anything else.

The ruptured face would have its purpose in her life, so she had come to count it as a blessing. At least he wasn't out and about with the wild ones, driving a car and cutting his hair in the English style the way Ike Stoltzfus's boys did. Shameful the way they carried on.

Cathy was far too engrossed in her own life to ask about Amos's new job. She kept up a lively account of her weekend, telling them about the place where the youths' supper had been the night before and who was there, giggling about the guys who'd given her attention. With a wave of her hand, she informed her mother airily about each one, the sheep's eyes with which they confronted her, blushing, to relate some bumbling story without substance.

Cathy was growing into her beauty, all her features symmetrical, the heavy waves of shining hair arranged in the latest fashion, the tiny heart-shaped covering all but sliding off her head. Her clothes were sewn with style in mind, her mother copying the "cool" girls' way of creating tight sleeves, the hem of her dress only a few inches above the floor, her black apron belt the widest of them all. A natural leader, Cathy was confident, aware of her own impact on those around her, absorbing admiring glances, walking into a room as if she owned it.

And her mother listened to her stories with glittering eyes, pride heaped on pride, fully aware of having come to the pinnacle of long-sought-after popularity. Finally, she did not have to feel as if she were way behind her peers, having produced this gorgeous child who would always make her way in any crowd. The epitome of attainment, the light of her life.

Cathy made her very happy, that was simply the truth. She was everything she herself had always wanted to be, blossoming like a rare lotus among drab flowers, the girl all the boys wanted.

And so she listened with rapt attention to the exciting encounters with boys, the dates she accepted, the horses and volleyball games, restaurants and quiet conversation. Inevitably, Cathy broke up with Jason or Samuel or Mark, shrugging her shoulders and tossing her head, saying he was dull, or wore ill-fitting clothes, or drove her crazy with his undying devotion, his smarmy ways.

At eighteen years of age, Cathy was still single, but that fact didn't bother her at all, knowing she could have any guy she wanted. They just weren't her type.

And oh, how her mother's heart thrilled, although she would bow her head in mock humility at quiltings and coffee klatches, saying how she had her hands full with Cathy, the way she was inclined to comb her hair in the latest style, not listening to her voice at all.

When Lydia had started running around, at the end of the nineties, she hadn't come from much, never felt the ease and confidence of her own daughter. Her parents scrambled to make a decent living on the farm below Nine Points in Lancaster County, the outbuildings leaning wearily on their foundations, the steel barn roof showing streaks of rust. Sliding doors flopped on aging hinges and fences sagged, barely keeping old mules and tied horses in the allotted pasture.

Lydia's father, Abner, walked slowly, living in a world of good will toward everyone, humans and animals alike. No matter if the cows weren't top producers, the milk check still paid the bills, so that was enough. He wasn't interested in the latest methods of dairy farming. All that costly fertilizer and new-fangled cow feed just didn't jibe with him.

He watched hawks, was fascinated by the vernal pool down where the low fields converged to a natural pond, the grasses, native shrubs, and trees creating an oasis for wildlife, the waters teeming with amphibians, migrating ducks, and geese. He recognized the slick mudslides of muskrats and would not allow the boys to set traps.

Lydia lived in a constant state of frustration, ashamed to bring her friends to the worn farmhouse. Her mother, Rachel, lived a life of sweet contentment, washing in an old-fashioned *kesslehaus* where her Maytag wringer washer stood on a cement floor, a large cast iron kettle built into a brick encasement with a small door underneath, where split chunks of firewood were burning and crackling, heating the water to do the twice-weekly washing.

She sang German hymns and English ones, praising her Heavenly Father in a clear soprano, her needs few, her life in simple harmony with her kind husband. They raised a family of eleven, with Lydia the only child who chafed at restriction and joined a group of youth unsuited to one of theirs, or so Abner told Rachel, who bit her lower lip and nodded, spending longer time in prayer.

Rachel had no desire to copy the latest style, or to sit in the church and compare her own covering with those of others. She was content to wear whatever she deemed respectful, tied the wide strings beneath her chin, wore plain, dark colors, and felt that rare attachment to peace in her own heart, love for everyone in her circle of life.

Lydia was finally asked by John Beiler's Raymond, who was not the kind of chap they would have chosen for Lydia, the way he cut his hair and had all the fancy rings and attachments to his harness, his horse just a bit too high-spirited. But they placed their trust in God, gave them the blessing, and prepared the wedding feast.

Raymond soon won them all over with his easy nature. At family gatherings it was he who was seated with the old grandfather and his father-in-law, eyes shining with good humor as he related hilarious accounts of his life, the old man guffawing unexpectedly, slapping his knee in delight. Yes, their patience had been well-applied, and for this they were thankful. Lydia often had the pinched look of a truly discontent woman, but then she'd always been like that, really. And Rachel loved her daughter with mercy and grace, was with her when Amos was born, and stayed an extra night for all the poor thing had gone through.

When Amos was a teenager, Lydia's parents became terribly ill with some kind of flu or COVID, the disease all but taking their lives, leaving them in a state of weakness for quite some time. The family pitched in to help out with the cleaning, washing, bringing meals. It was that winter that Lydia brought Cathy to stay for a day, to help wash the walls of their apartment, and the old couple sensed a misalignment, a crack in the foundation of the simple life.

Cathy sniffed at meals and only helped when she wanted to, with Lydia completely oblivious to her disrespect. There was a general air of haughtiness in which Cathy moved, a twist of her hips, a shrug of her shoulders as her mother pointed out a missed spot on the wall.

Patience and love were applied, a dash of grace, and the day went smoothly enough, but Rachel was tight-lipped, anger and concern barely hidden behind her eyes. She confronted Lydia with kindness, but asked if she was aware of Cathy's headstrong nature, and wouldn't it be a help if she was to rein her in a bit?

"Yes, Mam. I agree. But she has many talents and it's so much easier dealing with her than poor Amos. He has such a hard time in school, and his appetite is out of control. The children at school are less than kind, Lavina says. Cathy says it's not bad, and I pity her, having to put up with Amos."

They parted that day with frostiness, a certain cold atmosphere between them, like a dripping icicle causing discomfort on both sides. Rachel sat down a few days later and penned a long letter of warning against favoritism, exhorting Lydia to be kind and understanding with Amos and to hold Cathy to a standard fitting of a girl her age. This created more rebellion in Lydia, who threw the letter into the trash can, covered it with potato peelings, and told herself that her mother had no right to tell her how to parent. No one else could understand how difficult Amos was, what she put up with day after day. How dare her own mother judge her like that?

Chapter 3

Amos went to work every day and slowly learned the art of managing a growing business, the demands of a retailer. He kept quiet, his face averted as much as possible. Fully aware of his ungainliness, he bumbled from the warehouse to the back room, lifted fifty-pound bags of flour and sugar, brown sugar and oatmeal, his mind often dreaming of a better life, a better body and face, a quick, responsive mind, hair staying in place, clear skin.

He dreamed of having Katie Fisher for a special friend and watched for signs of reciprocation in spite of knowing it could never be.

She was friendly, but then, she was friendly to everyone. She was a happy girl with a quick smile and she was increasingly inhabiting his thoughts, the only thing he had to look forward to each day.

A year went by, then another, years of disappointment and emotional starvation. At eighteen, he was told they no longer needed him—nothing personal, nothing he did wrong, simply no niche for him to occupy.

The hurt was unexpected, a dagger of failure.

He left that day for the last time, his head lowered, his eyes on the floor. He wanted to say goodbye to Katie, but she'd gone home early. He resigned himself to their friendship—if it could even be called that—being over, along with the job.

The day was hot, the sky brassy with unleashed summer storms, the drought creating a stark landscape of olive-colored cornstalks half-formed, like pineapple plants, the soil cracked and parched. Dry, brown weeds rustled in the hot winds as he pedaled his scooter up the small incline, his heart like a stone in his chest, the sweat already forming on his upper lip. He dreaded going home, dreaded facing his parents and sisters. He wished he could crawl away under a tree and stay there.

He felt caught in a situation beyond his control, living in a body he had not created, with a family who was ashamed of him. What had he done to deserve any of that? He had no friends to speak of, never had a social life. It was a fruitless existence, and he felt powerless to change anything about it.

Wearily, his thick hair soaked with perspiration, he wheeled his scooter up the drive to the white house with the black shutters, the large urns overflowing with red geraniums and trailing ivy, the black porch rockers sitting elegantly—a real testament to his mother's determination.

He parked his scooter in the barn and carried his lunch into the kitchen to find his mother and Cathy deep in a serious conversation. He set his lunch on the counter, opened his mouth to say hello, then closed it again. They laughed softly, and his mother turned to acknowledge his presence.

"Oh, Amos. How was your day?" she asked, searching his face for signs that the acne was disappearing somehow. It hadn't improved even slightly, and she felt the familiar disappointment and disgust.

"I was fired."

"You were what?"

"They fired me."

"Amos, whatever for? I thought they liked you. I thought you were doing a good job. Were you goofing off?"

He gazed at his mother through hooded eyes. "Of course not."

Cathy turned, stuck out her lower lip to blow away stray hair. Her eyes were not unkind, but her mouth smirked.

"I heard you were being a creep to the girls. Sarah said she heard you touched one of them, grabbed her or something. I hoped it was just a rumor, but apparently not. You need to get a life, really."

Already fully aware of his own failure to be a "normal" guy, and already struggling with the raw shame of thinking so much about Katie Fisher, a cauldron of anger boiled up and over, a riptide of rage. He would never have touched her. Not in a million years.

He placed both hands on the table, palms down, leaned forward, and opened his mouth. "You actually believe that, Cathy?"

She shrugged as if she couldn't care less, but her eyes were wide. His mother quickly turned her back, stirring with rapid motion.

"Alright, I'll get a life. I will. But it won't be here with any of you."

That was all he said, but he was breathing hard as he went upstairs, blindly taking the steps one at a time, the thought that this was the beginning of the end forming as clear as crystal.

He stood in front of his dresser, breathing, breathing. The face looking back at him was monstrous, crosshatched with infection, the color between a dark maroon and sickening yellowish-pink. He examined the small brown eyes set too close to a wide flattened nose. A groan of despair escaped him, a sharp intake of defeat.

As he showered and donned clean clothes, his mind was churning, kicking up layers of dust and dirt, the accumulation of years of failure and embarrassment. He had a hefty savings account.

Without a social life, no interests to speak of, he had socked away nearly all his paychecks. He didn't know if it was enough to get his own place, but he would find out. Yes, the thought of going out on his own was terrifying, but he would shore up his courage, somehow. He had to.

But that night at the supper table, the courage slipped away like water over rocks.

"Mom says they let you go at the bulk food store," his father said. "Did they give you a reason?"

He wiped his mouth, turned his eyes to his son, whose eyelids already fell.

"No."

"There has to be something. I mean, Rueben is a good guy."

Amos swallowed, nodded. "He just said they don't need me. There wasn't anything . . . no other reason."

"I see." His father hesitated. "So, do you have a plan? Any idea what comes next?"

His mother broke in. "You need to start going with the youth."

He recognized a crackle of fear in her words, a certain anxiety. It awoke a sense of satisfaction in him. Let her worry, let her turn her attention on him for once in her life. Just this once, let her think about him more than the esteemed Cathy.

He leveled his gaze at Cathy, and she met it halfway. He saw the mockery in her eyes and a hot rage boiled up inside him.

His father's voice came again.

"Amos, I hope you're not actually thinking of leaving home. You're not ready to make your own way. You need the stability of family, a house, good meals."

When Amos didn't respond, he continued.

"You don't have a job, Amos. How would you survive on your own?"

His mother chimed in. "You wouldn't. It was just an outburst. You know you wouldn't make it a week on your own."

Amos toyed with the flat side of his knife, drawing it over the rounded edge of the table. Her words felt familiar, even though the context was new. How many times had he absorbed her reminders that he could not, now or ever, achieve anything? He would bumble slowly through life leaving a string of failures in his wake, the debris of a wrecked existence.

But this time, he felt a new urge to push back against her words, to prove her wrong.

"I have money in the bank."

"And that is where it will stay."

The sharp admonishment of his mother created a powerful urge to disobey, this once.

He knew it was wrong, this hot rebellion, knew it wrong to hurt his parents, but the idea of an independent life had been planted in the crevice of a bare, cold heart.

He left the table, walked out the door, down the driveway, and turned left, on his way to town. He continued past the propane business, past the car wash and the row of derelict houses.

His thoughts were like scattered birds, each one flying off in different ways. He began to think Cathy was right about why he was fired, and the thought brought a burning shame so deep he could not face the remembering now. He loved Katie Fisher, but had no idea what to do with the strong emotion, and certainly no courage to tell her. For two years, he'd harbored this ache, this hopelessness.

He walked past Laycer's Hardware, then the bank, the day beginning to cool as the sun lowered behind three-story buildings. Vehicles moved past, engines revved. A horn blasted.

He stepped aside to allow a heavy middle-aged man to step past, two big dogs on a leash, their heavy pink tongues lolling with the heat. He avoided the man's eyes, out of habit.

He heard low, pulsing beats, turned down a side street toward it, drawn in by the pull of anything to take his mind off his troubles. Light poured out of tall windows, the door propped wide open. He hesitated, stopped, then leaned against a brick wall.

The music created excitement. He was aware of his own pulse. He turned to see and hear more.

A neon sign blinked above the door. SCOTT'S FITNESS.

Fascinated, he walked closer. The music was louder, more insistent. He peered inside, quickly, then stepped back. He saw men lifting weights, running on treadmills. He blinked, swallowed nervously, but could not manage to step inside. He was obese, Amish, and ugly. This was no place for him. They'd make fun of his appearance, for sure. He turned to walk away.

"What's up, man?"

Startled, Amos turned, lifted eyes clouded with shame.

"Uh, nothing. I mean, just, you know, walking past."

"Okay. Hey, I'm Scott." He jerked a thumb to the sign.

Amos mumbled an acknowledgment, turned to go. This was the beckoning of the devil. How often had he heard the phrase, "If you give Satan your little finger, he'll take your whole hand?"

"You're welcome to come in and check the place out," Scott extended a hand. Amos looked at it, then slowly took it, the grip clenching as a vice. He stepped back, laughed, an embarrassed sound.

"You look like you could build some serious strength."

Scott's face was wide, his blue eyes as calm and serene as a summer pond. Amos became aware of the startling discovery that no one had ever looked at him like that. Scott didn't see the horrible skin, or the fumbling oversized body, but instead saw potential—the potential for strength.

"I don't know. I probably wouldn't fit in."

He played with the edge of his suspenders, pulled at frayed edges.

"Amish?"

Amos nodded.

"This kind of thing go against your beliefs?"

He shrugged, felt a deep shame. "Not exactly. I mean, I don't know . . ."

"Don't want to offend. I'm a Christian myself. But come on in if you like."

He held up an arm, waved it over his head in a sideways movement.

Amos followed him into the large room, blinking uncomfortably in the glare of overhead lights. Music pulsed, and everywhere he looked there were men lifting, straining, pulling cables, all kinds of body building equipment.

Eyes turned toward him. Scott was waving him over. He panicked, turned on his heel, and hurried out. He actually ran down the sidewalk, feeling his stomach and hips jiggling, his knees straining.

No, he could not give into something as sinful as that. He must return home and obey his parents.

He was hired at H&R Builders. It was the end of summer, which came in on torrents of rain, leaves on swaying trees bending, torn to shreds by attacks of hail, thunder, and lightning. He'd only been working a couple weeks when he fell off the scaffolding, tore a muscle in his thigh, and was laid up for a month. Toward the end of that time, when he was mostly healed but still couldn't work, he decided to join the youth, incorporate himself into the social goings on of the Amish youth. He was desperately bored. If nothing else, maybe it would make his mother happy.

Dressed in his Sunday best, wearing a nice wool coat, he hitched up and drove to Elmer Stoltzfus's, where Cathy had gone. He'd stay out of her way, definitely.

Unlike the fitness place, which was never far from his mind, he would fit in here. These were Amish youth, some of them acquaintances from church.

As he arrived, his horse shied from the cows on the left, took a sharp right turn, and went down a narrow incline straight into a whiteboard fence, where the front wheel became hooked on a post, the horse lunging and rearing, wild-eyed.

Amos climbed out the opposite door, deeply embarrassed at the cluster of well-meaning onlookers, young men loosening traces, some going to grab the reins of the terrified animal.

"Sorry, sorry," he kept repeating.

"Hey, you're okay. No problem."

The girls lost interest and hurried off to the volleyball game. A few guys righted the carriage while he led the uninjured horse to the barn. He stood, aware of every number he had ever seen on the scale, his hands in his pockets, trying to widen his chest while drawing in his stomach.

He listened to the boys talk, watched cigarettes being lit, smoke inhaled and blown out again. It looked cool—amazing, actually—but he shook his head when one was offered, afraid of embarrassment. He couldn't do anything else right, and doubted he could smoke, so he stood quietly, listening carefully.

No one quite knew what to do with him, obviously ill at ease and terribly shy, so no one made overtures, except for the offering of a cigarette. Cell phones appeared, social media was discussed, hilarious accounts of videos they'd seen. But Amos had never used a cell phone and had nothing to contribute. He smiled from time to time, even laughed awkwardly.

They all moved through the barn door, so he followed. He realized they were going to watch the volleyball game. There was a ring of lawn chairs set up for the parents and their friends. The boys greeted them all with handshakes, friendly words.

Amos followed, the last to shake hands. He was unable to speak, he was so frozen with anxiety. As he turned away, he heard a middle-aged woman with graying hair say, "My oh. Was that Raymond's boy? He's quite a sight, isn't he? Poor guy."

Hot shame like boiling oil sluiced through him. He was blinded with tears but desperate not to let them roll down his cheeks. He lowered himself on the grass, blinking furiously, and pretended to watch the bright forms of the players, the white volleyball pounded from side to side.

He was no longer there, however, but somewhere in a place without others, a place within himself that was a flat, endless desert of self-loathing.

He'd been a fool to come. He did not belong, and never would.

Once his emotions were back under control, he thought he should find someone to talk to, but he didn't know how or with whom. No one noticed him, no one cared to strike up a conversation. He stood up and walked around a little, standing near one group of boys for a while, then moving to another. Once, he thought someone had spoken to him, and he nodded and said, "Yeah," then quickly realized he was talking to someone else. A wall of shame unraveled like a scroll.

When he filled his plate in the long line snaking past tables laden with delicious casseroles and salads, he overloaded the paper plate, which buckled in the center, his food sliding off and landing on his shoes and down his trouser leg.

"Whatever," he mumbled, looking around for napkins, paper towels, anything.

No one said anything, no one knew what to do, so they all filed around him, leaving him stranded on the spot, his food an island around him.

He felt tears gathering as one of the adults efficiently wiped the food from the floor and took it to the garbage. Amos turned and moved as quickly as possible out the door, away to the barn and his horse.

Hatred welled up inside. Hatred for them all, followed by the realization he could never fit in. Some youth were admired for their appearance or good manners, some appreciated for their lineage, that long line of respected and revered family that had no losers in the whole bunch. He was neither.

He would never go back.

He was back at work at H&R Builders for two months before they told him kindly he was better suited for shop work.

His father frowned at the news, cleared his throat, and looked away. His mother threw her arms out, her voice shrill with anxiety as she raved on about his shortcomings.

For the next few weeks, his mother tried to do something about his weight. She served him vegetables and diet raspberry tea and gave him the table of measures from Weight Watchers. But when she wasn't looking, he ate how he pleased, sugary foods a comfort that nothing else in life gave him.

At nineteen, unable to land another job, he decided he was being discriminated against for his weight. There were laws against that, and he told his parents so. Cathy burst out laughing, Lavina held a hand over her mouth, and his mother rolled her eyes. His father took his words seriously, mulled them over, and agreed with him. "You may be right," he said. "But you know we don't get involved with legal battles like that. It's not our way. If you want to do something about it, find a way to lose some weight."

Amos answered an ad in the daily paper for a groundskeeper. It was an elderly couple, Joseph and Lila Brown.

When he showed up at their doorstep, the white-haired couple peered up at him, then opened the door and let him in.

He had to restrain himself from gawking openmouthed at the winding staircase and wide hallway with sunny rooms on either side, windows from floor to ceiling, imported rugs and antiques. They treated him with courtesy he wasn't accustomed to, calling him sir, inquiring about his faith.

They were refined, mannerly. Joseph spoke softly, and Lila rang for tea, a portly maid bringing a silver tray.

"Yes, we need a groundskeeper. We have four acres of lawn and gardens. It has fallen to neglect, I'm afraid. Last year we had a few local young men help out, but they proved a bit inexperienced. We're willing to train, willing to show you the ropes, so to speak."

Amos nodded, his eyes intent, desperately wanting to work for these kind people.

"Since we are getting on in years, we want someone who will live on the premises, in the gatehouse, to be exact. As you pulled in, did you notice the small house at the edge of the lawn?"

Amos nodded, his mind racing.

"The ideal thing would be for you to stay there. A guard of sorts."

"It'd be wonderful if you could," Lila interjected. "So wonderful."

"I will speak to my parents," he said almost giddily.

Joseph nodded, drained his tea.

"We would be delighted. As I said, mowing, trimming shrubs, pruning. Hopefully you could move in as soon as possible. Check in on us occasionally, too. We need a bit of care, maintenance, if you will, just like our property."

They offered him the job on the spot, naming an hourly wage that took his breath away. He'd even be paid to sleep, a watchdog. Finally, God was on his side. Finally.

He turned to look at the house on his way out, the late winter sun slanting through evening clouds. The golden hour, when the yellow painted brick turned to gold, the long black shutters holding the windows in a warm embrace, the wide verandas running every side of the house. Three stories of pure old majesty.

He saw the unkempt shrubbery, massive oaks, maples and elms, a climbing wisteria like clutching arms needing to be removed.

Yes, he would do this. The elderly couple had not seen his size or his face as a drawback, had never mentioned it if they did, and he already loved them for it.

At dinner, he announced he'd gotten a job as a groundskeeper for an elderly couple.

His mother raised an eyebrow.

"Whereabouts?" his father asked, cutting into a slice of spicy egg custard pie.

"Just out of Rainsburg. Close to Route 30, before you go up over the mountain."

"What will they pay you?"

"Thirty dollars an hour for ten hours, ten an hour through the night."

His father's fork stopped mid-air, the quivering egg custard sliding off.

"What? The night?"

"Yes. I'm moving into the gatehouse at the edge of the property, where the drive begins. They want someone who can stay as kind of a watchdog."

He could see his mother's mind calculating, counting dollars. "Well. That's quite something. Since you're not twenty-one yet, you can send half your money home, the way you should."

He could see she was already counting on a new sectional sofa, a rug.

Amos took a deep breath, bit his lower lip, gathered all his strength.

"No, Mom. I have to refuse. I may as well tell you now, that . . . that I'm not planning on being Amish anymore. There is nothing to hold me here."

He watched both their faces lose color, taking no pleasure in their shock. When his mother's hands went to her face and she shook with rare sobs, he felt nothing. His father's temper flared and bitter words were spoken, and still he felt neither satisfaction nor shame.

He had always been an outsider, had always felt adrift, never part of their community. Not even a part of the family.

"But you can't," his mother sobbed. "You'll be lost out in the world, you will. You'll end up with the pigs, eating their slop."

"They don't have pigs," Amos replied seriously, and Cathy snorted.

"Cathy!" their mom reprimanded sharply, and perhaps for the first time ever, she felt her mother's disapproval. A slight pink rose in her cheeks, and she turned away, crossing her arms.

Chapter 4

"Think of the prodigal son. Think of it, son."

When had he ever been called "son?" When had they truly cared what was best for him?

He knew this reaction was just because their pride was hurt. People would consider them unfit parents, their son having gone astray. Folks would shake their heads, wondering aloud where they'd gone wrong.

The shame and humiliation of it was unbearable to Lydia, in spite of the reduced grocery bill, the smaller loads of laundry she was already considering.

"You can have the job, Amos, and still be Amish. They have nothing against your beliefs, do they?"

She was whining now, thinking how love for parents should provide a better bond than this. The ties that bind should mean something.

She heard the sound of raindrops on the kitchen window, and a great cloying sadness enveloped her.

She took a deep breath to steady herself.

"But Amos, think of the future generations. You can't know what you want at nineteen. You should have joined the church last year."

"Well, I didn't. Sorry."

His father cleared his throat. "Amos, I feel you're making a terrible mistake. We have loved you, fed and clothed you, given our lives for you, and now you reject it all."

"I am not rejecting you. I still appreciate you. But no, you have not always loved me. I was the one you were ashamed of, and you know it. So I'm striking out on my own to a place where I have a chance to make something of myself."

"Oh, what will people think?" his mother groaned.

"Does it matter?" Amos asked.

And so the conversation crisscrossed the kitchen table, his mother putting on a grand display of tears, his father sinking steadily lower in his chair, his countenance rife with displeasure.

Amos decided to make one point very clear. "I'm sorry, Mom, but I'm an adult now and feel as if I deserve my own paycheck. You and Dad can make your own living. Once I'm out of the house, I'm sure you'll be relieved to have one less mouth to feed."

THE REMAINDER OF his days at home were fraught with turmoil. Cathy and Lavina were furious, had no understanding or mercy, took pity on their tearful mother, told him he was bringing sadness and heartache to the whole family.

Mostly, he said nothing at all, just stayed out of the line of fire as best he could, packed his few belongings in cardboard boxes and plastic totes, purchased a cell phone, applied for a Visa card, and bade his parents goodbye. When his driver arrived, he felt as if he was stepping into a new life.

HIS MOTHER WATCHED him fold his ungainly weight into the pickup, his hair untamed and much too thick, his inflamed face even redder than normal. She felt the tears slide warmly down her cheeks, and thought it would be easier if he'd never been born.

Now they had a son out in the world with the English and would have to carry that label the remainder of their days.

The guilt crept up on her like fog rolling in. His words poked through her justification, that alibi as weak as runny vanilla pudding.

No, she had not always cared or loved. She had not. Yes, she had been ashamed of who he was, and God help her, had thought far too much of Cathy. Still did. And so her nights turned into restless, guilt-ridden hours, her circling thoughts wearying her soul. Raymond drew into himself and refused to speak of Amos. He became irritated with her endless crying and told her she had to get ahold of herself.

She didn't go to church for a month. Instead, she stayed home and drank coffee and pitied herself immensely. She felt as if she was being chastened beyond endurance. She wondered if he could even pass his driver's test. Probably not. He was so hopeless with stuff like that. Well, the minute he drove a vehicle into her driveway she would just die. Probably have a stroke.

When she finally went to church, she sat on her folding chair and cried copiously, releasing soft sighs into her sodden handkerchief and looking around discreetly to see who took notice. Ah, the Lord was being harsh, but she would remain courageous. King David had a disobedient son, didn't he? And David was way up in God's favor, far more than herself, so who could tell?

And so her thoughts crept through her head as she sat in church, her face lowered as a cyclone of regret, self-pity, shame, self-blame, justification, blame on Raymond, and shattered pride spun in her head, all of it wreaking havoc on her thin spiritual life.

Her eyes searched the benches where the single young men were seated, imagining Amos sitting in his usual spot, so extremely large and bulky, so odd-looking. But how glad she would be to see him there.

A deep well of sorrow sprang from her soul, and she lifted a soggy handkerchief to her streaming eyes.

Well-meaning friends sat with her, inquiring about her welfare, but that served only to make her feel worse than she already had, so she kept her lips pressed into an uncompromising line and said nothing, except for a few clipped answers.

She tried opening the conversation with Raymond on the way home, but soon realized he simply did not want to talk about it.

Well, men were just pitiful. They had no idea how to fulfill the emotional needs of a woman, the way they went through life talking only about their work and hunting. Horse sales. Wages. That was it.

A certain irritation welled up.

"Why won't you talk about Amos?" A sniff, a soft whine.

"What is there to say? He left. He never joined the church, so we don't have to worry about *bann und meidung* (excommunication and shunning). He'll come for visits."

"But he'll be in English clothes. Driving a car."

Raymond shrugged. "Isn't that mountain pretty?" he asked her.

"I don't want to talk about the mountain," she snapped.

When he said nothing, she decided she was going to show him who was who, and wouldn't speak the remainder of the afternoon. She stuck her nose in a book, one she'd read more than a few times, absorbing very little as her mind raced on.

Raymond loved coming home from church. There was something so soul satisfying in unhitching, stabling the horse, giving him a bit of hay and a long cold drink of water, then walking to the house for an afternoon of coffee and popcorn, sitting side by side with Lydia in their brown recliners. A great love for his wife colored his days with rare contentment and happiness from the first day of marriage.

He felt sorry about her suffering but thought it best not to encourage the flow of churning words that took away his own peace and calm and trust in God.

Yes, she was a good woman, the way she worked and turned this place into a lovely home. Nice things meant so much to her, and she did a great job of earning money to buy them.

Now wasn't that something?

And yes, in Proverbs you could read how the wife went out and considered an acre, and bought it. She made things with her hands and sold them and her husband was proud of her.

As he was of Lydia, his helpmeet.

Amos was a good boy, in his own way. Yes, he was bitterly disappointed in his decision to leave the Amish, but a great mercy welled up in his gentle soul. Amos never had an easy life, his appearance and lack of social skills, his dyslexia in school, and to top it all off, his sister's popularity likely doubled his sense of failure.

Ach, he didn't understand the ways of the Lord, but he could praise Him still, rest in His wisdom. He had no idea what would come of all this, but it wasn't in his control.

He would love his wife, and when Amos came home to visit, he'd love him as well. Yes. He would.

When Amos arrived at his destination, he was overcome with anxiety threatening to take away all he had gained. His heart pounded in his chest as he instructed the driver to park at the gatehouse. He felt as if he was intruding as he lifted the boxes and totes, paid the driver, and watched him drive off.

He was a speck. A small black blip in the circle of life. He grasped his cell phone, his thick fingers shaking as he dialed, and jumped when Lila Brown answered.

"Yes. Uh, I'm here."

"Who am I speaking to?" she asked, in the low melodious voice.

"Uh, Amos. Amos Beiler."

"Oh! Oh. Of course. We'll be right down."

He stood, surveying his future home. The small brick structure had been painted in the same pale lemon yellow, matching the big house. The black shutters supported the many paned windows, of which there were two on either side, the door painted black, windowless. Overhead, massive oak trees spread their branches as if to shield the small house from the worst of the elements. The brick walkway was banked by curling brown oak leaves. Old shrubs grew haphazardly, the dying portions broken and twisted, a bed of leaves like an old blanket at their roots. He walked to the back, lifted his eyebrows at the sight of a brick enclosure, a patio of sorts, with broken Adirondack chairs streaked with green mold, sagging with neglect and old age. Huge cement urns contained limp brown plants straggling over the side. A gray plastic Walmart bag was caught in a corner, half-covered in decaying leaves.

A sense of homecoming enveloped him, and he swallowed the rising lump in his throat. Could this actually turn out OK? Yes, the place needed some TLC, but there was so much potential. He had a sense of discovering hidden treasure. To stumble onto a place, to feel the connection, the sense of having arrived . . . was it only a mirage, a dream that would vanish too soon?

He heard the sound of tires on gravel and turned to greet his employers. He should not have been back there nosing around.

"Sorry," he mumbled.

"Well, hello, Amos. No need to be sorry."

They both stepped off the golf cart and greeted him warmly, extending gloved hands, both surprisingly fit as they inserted a key, flung open the door, and ushered him in.

When the light was switched on, he took in the disrepair, the damage rodents had done, the musty odor, sagging furniture, and streaked, water-stained walls. His heart fell to his stomach, followed by a rising nausea. He couldn't repair this. He had no skills, would bumble the job.

He should not have come. He had no idea where to start. He wanted to tell Joseph, but his mouth was dry with fear. It was his arithmetic book, falling off the scaffolding at B and H Builders, the cut bags of sugar, his red swollen face. Failure barked at him, defeat advancing with opened jaws.

"Now, Amos, this doesn't look like much, but I assure you, a strong fellow like you will soon have this whipped into shape. This will be our project for the coming winter. Lila and I will do all we can. In fact, it's invigorating for us, gives us a boost of energy, thinking about this, and we appreciate a strong young fellow. Yes. We'll get along great."

Too miserable to speak, Amos nodded his head, blinked back loathsome tears.

"Now, since this is worse than we thought initially, we'll give you a room in the main house till the repairs are finished. Would you be okay with that?"

Lila's small, wrinkled face was capped by tendrils of white hair, her stocking cap pulled low on her forehead, her eyes alive with anticipation, as if she wanted him to stay with them.

She was so small, bundled into a heavy woolen coat, her feet encased in sturdy hiking boots laced with wide red laces.

He blinked. "I don't know. I mean, are you sure?"

"Well, of course we're sure. You can't live here. Not for the winter."

She peered up at him, her eyes filled with kindness, her face alight with welcome.

Joseph, tall, stooped, his thin frame giving away the years, repeated the invitation, mirroring Lila's welcome. Amos felt as if he needed to reach out, touch their expression, run the tips of his fingers along their faces to see if it was genuine, to see if they meant what they were saying. When had he ever felt truly welcome?

He'd always known he was irksome, an annoyance. He found himself remembering times in the buggy, Cathy yelping and tugging at her skirt, telling the parents Amos was too big to sit back there. *Get over, get away from me.* When he sat down on the bench beside her at the supper table, he felt her bristling, felt unwelcome. He'd learned to live with it, had never really expected anything different.

"So here's the plan," Joseph was saying. "We'll get a dumpster, throw everything out, go to Lowes for cleaning supplies and paint. We'll need to have a repairman out to check the furnace, have the water heater replaced."

His voice cracked and broke. Lila slipped an arm through his, laid her head on his arm.

Embarrassed, Amos looked away. He had never seen his parents touch each other, had never witnessed a display of marital affection.

"I'll have to tell you, Amos. We had a son. Only one child, and he . . ."

Here his voice broke again. His chin trembled. He lifted the steel-rimmed glasses, wiped his eyes. Lila patted his arm.

"He lived here for a while. A short time, actually, after he came home from Iraq. He had PTSD."

"Post-traumatic stress disorder," Lila explained.

"Yes. He was in a bad way the following summer, and we got him the best doctors, the best therapist, but he slid slowly into a state of mental illness. It was a shock when he wrecked his car on the turnpike. An eighteen-wheeler drifted into his lane, sideswiped him, and God in his great mercy took him Home to be with Him."

As if he was relieving the sorrow, the light in the old man's eyes faded, his voice trailed off.

"His name was Bradley, but we all called him Bud, or Buddy. We have many happy childhood memories from when Jim, the one who took care of the grounds, lived here in the gatehouse. Jim and Bud were best friends. He'd trail him like a puppy, everywhere he went. Cousins came for sleepovers, and Jim would start a fire here in the backyard, roast marshmallows," Lila related, her voice subdued.

Amos felt awkward, as if he was witness to a secret sorrow, one infused with an inseparable bond of lifelong grief. He wanted to offer words of comfort, but knew he would say the wrong thing. He always did. So he nodded, shoved his hands in his pockets.

"We were against him joining the Army, but we realized early on he had his heart set on adventure, going out, away from here. Perhaps we stifled him—the doting, overly dedicated parents."

Joseph sighed, lifted his shoulders, let them fall.

"We became bitter, let the place go for many years, railed against fate, against God. Our only son."

He shook his head, as if the accident was fresh in his mind. "But God didn't let us go. He called us back, bit by bit. We no longer attended church, never went out except for necessities, only saw friends infrequently."

Lila took up the story. "It was a time of bitter sorrow, but God in His mercy looked down on us and remembered us. Slowly we healed, began to watch evangelists on television, resumed our faith on shaking legs. Time has a way of healing old bitterness if we open our hearts to the light.

"Well," she added briskly, "we'll give you a case of depression, Amos. Now tell us what you would like to do with this place."

"I have no idea. I mean, it will cost a lot, won't it?"

"Don't worry about money. We want to do this right. It's our winter project."

They took him and his belongings to the big house, and Amos was overcome with shyness, awed at the wide cement steps leading to the wide porch, the massive oak doors with sidewalls, the old luxury of a well-preserved home with an abundance of money to purchase beautiful things. He thought of his mother, the need to fulfill her desire for a lovely home, the small amount of money she used to buy contentment. A thin veil of affection wafted through him for a second.

He was given a tour of the house, the vases of flowers, the original paintings, the handmade imported rugs. He had never imagined such opulence, so much money.

His room was on the second floor, toward the back of the house, a large room with three low windows and heavy cream-colored drapes matching the quilt on the king-sized poster bed. The rugs beneath his feet were as thick as new grass in spring, the floorboards between them glistening with lacquer. There were sprays of flowers in heavy vases, at least seven or eight paintings, cherry dressers, and a tall piece they called an armoire, something he'd never heard of.

The bathroom was tiled in black, with white walls, an old-fashioned claw foot tub, the floor covered in more imported rugs in all kinds of colors and patterns. *So thick, so expensive*, he thought.

Lila flitted around like a small frantic bird, opening doors, showing him where to store his things, with Joseph beaming from the doorwas.

"Here is extra soap, shampoo, toothpaste if you need it. Towels, washcloths. And please don't be afraid to ask for things. We want you to be comfortable."

Amos nodded, tried out a smile, thought of his yellowed, crooked teeth. He needed to go shopping but was ashamed to say it.

All he owned—his whole wardrobe—was Amish, homemade clothing.

Nancy Farmer was the cook and housekeeper. She had been there for more than thirty-five years, so was actually part of the family, although they warned him that Nancy was no pushover. She wanted things organized.

The old couple made their way downstairs, and Amos was left to heave the totes and boxes upstairs, his breath coming in ragged gasps after the first one. He couldn't help but feel a certain thrill, as if he stood on the threshold of an expanding world, one lit by electric lights and promise of better things to come.

As he lifted his button-down shirts and put them on hangers, he felt the old sense of shame drawing him down, pulling him away from the dawning of a new day. Who, really, did he think he was?

He was a joke. He'd never be able to please this old couple.

He thought of his bare feet, those white, flat feet with crooked toes padding across these wonderful rugs, carrying the obesity, the pale, wobbling body he had created by his wolfish appetite.

He snuffled when he ate, Cathy informed him. Breathed out of his nose, like a pig in its trough. He would have to be very careful in the dining room tonight.

Suddenly, without warning, he wanted to go back. He wanted to tell Joseph and Lila it wouldn't work. He needed to go home, didn't have the capabilities to carry out this job.

As he laid his broadfall trousers in drawers of the tall dresser, he thought how terribly out of place he was, thrust into a world in which he would only be defeated again. He lifted out a pair of socks, worn at the heel, and felt despair. Three pairs of shoes, all worn on one side of the sole, attesting to the weight pressing down on them.

In the bathroom, the cruelty of overheard lights. The hair. The ruined skin. Small brown eyes.

He turned away, lifted items from a tote, placed them in a medicine chest.

He walked across his bedroom, stood at the windows, his hands behind his back, gazing through tree branches across the expanse of unkempt lawn and garden. A roof with two wide chimneys rose from a line of trees, of brown fields, the blue sky with a smattering of white clouds blown by the early winter winds.

So, his life had come to this at the age of nineteen. Most young men his age had a girlfriend, or at least someone they were interested in, perhaps a few. They had good jobs, a firm foundation beneath their feet, with no doubt they'd be incorporated into the mainstream of the Amish community. They would attend the same church their parents had before them, or move to another community after marriage, but still obey the same rules, the same way of life, the ties that bind, secure, loving, and without doubt. He wanted the same thing. He wanted to be Raymond Beiler's Amos, date a nice girl, get married, and make his parents proud. But that was impossible. No girl would have him.

He must always remember this, never allow himself to think thoughts of love and marriage. It must be this way. He thought of Katie Fisher, mortification sweeping through his soul. He knew he had never touched her in any way, still could not understand where that horrible rumor had started.

He didn't know if he should stay in his room or go downstairs. He sat down on the bed and lifted his phone to check his messages, and of course there were none. Who would try to contact him? So he scrolled through a few sites, then shut it off and pocketed it. He went to the top of the stairs and hesitated. Should he go down? What if they were napping and didn't want to be disturbed?

As if on cue, the portly housekeeper appeared. Amos stepped back.

"Hey!"

Amos stayed where he was.

"Hey, you up there! Lunch is in the kitchen."

Amos forced himself to go to the top of the stairs.

"Oh, there you are. Come on down." She bent her body sideways, made a swooping motion with her arm, then turned and moved off with a funny swaying motion.

Amos made his way downstairs, followed a wide hallway to what he hoped was the kitchen. He was aware of the smell of fried meat.

"Come on in."

He blinked at the ceiling lights, gawked at the large room, the amount of white cabinetry. Again, he thought of his mother and how much she appreciated nice things. Beautiful woodwork, a huge ornate island with fancy barstools, a refrigerator as big as his father's harness cabinet in the barn. Solid oak floor.

"Hello. I'm Nancy. You must be the new guy."

"I . . . yes. I am."

"Amos?"

"Yes."

"Well, Amos, we may as well get to know each other, 'cause we're stuck here together."

She stopped, came closer, lifted her head to peer through her bifocals at his face. He felt the color rising.

"Whatever," she muttered, as if to herself. Then, "You want to do something about that skin?"

He shrugged almost imperceptibly.

"My daughter Reilly had a face like yours. Possibly worse. There's a name for it. I have just the place for you."

He wasn't sure whether to feel insulted or grateful. He knew his skin was awful, but did she really have to bring it up so boldly? On the other hand, maybe she really did know someone who could help. Before he could formulate a response, the moment had passed.

"Okay, here's your grilled ham and cheese. Potato chips. Diet or regular Coke?"

"Regular's fine."

He stood uncertainly. Should he sit or wait to be told?

Chapter 5

WOULD HE FIT ON THESE FANCY BARSTOOLS? HE FELT LIKE A BUFFALO.

"Sit," she said, moving her hand in a downward motion.

He slid on, righted himself, blushed achingly.

"Okay, so I used to wear a black dress, white apron, you know? No more. I told Lila those days are gone. Now I wear this." She lifted one short leg, held the fleece of her sweatpants, and tugged.

"T-shirt and my stocking feet. I'm fifty-two years old, and no skirts and shoes for me. Hope you don't mind."

Amos had just experienced the sandwich, unlike anything he'd ever tasted, and he was fully absorbed in it. He chewed, swallowed, then smiled and told her it was fine with him.

"Good. And I won't say anything about your clothes. You really do need to see a doctor though."

He wanted to tell her how wonderful the sandwich was, but knew he wouldn't be able to get the words out in proper form.

She kept talking as she poured a cup of coffee, added a splash of heavy cream and a long pour of sugar, telling him about his new employers, the history of the place, their son.

Amos drank his Coke, finished the potato chips, wished for another sandwich, but knew one was enough. Nothing else was offered, so he sat and listened as she talked.

He learned how to apply a paint roller, how to draw a trim brush down along the woodwork. He scoured cabinets, applied fresh paint to them, scrubbed floors, and washed windows.

The old couple took him along to purchase the necessary items of furniture, brought rugs and towels from the big house.

He went to a barbershop in the next town over, where he felt safe, not wanting to offend the Amish people he knew. He came away with his hair cut close to his scalp, longer on top, and hated the face looking back at him.

He went to Walmart, spent a humiliating evening in a poorly lit dressing room trying on different sizes, belts as long as a room. He tried T-shirts and plaid flannel shirts, everything too small, sizes embarrassing to see on the white tags. Was he really that big?

He had never felt quite this extraordinarily huge. He took note of his pale, flappy arms. The soft hands.

The day came, just before Christmas, when the gatehouse was completed, curtains hung, dishes stacked on shelves, the water running hot and cold. His small bedroom held a queen-sized bed with a very comfortable mattress, a dresser with a mirror, and a built-in closet, one Joseph had led him through, building it step by step, Lila looking on as he worked.

His second paycheck's arrival prompted him to ask Nancy about the doctor she had mentioned, and she nodded, chewed, swallowed, lifted one finger and tapped her phone, then held it up for him to see. He felt a stab of accomplishment, lifting his own phone to show he had entered the number and would contact them, certainly.

True to Nancy's predictions, they were often together at lunch, for breakfast or in-between, managing things without relying too heavily on Joseph and Lila, who often rested in their room during the day.

He borrowed a laptop from Nancy and studied for his driver's permit, but found it extremely challenging. He was hopelessly inadequate with the computer, his lack of self-esteem his biggest hurdle. He agonized every week, trying to make sense of the many regulations, dreading the actual test, pushing it away whenever he thought about it.

In January, he finally asked Nancy to help him, if she had time, please. And if she didn't mind.

Nancy said she was more than happy to. He hated bothering her, but her guidance made all the difference. He took the test and passed, came home and high-fived her, his best friend in all the world, he told her.

Nancy accompanied him to the dermatologist, insisting that he drive now that he had his permit.

Driving her car was both terrifying and exhilarating, gripping the steering wheel with hands positioned the proper way, timidly pressing the gas pedal, holding up traffic, then braking too hard, lurching at crossroads.

They walked into the waiting room together, and sat until his name was called. He had never felt worse about himself, meeting the slim, dark-haired woman named Dr. Emily Scheller. She was perfect, one of God's best creations, he figured, and in comparison, he felt absolutely miserable.

Dr. Scheller did a thorough examination, asked questions, and did a few tests. She explained that skin conditions were created by a variety of circumstances, often hormones, stress, eating habits, genetics. But as he was aware, his skin was acutely infected, which by all appearances had been going on for some time.

He nodded, bitterly thinking of his mother, his father's complacency. Cathy's smart remarks. Had his family ever loved him?

He supposed they had, in a way. But mostly they were disappointed in him. Maybe love and approval were two different things, but it was hard to separate them in his mind.

Could he really blame them for being disgusted with him? How many times had he shuffled around on his soft feet and snuck entire bags of cheese curls and sour cream and onion chips into his room, drank thirstily out of the bathroom sink faucet, belched, and flopped on his bed. In those moments, he loathed himself, so why shouldn't they?

The doctor prescribed him an antibiotic for infection, another pill for inflammation, and told him what face wash and cream to buy at a drugstore. He left feeling hope like he never had before.

He walked into the local drugstore with the prescription, handed it to the pharmacist, smiled, and nodded at the cashier. He felt more normal than he could ever remember. For one, he was dressed like other people. The only thing drawing attention was his face, and his large size. And soon enough, maybe it would only be his size, which suddenly didn't feel like as big a deal.

He received a heartbroken letter from his mother, accusing him of staying away on Christmas Day, purposefully hurting them all, complete with a list of Bible verses he was choosing to disobey.

To hurt your mother was a curse, first and foremost, and he was most definitely guilty of that one. He read on, shook his head, thought, *Really? What about the mother hurting the son? Isn't that a sin, too?*

How many times had he felt belittled, mocked, inconsequential, a shame to the family, a failure in every single way? He realized how little he missed his old life.

After a month, he went to the pharmacy in Rochester for a refill, although he still couldn't see any changes in his skin. Not to speak of. As he turned to leave, he bumped into an almost familiar face, the guy from the gym. There was instant recognition.

"Hey, Amos, right?"

"You're Scott."

"Yeah!" The blue eyes flattened as his smile spread wide, crinkling the corners. His hair was cut short, his shoulders sculpted beneath the heavy sweatshirt.

Puzzled, he looked at Amos. "You left the group?" he asked. Amos nodded, feeling the shame. His hand went to his suspenders, found them missing, dropped to his side.

"The parents okay with that?"

"Well, no. Not really."

His brown eyes flattened, dulled, his jaw solidified as he thought of his family.

"I'm sorry about that. But hey, look, if you need a friend, stop by the gym sometime. We'd love to have you."

Amos nodded, curt in his manner. He had no inclination to join a group of bodybuilders. It would just be one more way to feel inferior.

He was living comfortably in his own house, far beyond anything he had ever imagined. He was more at peace than he'd ever been in his life. A thin, fragile peace perhaps, but it was certainly an improvement.

During the day, he shoveled snow, pushed the driveway open, collected fallen branches, and in February, trimmed grape vines, surveyed the vast area he would be expected to manicure, maintain.

He ate his dinners in the dining room with Joseph and Lila, and learned to eat slowly, with the proper fork, and to enjoy a glass of red wine with his pasta. The meal always lasted longer than an hour, while Joseph relayed endless stories of his life as a professor of history at Bainbridge University. Lila had been a lawyer in Williamsport for thirty-three years. He sat and listened, amazed at the enormous scope of their lives, the travel, the people they knew, the amount of money they earned collectively, though he gathered that it was Lila who brought in the most income.

They asked him to accompany them to church, the beloved old building in the center of Rochester, but he always shook his head. It wasn't the thought of being a traitor to the Amish, it was just not something he wasn't interested in at that point in his life. He couldn't explain it, even to himself, although he knew how he felt about God, and that was nothing he needed to disclose to anyone.

One evening, Joseph wiped his mouth with his napkin, cleared his throat, and asked if he was happy living there in the gatehouse.

Amos looked up, surprised. "Yes, I am."

"Well, we hope so. If there is anything you need, please don't be afraid to ask. You have made us very happy, just knowing you're there, knowing you'll hear the alarm if there's anything odd going on."

That evening, he noticed a slight change in his face. The red was turning into a tanned, pockmarked red, the pockets of pus draining away. His skin was actually peeling. Then he thought of the glare of the sun on snow, being out in the cold, the antibiotics. In disbelief, he smoothed his face with his fingertips, over and over.

Could this be possible?

He loved his small kitchen, purchased a few cookbooks, went online to find recipes. He never went home, but wept sometimes, when he felt especially lonely on Sunday. The only person he missed was Lavina. She had been genuinely goodhearted as a child, but he supposed Cathy had taken care of that by this time.

In March, the snow crystallized in the stronger sunshine, rivulets of water seeped from beneath dirty piles of snow, and the crocuses pushed up through soggy, half-frozen soil. Suddenly there was so much to be done it threw him into a state of fine-tuned anxiety. He raked piles of soggy leaves, hacked, cut, and mulched for several days, developed horrible cramps in the backs of his legs, and realized he was not cut out for this kind of work.

He told Joseph as much, who looked up from his book, told him Rome wasn't built in a day, and said, "keep calm and carry on," chuckling to himself.

Lila gave him potassium pills and a hot water bottle.

Nancy told him to lift some weights. He was like a baby seal, all flab and blubber. But she was laughing, teasing as she said it, folding a mound of fried minute steak and cheese into a roll, flopping a pile of sautéed peppers and onions on top before sliding the plate across the countertop.

He was in agony that night, repeatedly walking the floor to get rid of the cramps. He thought if the alarm went off, he'd be useless, chasing an intruder on these legs.

The following day, Joseph and Lila donned sweaters and caps and drove the golf cart around the property with Amos on the back, instructing, encouraging.

"This can't all be accomplished in one summer, Amos. Just do what is possible each day, and we'll give you a list to get through the maze, alright? You're doing a great job. However, before July, you'll have to learn how to trim shrubs properly, so we'll have Alfie come by. Alfie Hatter. He used to be an assistant to Jim. I think you two will hit it off rather well, seeing how quiet you are, and Alfie quite opposite."

As the days lengthened, the sun's power became more intense, which was very healing to the infection in his face. He could see a difference each week and was elated when the doctor said the antibiotics could stop. He gave him a different prescription for a new cream, plus a moisturizer.

He could hear Cathy's opinion in his head. *What a baby. Moisturizer. Really?* But he applied it without fail and after a few more weeks could hardly believe how smooth his skin was becoming.

He was clipping dead branches from apple trees in the overgrown orchard on a sunny, windblown day, dandelions and violets in a riot of color, dry brown grass rattling with last year's growth, the new shoots bravely pushing the old out. He wondered how he was expected to mow through this overgrown mess.

He thought of his mother, wondered if she had her garden planted. His mother's garden was the most picturesque in the valley, the way she mixed plots of herbs and flowers, the rows of peas and red beets laser straight, the chicken wire on wooden posts to support the heavy pea vines. She was a hard worker, that much was true. Especially when it came to anything that would impress onlookers.

He'd go home soon. After he acquired his license, he'd go. Not that he looked forward to it, but he owed his parents a visit.

He looked up to find he was being observed. A jolt went through his chest.

"Hi."

"Uh, yeah. Hi," he answered, reaching for his suspenders, his hands again falling to his side.

"Who are you?"

"I'm uh, I work for Joseph and Lila Brown."

"Oh, you're the guy in the gatehouse. Cool."

She was tall, wide, and appeared to have stepped out of an outdoor magazine, her camouflage bill cap pulled low over thick, tawny hair like the mane of a lion.

"Yes."

"Your name is . . . ?"

"Amos. Amos Beiler."

"You from around here?"

"No . . . I mean, yes. But I come from the Amish."

Her eyes narrowed and she tilted her head to one side.

"So, you're not Amish now?"

"No."

"And why is that?"

He did not know how to answer her question, so he stood silent, feeling the old rush of embarrassment, which inevitably led to defeat. He was too dense, too slow, too bumbling to come up with a witty answer the way a normal person would.

He shrugged.

"You don't say much, do you?"

Her eyes beneath the bill of her cap were light in color, but he didn't know if they were blue or green or gray. She seemed to be at ease, without any knowledge or caring of how she appeared.

"I guess I don't."

She turned, pointed to the two chimneys. "I live there."

"Oh. I see those chimneys from my house, but only in winter."

What a stupid statement. It wasn't even really true. He saw those chimneys from the upstairs bedroom when he slept in the big house, but he had no idea why he'd blurted out that half-truth.

He was not fit to talk to anyone, especially girls.

"Yeah, well, you know the life of the privileged. That's why I roam the fields. Wealth and all the craziness makes me go . . ."

She twirled a finger beside her ear.

He smiled, but could think of nothing to say.

"I'm Skye. Skye Madeline Larkin."

He nodded. He didn't know anyone named Skye, and she was so English and so confident that his thoughts simply left.

"Yup. Larkin, Windsor, and Scott. My dad's law firm. Meting out justice. Helping the unfortunate."

She snorted unbecomingly, shook her head.

"I don't know anything about that," he said, then wished he could reach out and take the words back.

"Lucky you. So, you're the gardener?"

"Yes."

"Interesting."

She sighed, looked around, tugged at her sweater, then began to move away. "See you around."

"See you."

He watched her go, the long strides, the rounded shoulders, wide across her backside. He couldn't help watching her. That was something he just did, even with Joseph and Lila. It was interesting, the way people moved away from you. Some were energetic, brisk, others were slow and relaxed, their gait a sort of amble, while this girl's movements were bored, aloof. Could a movement be cynical? Hers was.

He found himself whistling as he created a sandwich for lunch, then another. He was always ravenous, always wanting a snack, a piece of cheese, a handful of crackers. He should go on a diet the way his mother and Cathy wanted, but he knew he could never stick to it.

He looked in the mirror as he shaved, grateful for the improved skin, but he would never be able to change the nose, or the small, narrowed eyes, the slash of a mouth.

And now, meeting this girl named Skye, he recognized again how inferior he was, how slim his chances of ever having a girlfriend. Oh, he knew folks said it wasn't about appearances, but that simply wasn't true. He'd just stay alone all his life, erase any thoughts of dating, romance, or marriage. He'd have the old couple and Nancy Farmer, bless her heart. She was like a mother, only better.

Sorry, Mom. Sorry. I know you did the best you knew.

He found himself watching for Skye, taking any foolish excuse to go to the orchard, but after having mowed it twice and finished the pruning, he realized she didn't make a habit of walking the fields.

He bent the blade on the mower watching for her and had to take it to the barn and tell Joseph. It was the second blade in three days, and he was gracefully reminded of it. His face flamed with embarrassment, and he mumbled an apology.

"Don't apologize, dear boy. Just use a bit of caution."

He was buying groceries with Lila when he met Scott again and received another invitation to the gym. He offered him one free month and gave him a friendly punch on the shoulder, a flash of the blue eyes.

He'd think about it, he said.

That night he was awakened in the middle of the night by a sound he could not place. The alarm would be jangling if someone passed through the gates, obviously, so what, exactly, had awakened him?

He lay still, holding his breath. His window was opened four or five inches, but no breeze came through. His heart beat in his ears, his chest, down his forearms. Every nerve tingled.

Slowly, he heaved out of bed, crept silently to the window, and grasped the pull-down shade, drawing it inward to peer through the opening. The brick enclosures along the back of the house were empty, the bricks swept and tidy, the new chairs and table in place, exactly where he'd put them. He waited, trying to separate night from shadow, pale gray from starlight. There was a sliver moon.

All was fine.

He berated himself for being an idiot, imagining the sound, feeling afraid over nothing. But he could not get back to sleep till the sky was turning pink in the east. He felt confused, disoriented as he stumbled up the drive to the kitchen, where Nancy insisted on making his breakfast.

It was a beautiful morning, birdsong like liquid gold pouring out of opened beaks as the wee warblers and wrens sang their praises to the

Creator. Lilacs were everywhere, untrimmed and growing in profusion, great heavy piles of them in purple, lavender, and white.

Rose of Sharon bushes were in bud, the delicate pink flowers ready to burst forth by the gentle persuasion of the sun.

Amos saw none of this, only felt a sinister chill as he walked. He was almost certain someone had been lurking around that gatehouse, someone who tried to step quietly, sliding their feet on the brick walkway. He couldn't tell Nancy, the way she thrived on excitement or gossip of any kind. And it seemed silly to mention it to Joseph or Lila when he had zero evidence.

He rubbed his arms, shivered as he entered the kitchen.

Nancy had her back turned, lifting bacon from the frying pan on the massive gas stove.

"That you, Amos?" she called over her shoulder.

"Yup, it's me."

"How was your night?"

She opened the oven door, inserted a toothpick in muffins, then placed them on the counter.

"Not great. I kept waking up."

"Bad moon."

Amos grinned to himself, said he highly doubted it.

"Don't you believe in that stuff?"

"You forget I come from the Amish. We're very not . . . well, like that."

Nancy eyed him, then rubbed the palm of her hand across her right hip, massaging, her eyebrows drawn down.

"Pain is like an unwelcome guest. You have to live with it, learn to get used to it."

"I get cramps in my legs at night."

"Your legs aren't used to working hard. You need to toughen up."

Amos shook his head, reached for a muffin. She smacked his hand.

"Eggs, fruit, and oatmeal."

Amos drew a wry face. She laughed, and the usual sense of security, a place he belonged, rose within him. He honestly loved Nancy like his own mother. More, probably.

Why could she tell him to toughen up and it didn't hurt his feelings? She was truthful, but not in a way brought on the self-loathing, the bitter rebellion.

Was it just that he cared too much what his parents thought? Or was there something about family that made their words hurt more?

He always felt his mother's words like a knife, and his father never protected him, but allowed the words to hit him like a sledgehammer as he quietly went about his life as if they had never been spoken. He was alone, with no one to shield him from the constant reminders of his incompetence.

Nancy watched the expression on his face, asked if she'd hurt his feelings.

He shook his head. "You never do."

"Well, good. I certainly don't mean to."

She paused, broke another egg into a bowl.

"You're like a son. The boy I never had."

And Amos felt the fluttering of hope in his chest.

Chapter 6

As the world turned on its axis, the days became longer, the warmth of the sun like a fuzzy blanket, comforting Amos as he went about his duties. He often found himself leaning on the stone wall, gazing at the splendor of the softly hued yellow brick walls, the heavy black shutters flanking the length of many-paned windows. Three stories, wide verandas, dormers on the roof like eyes, guarding everyone's safety. The amount of green foliage on heavy old trees was astonishing. Oaks that appeared to be hundreds of years old, maples with untrimmed, dead growth, chestnut and sycamore, rows of hedges remaining with a minimum of care.

There were gorgeous lilacs in groups, old stone fountains without running water, flagstone walkways completely hidden by overgrown grass, rife with dandelion and thistle. Great swaths of daffodils, past their prime, leaned on each other like weary maidens, the green from their leaves already yellowed. Tulips swayed in the wind, flopped open, and lost petals, then disappeared in the tangle of brown clumps of grass remaining from the previous summer.

But it was the house itself that amazed him. He wondered who had built it, how grand it must have seemed in the early nineteen hundreds. How splendid the old automobiles must have been as they purred their way up the curving drive.

A different time, another era. He must find out about the history of this place, the wonder of someone establishing these gardens. In the freshness of a late spring morning, the dew in tiny diamonds on every leaf, the house backlit by the rising sun, he imagined himself on the veranda, his cup of morning coffee, strong, fit, having made his own fortune, lord of all his domain.

He could create this world for himself without shame or reproach from anyone. He could dream, aspire to inhabit a better world with hope and kindness. He would learn to be the best he could be, please his employer, be willing to start at the bottom of the ladder and climb steadily upward.

He took a deep breath, his chest swelling as he allowed himself the hope of early morning, the wonder of the rising sun and the grandeur of this wonderful place.

Joseph appeared silently, as his back was turned, scraping leaves and dead growth from the row of yews surrounding the stone wall.

"Amos, my boy."

He straightened immediately, said, "Yes sir."

The old man wore a plaid hat with a narrow rim, a wide leather band encircling the crown with a jaunty brown feather pushed into it. His outerwear, as usual, was immaculate, the trousers pressed, leather oxfords polished to a high sheen. He was holding a decorative walking stick, which he used to push through the wet leaves Amos had raked out.

"What a great opportunity for Lila and me, to see the old gardens restored to their normal glory. Yes. It makes my old bones feel young again."

Unused to compliments, Amos blinked uncomfortably, pushed a few dead leaves with the toe of his boot.

"But I forgot to ask how you are. Have you enjoyed a good night's rest?"

His blue eyes, shaded by the hat's brim, were a startling robin's-egg blue, alive, vibrating with the joy of morning.

"Yes."

"Good. I'm so glad. Lila had a bit of misery during the night with restless legs, but a sleeping pill did the trick."

He paused, looked around, then asked what the long, thin shovel was doing out here.

"It's an edger. I'm edging as I go. I mean, if that's alright."

For a long moment, Joseph looked at the deep edges along the length of shrubbery, then his blue eyes crinkled and he began to chuckle.

"You won't believe this, but I honestly never knew what it was for."

"My, uh, my mother edged. I mean, she used one just like this. Sometimes, I did."

"It's a great accomplishment, Amos. I have never seen better work. Carry on."

They made plans to order truckloads of mulch, to get the old garden tractor running. He was shown the plot where Lila wanted the vegetable garden, but today, after lunch, they would power wash the porches, the lawn furniture, replace the swings and urns.

Amos felt the old pinch of inadequacy. Never having used a power washer, he knew he wouldn't get it right.

The old garden shed was in need of repair, the interior dark, moldy. There was an odor of rotting wood, mice, damp earth, and clustered leaves blown through broken windows. Together, they heaved open the old sliding door, laughed at the sight of dust and cobwebs, broken acorns, and other debris small rodents used to make a home for themselves.

Inside, he surveyed outdoor tables and chairs, swings, an ottoman, decorative pots and urns, and hanging baskets. There were cement figures of turtles and frogs, rabbits, snails, birdbaths in all different shapes and sizes. Amos began to see the former glory of these gardens, the wide, shaded verandah, and experienced an eagerness, a sense of anticipation.

Joseph laughed out loud, picked up a small ornament and held it lovingly.

"Our whole collection. The times we had, Lila and me. Yes. We traveled, we bought things, our joy was our home. A haven for us, our retirement. And then old age renders it all useless. It's all just here, taunting us, reminding us we're no longer capable."

His eyes gazed across the winding driveway, as if seeing the home as it once had been, lost in thought.

"Ah well, it's all creature comforts, and a home is prepared for us, Amos. Think about it. Our Lord went before us, prepared many mansions for us, a place we can only imagine, but what joy and comfort He left us. Yes."

Uncomfortable with such talk, Amos cleared his throat, swallowed, grasped the handle of a shovel, tilted it forward.

He should have said something to verify the old man's statement, but didn't know about skating freely through life thinking you were going to enjoy mansions later, in eternity. What about hell and doing wrong things, being a sinner found unworthy on judgement day?

As Joseph rummaged through old plastic buckets and baskets, Amos remembered the church services of his youth, the times he was petrified with fear. The end of the world was a disastrous event looming on the horizon, fire and brimstone raining down on terrified people who lived in sin. Certain he would be among them, he wept with fear.

But that was in the past, and he felt his life was better for having put all that behind him. If this old man burned with religious zeal, that, of course, was completely up to him. But Amos wanted nothing to do with it.

A FEW TOWNS over, his sister Cathy sat in her mother's kitchen, blind to the glory of early morning light, birdsong, or the brilliance of splendid blue skies, spring breezes, or flowering lilacs.

Her face was unnaturally splotched with smears of red, her voice hoarse and eyes swollen as she slouched in a kitchen chair, her hair uncombed. Even in this state, in the blinding early morning sun, she was strangely beautiful, in a haphazard, relaxed way.

Her puffy lips were drawn into a pout as she watched her mother fry bacon, slice bread for toast. Her head pounded, her throat was dry and raw, but she could never admit it. These days, her mother pounced on anything even slightly suspicious and drew details out of her as if she were a prosecutor in a courtroom.

"So, Cathy, how was your weekend?" her mother trilled hopefully, her eyebrows raised in starched anxiety.

"Good. It was good."

The sound of her own croaking voice was mildly alarming, as was the white lie. Besides, the smell of eggs and bacon made her want to heave.

"My goodness, Cathy, you have a frog in your throat?"

She cleared her throat with all the theatrics she could muster, flapped a hand to her neck, and said she was getting a sore throat, she'd started with it last night.

Instantly, her mother took flight, raced to the bathroom for sea salt, then to the stove to draw the teakettle to the front burner and flick the proper knob.

"Warm salt water, Cathy. But it has to be sterile."

She turned, waiting for her to begin. She lived for Monday morning, lived to hear her daughter relate stories of the young men who noticed her, the compliments they gave her, who was going to ask her out soon, the antics of her friends. It was hugely gratifying, this pretty young girl whose beauty and personality were everything she had never been, a gift in her middle-aged years.

When Cathy said nothing, she felt a desperation, premonition like a shadow on a clear horizon.

"Is something wrong, Cathy? I'll make you a cup of tea."

"Nothing's wrong, Mom. You always go off the deep end every time I don't start to chatter the minute you think I should."

It was a rebuke, and her mother's face flamed with embarrassment. "Oh, well, I just wondered if everything went OK."

"I told you it was good, so what more do you want?"

"True, Cathy, that's true."

And Cathy knew the ball was in her court, right where it needed to be. If her mother knew the truth about her weekends, she'd have a fit. How could she admit to herself things were starting to go awry, her group of friends definitely trying out their wings, stretching boundaries, experimenting with *verboten* (forbidden) things? He parents were so gullible, never even slightly suspecting what she really did on the weekend, which was laughable.

As long as she was picked up with a respectable horse and buggy and dressed decently, she was allowed to disappear on Saturday evening and arrive home the next night, as long as it wasn't too late. She'd arrive home with the comforting crunch of steel-rimmed buggy wheels on gravel, have a nice talk with her mother the following morning, and she was left to her own devices.

Sometimes, when her mother felt there was a wild quality about her, a questionable remark, a smattering of swear words, Cathy would find a Bible verse on the back of the toilet tank, a blue card with an encouraging verse from Psalms, causing guilt and a certain sense of not being good enough. But this was quickly shrugged off and the card pitched in the trash can below the sink.

Only a small posse of rebellious youth knew the truth about Cathy. In this group was a young man who carried an aura of intrigue, with the looks of a famous model, the build of Greek mythology, and a magnetic draw. He inhabited her thoughts, tugged at her will, his eyes holding the power to lift her spirits to soaring heights or plunge them to the depth of raw despair. She had always thought herself superior to the opposite sex, branding them all with the same scornful bat of her lashes. But this boy was different. And now, because of him, she found herself riding in forbidden cars with questionable safety standards, her voice rising, strident in her desperation to be noticed, every single teaching of her parents evaporating like evening mist in the brilliant heat of a hot summer sun.

Her mother, on this lovely morning, having been put back in her place efficiently, served the breakfast, swallowed the rebuke, and sat down on the opposite chair with a fresh cup of coffee laced with hazelnut creamer and three graham crackers from Trader Joe's, which lifted her spirits. She'd learned about Trader Joe's from Kelly, the woman whose house she cleaned every other Wednesday for thirty dollars an hour. She first rode to the store with Kelly one afternoon when she'd finished cleaning. Kelly said she had to run out and get some groceries, and would Lydia like to join her? And so they left the driveway in a sleek, black Infinity, an expensive car, she was told. She kept to herself the fact she didn't know the difference between it and, say, a Honda. But it did feel nice. At Trader Joe's, she appreciated the men in designer jeans and leather jackets, smiled at elderly women exuding wealth from every pore.

After that first visit, she returned to the store whenever she could. She was an oddity, of course, dressed in her Amish clothes, but she always felt like *someone* as she filled her cart with huge organic blueberries, spiced chai tea she really didn't like, but served to Dan sie Becca so she would know she'd been at Trader Joe's. Becca was the pinnacle of, well, everything—home décor, latest fashionable pattern for dresses, nicest covering.

Another afternoon, Kelly took her through the drive-through at Starbucks, explaining all the amazing drinks, including the seasonal ones. Lydia had a good sense of the English language and could speak fairly well, of which she was grateful at these times.

Perhaps she was being a bit worldly, but as long as she dressed within the *ordnung*, she figured she'd be alright, as far as God was concerned. He was loving and showed great mercy, didn't punish unfairly for a bit of pleasure.

She just loved nice things, and how could she help how she was made? She loved to enjoy the wages she earned fair and square. She worked hard and deserved every penny.

She looked across the table at her daughter, dunked a graham cracker, and tried to rush it to her mouth. But it fell back in with a splash, eliciting a disparaging look from her daughter.

"You're disgusting, dipping those things in coffee."

"They're so good."

She quickly dunked another one and waited, hoping she'd get lucky and be able to hear some information about her daughter's weekend.

Cathy yawned and stretched, then slumped. She sighed, got up, and filled a large tumbler with cold water from the gallon pitcher in the refrigerator. Her mother watched as her long slender throat worked, swallowing.

"How can you drink that cold water so fast?"

Cathy shrugged, asked nonchalantly, "What's today?"

"Monday."

"No, I mean, what are we doing?"

"Well, there isn't a whole lot. The garden's planted already. We could go to the greenhouse as soon as the laundry's done."

"I don't feel like poking around in a dumb greenhouse."

"Alright. Okay. I'll take Lavina. Isn't she up yet?"

Another shrug.

Well, her mother thought. Today was not a day to glean anything from Cathy. She got up, emptied the remains of her coffee, and went to check on her washer, the pride and joy of her life.

She had always washed her laundry in a used Maytag wringer washer, then lugged the semi-wrung-out clothes to the clothesline and hung them out to dry. Now, someone had learned how to convert an electric washer to battery, and she'd saved and saved from her cleaning jobs and purchased one, the best buy she'd ever made. She could throw in a load of towels, return to the kitchen and do dishes, sweep the floor, or whatever, while her laundry washed, rinsed, and spun itself half-dry. The only downside was Raymond having to see to the battery charge.

Some folks had solar panels on their roof, but Raymond said it was too expensive, too modern. Let other folks invest in it. He felt alright without it.

She often thought of Amos with a mixture of shame and pity, wondering if he was fit to make his own way in the world. She didn't believe for one minute he'd leave the Amish for real, switch from all he knew to a culture he'd never understand, let alone navigate through the world with cars and cell phones and computers so confusing he wouldn't make heads or tails of them.

Ach my, poor Amos, she thought. The word "fluke" came to mind. What fluke of nature had created someone quite like him? He was not given much, by all standards of outward appearance. And so big and ungainly.

Yes, it was a sorrow, having him out in the world, with all the selfish pettiness, the greed and unkindness. She was so glad she was Amish, taught to live a godly life, going to church every two weeks and hearing a good sermon, giving her life to Jesus at baptism.

How well she remembered her baptism, the holy pouring of water from the cup in the bishop's hand, taken into the church as a lifelong member. Yes, she would stay true to the end, had always imagined reaping the good harvest they had sown as parents.

And now Amos said he wasn't going to be Amish.

Well, it hadn't happened yet. Probably wouldn't.

She didn't feel like hitching up a horse to go to the greenhouse. She decided to call a driver instead, so she walked across the yard to the phone shanty, the bane of her life. She simply hated having her black box in the phone shanty, but Raymond was so conservative that way. Things had to be the way they always were, according to him.

Lots of women brought their black boxes into the *kesslehaus* (laundry and canning room). But not her. She nudged a barn cat out of her way with the toe of her foot, then plopped on the cracked vinyl of the phone shanty chair, dialed, spoke, set the receiver in place, squinted at the list of drivers posted on the wall, and dialed again.

No answer.

After the fourth phone call, Betty Wains said she'd go, so Lydia hurried back to the house to change into a belt apron and put on her shoes and stockings. She called for Lavina, who answered from her room and said yes, she'd go.

Dear Lavina, she thought. As different from Cathy as day and night. Lavina took after Raymond's side. His mother, God bless her, the sweetest soul she had ever been fortunate enough to meet. No matter what, she always approved of everything her daughter-in-law did, was mild-mannered, loving to a fault, like Lavina.

God was good, giving her these two girls, the light of her life. As she pinned her apron, she noticed the width of both sides of fabric on each side, thought she couldn't remember if this was the apron that fitted differently or if she had put on weight. She must invest in a digital scale.

She was tidying the kitchen when the welcome crunch of gravel sounded, and Lavina came pounding down the stairs, purse slung over her shoulder.

"Morning, Mom," she called, the way she'd always done, even as a waking toddler, her eyes swollen with sleep, already forming a smile on her lips.

"Good morning, Lavina. Ready? Oh, what about breakfast?"

"I'll be fine."

"Okay, come on. She's here."

THE GREENHOUSE WAS owned by an Amish family from another district and was about eleven or twelve miles away, Lydia guessed.

She was in the mood to buy flowers and plant them, so there was a spring in her step as she pulled a cart from the long steel-sided slot, put her purse in the spot for children, smiled, greeted acquaintances, and was lost in the profusion of color, the sheer complexity of choosing an array of perennials, shrubbery, and flowers to complement the landscaping she'd already done.

She opened her wallet and counted her cash. The amount was disappointing, but then, she'd gone for groceries on Friday. She could write a check, but the mortgage payment was due in a week, so she better hold off. It was the story of her life. Never enough money.

Other women had far more. Some of them did. Not as many here as in Lancaster, but still. She grimaced at the cost of geraniums, could only wish for those gorgeous pots filled to the brim with begonias, and what were those purple flowers? She had to have them.

She'd borrow money from Lavina. She wouldn't mind. She was on her way down aisle C looking for a worker, anyone to answer her question, when she ran into Levi Stoltzfus sie Annie, a woman about her own age, with eleven children ranging from toddlers to teenagers.

"Annie. Hello," Lydia greeted her, as warmly as she felt.

"Why hello yourself, Lydia," she answered.

She reached into her old-fashioned carpet bag to retrieve a wrinkled and soiled handkerchief, and swiped blindly at the baby's messy face as he twisted from left to right, screeching indignantly.

"Here, here, Davey."

But Lydia had seen the carpetbag—homemade, it had to be. Why couldn't she carry a purse like other women? It irked her, almost. Had she no sense of style at all? Or having had eleven children, she simply didn't care?

But Annie was talking, so she quickly switched her attention to her voice, away from the awful carpetbag.

"I told myself no matter how busy I am this morning, I must plant a few geraniums, a few purple striped petunias. The asparagus is ready, has been now for a week."

"That's nice. Do you have plenty?"

"Oh my, yes. Load after load of horse manure will do the trick. Just mulch as thick as possible."

She lifted the carpetbag, rummaged furiously for the missing pacifier, located it, and popped it into little Davey's mouth.

Her eyes sparkled with happiness, the thought of her asparagus and a few geraniums all she needed.

As she moved on down the aisle, Lydia became quite occupied with her thoughts. She should be like dear Annie, content with so little.

She always had a mental list of things she wished to purchase, and after one item had been bought, there were a dozen more waiting. And never enough money.

She sighed, blamed herself, compared herself with Annie again, and felt quite miserable inside, but only for a short time. She found a young girl dressed in a tight pink dress and black bib apron, thought to herself how ill-fitting the dress was, before inquiring about the purple flowers. As she followed the helpful girl down the aisle, she couldn't help but notice the dimpled elbows popping from the too-tight sleeves. She thought if she was her mother she would not allow her to wear such tight clothing.

But then, she had Amos. Amos was way bigger than that girl. Oh, how she cringed, buying his 3X shirts at Kohl's. He was just so big. Before she could stop herself, she felt a sort of gladness well up inside of her, a feeling akin to relief, that he was actually gone and someone else was looking after him.

Yes, she had loved him the best she knew how, even if it wasn't perfect. Surely, she had.

But she felt guilty, somehow, inadequate. Later, she discussed it with Raymond. She'd always been kind about Amos's size, right?

When her patient husband hesitated only a fraction, she felt the heavy hand of doubt. But she was restored to her normal self when Raymond said she'd done well with Amos and that it wasn't good to continually place blame on oneself.

Chapter 7

Amos worked every day, raking piles of debris accumulated over years of neglect. At first, he couldn't stay on his feet for the duration of eight hours, his legs starting out with a dull ache, his feet eventually feeling as if they were accosted by pinpricks, a pain he had come to dread. But as time wore on, he stayed on the job for longer periods of time, resting his legs and feet for a few minutes here and there as needed.

The front of the house had been transformed, an amazing feat and one serving the purpose to launch his true calling. He never wanted or aspired to any other type of work, which seemed a bit mind-boggling in itself. He had, as a child, detested helping his mother in the garden, hated mowing grass, fought with Cathy about whose turn it was to push that awful reel mower.

He was shown the art of hedge-trimming, taught the right angle to hold the trimmer. He had an instinct to find the best turn to shape a holly bush or an azalea. He was nervous, berated himself after the first few attempts, but as he progressed, his confidence grew.

He loved the property, never tired of gazing at the beautiful old house, especially now, with the porch furnished and cared for. Urns were filled with cascading plants, ferns sprouted and grew from deep ceramic pots. Wicker chairs, cast iron tables, comfortable porch swings hung from massive hooks, cushioned and blanketed, Lila hovering like an elderly angel, praising, encouraging.

At night, he often wept for no reason. He didn't understand the deep ache from somewhere in the region of his chest. He just knew weeping was a part of his life, the forming lump in his throat, the tingling of his nostrils, and the tears forming in the corners of his eyes. No one knew, and no one cared, so he allowed the tears to form, his chest heaving with quiet sobs.

The encouraging words Lila spoke in that low gravelly voice of hers were sometimes like an echo hours later, causing the lump to form. He couldn't handle words like that. He believed her, and yet what was believing? Did he honestly think her words were truth?

He was actually quite incompetent, slow, and disgusting, his T-shirt always soaked with perspiration. Stepladders groaned in protest, the zero-turn mower creaked when he heaved himself onto the seat.

But his hands, much to his surprise, were no longer white and soft. One day, he sat on a crate in the warmth of the shed's south side, catching his breath, and absentmindedly spread his hands. The backs of his hands were honey colored, his fingers calloused where the watery blisters had broken.

He felt his upper arm, shook his head. No muscle to speak of. And yet, when he flexed his arm, he felt the beginning of a bulge. Who knew what might develop if he kept working ten, eleven, even twelve hours a day?

His face was still pocked with scars, deep indentations, but the flaming color and pus-tipped pimples were gone. When he stood beneath the brilliant lights above the mirror, he would turn his head from one side to the other, his fingertips exploring the damage the infection had done.

Every two weeks on Friday he had his hair cut at his favorite barber. For reasons known only to him, he called Amos Fred. "It's Fred on Friday," he would say when he walked in, which always made Amos smile.

"You should grow a beard, trim it close, Fred. Would hide some of that ruined skin," he said, from some region along the back of the chair.

Amos shook his head. "Don't think I could."

"Sure you could."

And so on. They discussed everything, or rather, the barber talked and Amos made short comments, but there was always an easy rapport, a give and take without anxious moments of self-loathing, afraid of saying or doing the wrong thing.

"How's the old folks?" he'd ask, and Amos told him, which would launch him into a history of the old Brown place.

Afterward, Joseph and Lila would take him out to dinner. He was painfully ill at ease in a nice establishment, felt like a great walrus, rolling from side to side as he walked, following the elderly couple ahead of him, blushing, averting his eyes. He would eat as delicately as possible, then make a huge sandwich when he got home.

Tonight, they decided to go to the old hotel in Lakeshore, a community an hour and a half away. It would be a nice experience for him, they said, so they reserved a table on the lake, beside the windows.

He dressed in his best black jeans, a dark gray shirt, and used hair gel and men's cologne. The image looking back from the mirror was perhaps a bit hopeful. Obesity was prominent, but the face, lined with a shadowy dark beard, was in fact, a bit hopeful.

Lila told him he looked handsome, which made Amos squirm. The thing was, if he stayed in the secluded cave of hopelessness, it was easier, in a way, than the enormous, crushing weight of hope, of imagining himself to be normal, of having to attempt having friends, a social life, possibly a girlfriend.

Joseph drove on the interstate highway at the steady speed of fifty-five, never more than sixty. On his left, cars zipped by steadily, tractor trailers growled as they inched past, while Joseph hummed softly, tapping the steering wheel in time to his music. Lila smiled and spoke to Amos in low tones as he sat scrunched up like a giant stuffed bear in the back seat.

It occurred to Amos that he should practice driving with the old '79 Chevy truck Joseph drove around the place, hauling debris to the burn pile by the orchard. But he was a coward, afraid to get behind the wheel and take charge. He could barely maneuver the tractor properly, often missing the right lever, stalling out, always driving with his heart pounding.

He wasn't raised around cars and trucks and tractors the way English people were. He was raised with horses and one pony his father bought for him. Jack was a small, shaggy Shetland the color of oatmeal with a heavy mane and tail, and a deep need to run as fast as possible all the time. He was so afraid of that pony his stomach rumbled whenever his father said it was time to drive him again. He would plead, beg to be let off, his breath coming in short, hard puffs, running to the bathroom for relief.

Inevitably, he had to hoist himself on to the seat of the pony cart, his lips dry and tongue swollen with hyperventilation. The reins were put in his hands and he was off with a jerk, almost losing his balance.

The worst part of the whole ordeal was slowing Jack, turning on the road, knowing he would sense the homeward journey and increase his crazy speed again. He slid sideways on the slippery upholstery, desperately pulling back on the reins with all his strength, despair creating a deep and lasting memory. The part about his father standing in the driveway, bent double, slapping his knee at the hilarity of it all, was far too painful to think about, so he seldom did.

Cathy took her turn, eager, confident, driving with her hands held out to shorten the pull when Jack shook the bit in his mouth, her back straight, a smile on her pretty face. "Real showmanship," her father said. If they weren't Amish, she'd be in the Horse Expo in Harrisburg, he said. Shook his head and whistled.

And Amos slunk off, knowing he needed to change his clothes. Deeply ashamed, he escaped to his room, rinsing his under shorts before putting them down in the bottom of the hamper.

He found a bag of Fritos, stole them back to his room, drank water from the bathroom spigot, and wished he was like Cathy.

Before he knew the word "defeat," he was well-acquainted with the concept.

Amos was so lost in remembering that he was surprised to find they had already gotten off the exit and were cruising slowly along a smaller road. Lila patiently read the GPS map, and Joseph nodded, said, "yes, dear," and they turned to a parking lot lined with cars.

Suddenly, Amos was gripped with fear. He was rooted to the seat with wave after wave of anxiety. He watched Joseph turn off the ignition, heard him speak to Lila, his voice as if in a tunnel. Lila pulled down the little mirror and patted her hair, then reached for the door handle. They both opened doors, got out slowly, the way of the elderly.

"You coming, Amos?"

He nodded, gathered courage, reached for the door handle. He had to go. Dim lights, crowds of people, waiters moving among them. He followed, a sheep led to slaughter. He told himself he could do this.

And he did.

As dessert was served, he looked at his slice of cheesecake, excused himself, and made his way to the restroom, his stomach heaving. He arrived in time to deposit all he had eaten, deeply ashamed of the men who came and went. He averted his eyes as he rinsed his mouth and washed his hands over and over.

When he reached their table, he was distracted by the evening sun on the glassy surface of the lake, the sky above it like an artist's rendering. Dark blue, pink, rose, orange, and a soft yellow reflected in the lake, a kayak slowly moving through, the occupant raising and lowering the paddle as he propelled his tiny craft through the water.

When they asked if he was alright, he nodded and managed a weak smile. He slid into his chair and took a sip of Coke. He felt the color rush back to his face, steadied himself.

He became aware of the passing diners stopping at their table.

Joseph rose to his feet, extended a hand, said, "Mr. Larkin." Greetings were exchanged, small talk followed. Lila rose, hugged Mrs. Larkin, extended a hand to Skye, the girl from the orchard. A young man was at her elbow.

He hoped to be invisible, of no consequence, passed over. He was only the gardener, the groundskeeper.

"Yes, and this young man is Amos Beiler, the new occupant of our gatehouse."

Was he supposed to stand, or remain seated? He felt the beginning of panic, but shoved his chair back and stood, meeting the hand thrust toward him.

He felt like a thousand-pound lump of flesh, but mumbled a small hello. She stepped forward, and he had a hazy glimpse of tawny hair, a white sweater, a smile.

"Hello, Amos. I believe we've met."

"Yes."

"How's it going? I haven't seen you in the orchard."

All he could manage was a thin smile, a nod.

"Are you still trimming?"

"Uh, yeah. Yes. I'm just not in the orchard right now."

Mr. Larkin said the place was beginning to look the way it used to, back in its glory days. How about sharing your landscaper?

Everyone laughed. Skye looked at him, but he quickly lowered his eyes. There was talk of a coming rain, residue of a hurricane on the coast, and they moved on. Relieved, Amos sank back in his chair and accepted a cup of coffee, ashamed of the pronounced tremor in his hand.

In the safety of his gatehouse, he paced restlessly, unable to think of sleeping. Maybe it was the Coke and coffee. He should have had a water with lemon, the way Joseph and Lila had.

His thoughts were consumed with his stupid reply: "I'm not in the orchard right now." Of course he wasn't at that moment. It was a hopelessly Amish phrase, "*Net graut nah.*" The proper English phrase would have been, "I'm finished with the orchard for now."

Well, nothing could be changed now. He would always stand out, unable to fit into this new culture. He had never known you were supposed to stand up to greet someone. Why did they do that?

What he needed to do was read up on manners, learn how to navigate this maze of strange ways.

Who was the young man with the Larkins? He couldn't remember an introduction, but was certain there had been one.

He was hungry now, so he reached for the box of Wheaties, the gallon of whole milk. He added a generous amount of sugar to his bowl, then sat at his small table, shoveling cereal into his mouth with a tablespoon, greedily, snuffling from his nose. He had no idea he was eating too fast or too much, it was simply the way he ate when he was alone, his intense hunger driving him.

Satisfied, he pushed back his chair, burped loudly, and shuffled off to bed, where he collapsed, then lay awake as he relived his evening. He decided he was not made to be a social person. Not now, not ever.

Was it something he could change? Would a counselor be able to help? But he didn't really have to be a social person, did he? Being in the company of anyone was stressful, the way he never knew how to reach the proper words, to smile and reply in an appropriate manner. It was hard work, and it took a toll on his nerves.

He lay very still, breathed in and out slowly to relax, but nothing soothed his jangled mind. Slowly, he became aware of the sliding, scraping sound on the back patio. He held his breath. Yes, there it was. Silently, he rolled out of bed, grimacing as the bedsprings creaked, then stood, listening.

A dog? A larger creature? Cats made no sound. His heart pumping furiously in his chest, he made his way to the window, separated the wooden slats of the blind, and peered through.

His eyesight slowly took in the light and shadow, shapes of bushes and trees, the chairs and fire pit. Along the perimeter of the yard, where the rugosa grew untamed, he detected a moving shadow, darker than the trees. His fear was an electrical current through his entire body now. Cold chills raced up his spine. He was the watchdog of the property, supposedly, cowering behind window blinds, helpless and trembling.

He bit down on his lower lip as a figure emerged, a dark hood thrown over a man, the dark-clad legs scissoring as he moved along the hedge, then stopped. In an instant he turned, the black hood drawn well over his features.

Amos froze, afraid to move, afraid to show his face, or back away. What if he detected a movement of the slotted blind? He couldn't take his eyes off this man, for the safety of Joseph and Lila, as well as himself.

The intruder backed away, bent his frame, and vanished between the rugosa bushes.

There was no moon, only faint starlight, and no breeze, so the back yard took on a strange, ethereal quality. A portrait in gray and black. Amos was shaken to the core, afraid to go back to bed, afraid to remain standing.

Defeat caught up with him, held him in its maw, that gaping place in which he would inevitably plunge.

Coward. Chicken. Crybaby. Every cruel taunt he remembered rose to mock him the way it always had. Slowly he let go of the blinds, stepped back, and sank on his bed. He rested his elbows on his knees and put his face in his hands.

He would tell Joseph in the morning. He would leave. Resign. Quit. He wasn't fit for the job. He couldn't deal with a stranger prowling around. If only he was stronger, like the men he'd seen in the gym, but he was far too heavy to think about muscle building. Slowly, his thoughts slowed, cooled. His body relaxed, and he lifted his face from his hands, held out the covers, and rolled into bed.

In the morning he told the old man first thing, without procrastinating. He explained about the man, mentioned he thought he'd heard him once before, and finished by saying he really was not fit to be their guard.

Joseph pondered his words, stroking his chin, then shook his head in bewilderment.

"I have no idea, Amos. Who would need to prowl around the gatehouse late at night? I presume you have no mortal enemies?"

His blue eyes watched Amos intently, could see the lack of guilt, the softness in the small brown eyes.

"Not . . . no one I know."

"I believe you, son. Well, I'm going to let the police know. A man with a hood pulled over his face is up to no good."

Amos was ashamed it hadn't even occurred to him to call the police.

For a long moment, Joseph was quiet, then he clapped his hands, his wrinkled face breaking into a smile.

"I have the solution. Yes. A dog. We'll get you a dog."

Amos groaned silently. He did not like dogs. They all viewed him as a large steak, a tasty morsel of gigantic size. He was terrified of every large breed, afraid of middle-sized ones, very uncomfortable around the little balls of fluff gladly sinking their tiny canines into the backs of his heavy calves.

"But. I don't know if it will work," he murmured.

"Sure it will. We'll make sure it gets trained at a good obedience school. And it can stay with you in the gatehouse. It is exactly what we need. Yes."

Once more, Amos tried to persuade the old man a dog wouldn't help, large or small, but Joseph was determined to take care of this problem in his own way. He'd talk to Lila and get this new plan underway.

These days, Amos's work largely consisted of mowing, sitting on the gigantic zero-turn mower, wide swaths of fresh grass clippings creating a certain sense of accomplishment, the scent of new-mown grass a delicious aroma, the beauty of landscaping fully appreciated and enjoyed. As he drove at a good speed, he realized the heat of the midsummer sun, the blue of the sky above him, and thought he might be experiencing something close to happiness.

Perhaps life was like that. You couldn't expect a silver platter handed to you, one loaded with good things, but maybe you could find a small white flower in the thorns occasionally if you looked hard enough. A freshly mown lawn sweeping up to the shrubbery, the trees like benevolent guards, the beauty of the yellow house itself—all of it created a newfound sense of well-being.

He decided to go home and visit his family, if Joseph would be so kind to give him a ride. Joseph agreed enthusiastically, saying he would bring Lila, meet Amos's parents, then spend some time in town, leaving him to visit alone.

When the day came, Amos pushed back overwhelming apprehension, dressed carefully, and sat in the back seat, biting the inside of his cheek, pushing it in with a fingertip, watching as the landscape went by too fast.

Did he really want to do this?

The home place appeared as usual in the light of evening, the time when the summer's heat was beginning to lose its strength. The house seemed quite ordinary, smallish, the black shutters against the white siding a tribute to his mother's good management, the yard mowed and trimmed, the garden weeded.

There was no comment on the old couple's part, so Amos cleared his throat nervously, and invited them to accompany him to the door. He found his parents on the back porch, where his father stood eagerly, clearly happy to see him. Amos introduced Joseph and Lila, who both shook hands with him.

His mother, however, remained seated, her eyes wide in disbelief, her mouth set in a prim line of disapproval. Here was her son, insolently appearing on her porch, with English clothes and a haircut, a beard. Really? A beard. Well, if this didn't beat all.

Well, sort of a beard. A trimmed line of dark brown. He was as big as ever. He looked ridiculous in those jeans. Who did he think he was, coming here to his own home, his Amish home, like that?

Angry red crept to her face, and shattered pride oozed out of every pore. She wanted to slap him.

Joseph did not shake her hand, but gave her a small bow, while Lila's smile withered on her gentle face as she received the popping anger on the face of Amos's mother. Realizing they would not be offered seating, they turned to Amos and said they'd be on their way.

"Thanks," Amos said, looking deeply into Joseph's eyes.

"Yes. A few hours?"

"That's fine."

The silence on the back porch was broken by the slap of the wooden screen door, and Cathy sashayed across the wooden floor, her hips thrust forward, her head held high.

"Amos!" she shrieked, her voice high-pitched, mocking. "Whatever is up with you?"

He shrugged, smiled sheepishly. "Hi, Cathy."

"How did you find jeans big enough? Really? Why'd you grow that cheesy-looking beard?"

He smiled, tried to take the joke. She was just being Cathy and he could take it.

"That's quite enough," her father said quietly.

His mother sat up. "She wasn't doing anything wrong, Raymond. Amos, you have a nerve, coming here like this. Don't you feel any shame? You should. You are English, disobedient, gone the way of the world. Don't you feel any remorse at all? You have no love for us, coming here looking like that. You know what the Bible says, 'Cursed is he who grieves his mother.'"

There was nothing to say, so Amos sat in a lawn chair and lowered his eyes. The shame was so deep, he felt dead, as if his heart had stopped beating entirely. He shouldn't have come at all, should have known better. He tried to think of something to say, but his mind was a blank, black space, devoid of emotion.

"You have no idea how I have cried and prayed to God on your behalf, Amos. Do you think any of this is easy? Going to church and sensing the community's disapproval for us, because of you. All of our happiness has been replaced with sorrow, our days and nights are cold and hard, long with thoughts of you making our life miserable."

When she paused for breath, his father broke in quietly, his voice gentle. "Tell us about these Browns, Amos."

Amos lifted his eyes to his father's, blinked, then opened his mouth to answer, but the strident voice of his mother broke in.

"There, Raymond. Right there is our whole problem. You won't stand with me when I try to discipline this boy. You never did and you never will. Who wants to talk about that old couple when so much more is at stake?"

Her eyes flashed with indignation at Raymond's attempt to restore a sense of normalcy, a willingness to hear about the life his son had chosen. Amos felt caught, trapped between his mother's absolute disapproval and his father's weakness. From the corner of his eye, he saw Lavina slip through the screen door and sit beside her mother, her eyes wide at the sight of him.

"Hi, Lavina," Amos said softly.

She lifted a hand, said, "Hi."

"Mom, just chill for once," Cathy said, already tired of the drama.

"I'm not going to, Cathy. For once, I'm going to have my say."

What followed was a lengthy diatribe of put-downs, accusations, martyrdom, and heartache, a spoken word put to every negative emotion he'd come to know as he grew in years. He had never been good enough, had always been a disappointment, had always caused her shame and heartache.

He watched his father draw into himself, watched the drapes of weakness close over his face, and knew his mother was winning. Again. She always won.

"You have nothing to say, do you? You have nothing with which to justify your actions, right?"

A storm of words circled in his mind, harsh words kept locked away in his innermost being, words that should be released but would only heighten the suffering she was enduring. Yes, he had hurt his mother terribly, but hadn't she always hurt him? He felt the beginning of disdain, the rooting and sprouting of real truth, one he believed would always need to remain tamped down, buried under layers of his own hurt. For a shocking moment, he realized he hated her. He did not hate his father, or Lavina, but Cathy was in the same category as his mother. His jaw set, his eyes hardened, he slowly became aware of the awful growth taking over his mind.

He knew it was wrong, but had no power to withstand its steady advance. "Honor thy father and mother," he'd been taught. How? Was a person exempt from this if they weren't godly parents? He didn't know.

"Amos, seriously though, with your face. It doesn't look as bad as it used to. What happened?" Cathy asked, scattering his thoughts.

"I went to a skin specialist," he said, avoiding his mother's glare.

"Mm. Huh. I guess you had money to pay for it."

"I did."

"How much do you make?"

Cathy had the same glitter in her eyes, the same greed for money that his mother possessed.

"I make good wages."

Here his mother broke in again, berating him. By the time his visit was over, the overwhelming guilt and shame had turned steadily into disdain for his mother and Cathy and contempt for the curdling, sour-milk weakness of his father, who never rose to meet the thrown knives his wife directed at his son, leaving him alone as they were firmly embedded in his heart.

Chapter 8

After the visit with his parents, he threw himself back into his work. He took his driver's test twice and failed both times, anxiety getting the better of him. It was Joseph's urging to give it a third try that got him back behind the wheel.

As he sat in the small black car, the proctor in the passenger seat beside him, he told himself he was driving the mower, zipping around trees and along embankments. But he felt much too big, stuffed behind the steering wheel, his stomach pushed against it. The proctor helped him adjust the seat, tilted the wheel a bit, his face kind. Joseph had told him before how important it was to be comfortable, to take deep breaths, to calm himself. He'd told him to pretend he felt confident, even if he didn't yet. Sometimes pretending was the first step.

With every passing car, every stop sign, he told himself he was just on the mower, the sun bright overhead, the scent of fresh grass, that feeling of accomplishment.

And he did pass. He walked out of that building as a licensed driver of a vehicle in Pennsylvania. It didn't matter about his face looking like a frightened whale, it didn't matter he was the homeliest-looking young man who ever obtained a driver's license, he had nailed it. Even the parallel parking.

He waved at Jospeh, felt tears well up as the old man thumped his back and congratulated him. For the first time since he'd known Amos,

Joseph saw a real smile encompassing his eyes, changing his face completely, his appearance without the beaten demeanor.

As they drove home, he told Amos how proud he was, how he'd not given up. Amos told him he'd remembered his words about pretending to be confident and that it had made a difference.

"You know, Amos, what an attribute that can be. So many young people nowadays think they know everything. Not to be cynical or judgmental, but it's refreshing to know you took seriously what I said, and for that, my boy, I congratulate you."

And Amos felt his heart swell, his shoulders lift to new heights, and thought if there was a God that cared about you, he'd be a lot like Joseph Brown.

That evening, they had a celebratory dinner on the wide front porch, with Nancy going all out with an array of summer dishes. She was a skilled cook and seemed glad to have someone appreciate her work.

The evening was warm, but there was a soft breeze lifting the throws by the fringes, rocking the fig tree in its enormous clay pot. Robins hopped on the lawn and bluebirds fluttered in for mealworms from the wooden feeder. Sparrows and house finches chirped and twittered in the late-blooming lilacs, while the clear whistle of a cardinal broke through the warbling of a nuthatch.

Amos rocked slowly, balancing a plate of stuffed mushrooms and macaroni salad. He felt a soaring of his spirits, as if there was a glimpse of possibility somewhere on the horizon. He smiled at Nancy's constant chatter, but narrowed his eyes as the old couple brought him up to date on their search for a dog.

"I think you need to get one of those retired K-9 dogs. You know, the German Shepherds the police use," Nancy said, inserting her opinion in the usual way.

"Is that even possible?" Amos asking, hoping it wasn't. A German Shepherd was the last thing he wanted. He was deathly afraid of them. His uncle Leroy had one. When his large ears went forward and he lowered his haunches, lifted his nose, and let loose with a ferocious barking, it curdled his stomach and he felt weak and sick with fear. He loathed that crazy animal, took his cousin's taunting as a part of his own failure to be normal. He dreaded visits to his uncle's and stayed in the house whenever he could get away with it.

"I don't know. We'll check into it," Lila said, but he barely heard her reply, transported back to his fear of dogs.

Nancy eyed him from her porch on the white railing.

"You know, Amos, you need to get over yourself. Who doesn't like dogs?"

"Me," he said, grinning up at her. He considered another slice of carrot cake.

"Well, you were scared to death of the lawn mower when you started, scared of being alone at night."

"No I wasn't. Not till the guy came around. I'm over that."

Nancy laughed good-naturedly.

"No, you aren't. If you are, why are we getting a dog?"

And Joseph smiled at Lila. She winked at him, and reached for his hand. Amos caught this sweet gesture and felt embarrassment at the show of affection, something he had never seen between his parents, or parents to his siblings. He swallowed the nervousness the display of love invoked in him, knowing certainly he could never find himself in a relationship with a girl. He wouldn't know the first thing about it, and besides, who would ever want to hold his fat, clammy hand?

No one would.

THEY PURCHASED A German shepherd puppy, a ball of brown and black fur with bright blue eyes from an Amish farmer along Mercersburg Road. Amos felt his heart sink, every insecurity he had ever known rising up like hissing steam.

Joseph lifted the puppy from its crate, handed him over with both hands wrapped around his stomach. Clumsily, Amos held him. He smelled bad, his fur was matted. With all his heart, he did not want this dog. He didn't know anything about dogs, had no desire to hold him now, and certainly didn't want him in his house.

Amos was meticulous with his little house, a space all his own, and he created a sense of order and cleanliness around him. He was good with his laundry, kept his kitchen and bathroom spotless. This puppy would be nothing but mess, chaos, and disorder.

"He smells bad," he said drily.

"You can bathe him," Lila said sweetly.

Amos groaned, and they both laughed. It took them all afternoon to get the whimpering puppy clean, to establish the crate, the food and dishes, instructions on housebreaking, dos and don'ts of dog care reviewed.

He wanted to refuse so badly, but didn't know how. He knew the whole thing would end in defeat, same as everything he tried. Except the driver's license. A thrill of having done something right went through him like cold water, cleansing, replenishing.

That first evening he sat in his usual chair, reclining, the dog sitting in a corner, eyeing him warily. He should go to him, but he didn't want to touch him, really. He felt no affection for this odd little puppy, and felt sure it felt the same way toward him. Joseph shouldn't have made him get this dog.

He'd need a name, of all things. He couldn't think of a name, didn't want to. He'd have to be taken out, the housebreaking already begun. A crushing sense of responsibility weighed on him, so that he groaned as he heaved out of his chair.

"Come on, pup," he growled sourly.

The dog sat, staring.

Amos snapped his fingers, "Come on."

He tried to make his tone lighter, wheedling a bit.

The puppy made no move.

"Whatever," he muttered under his breath, then scooped him up and carried him to the door, opened it, and set him outside, half hoping he'd disappear. The puppy had no idea what he was meant to do, so he waddled around on his short legs, sniffed at grass and bushes, then sat on his haunches and stared at Amos as if to say, "What now?"

Amos reread the manual. "Don't bring him in till he goes." He sighed. This could take all night.

Much to his delight, the little fellow sniffed around some more, then did his business in a suitable spot before turning to go back in the house. Then, while Amos was in the shower, he produced a nice pile of dog doo on the rug by the door.

This was only the beginning, Amos thought, reaching for the roll of paper towels. He was caged for the night, and the minute the lights went out he set up a horrible racket, yelping and crying without any letup at all.

He thought of putting him in the small garage, or even outside. The night air was warm enough. He went out to open the door of his cage, fluff his blanket, try and settle him, but the minute he crept back to bed, the yowling started all over again.

Finally, after midnight, he reached in, lifted him out, carried him to bed, tucked him in a safe distance away, and turned his back. He didn't want to sleep with this puppy touching him. All that dog hair, and what if he had worms? Parasites. Could he help it if he didn't have a smidgen of affection?

He couldn't believe it when the whimpers turned into full blown yelps, as if someone had turned the volume on high. He groaned again, thoroughly fed up with this pesky little ball of fur and all it entailed. Reaching across the bed, he lifted him by his stomach, turned on his side and let him lie close to his stomach.

Amos sniffed, checking for dog smells, and found none. Beside him, the puppy felt as light as a feather, and he realized if he rolled over, he'd suffocate him. His breathing slowed as the puppy nestled against him, and the last thing he remembered was needing to make sure the dog got the required shots.

For the first week, he never got a full night's sleep. Neither did the puppy sleep in his cage. He slept with Amos, but no one knew, and he certainly wasn't going to tell.

He named him Fred. It was easy, the way he reminded him of Fred Atkins, the neighbor man when he was a boy. Those triangular blue eyes, the wide mouth. Fred suited him well.

He ran around the lawn and gardens as Amos worked, picked up ticks and fleas, dug holes until he was taught otherwise.

He was nothing but trouble, Amos decided, and that's why he didn't like dogs. But the old couple spent time with him during the day, allowing Amos time to do his work, and eventually things turned into a manageable pattern, although dog care was still only a duty, not a labor of love, definitely.

He purchased a used black pickup truck at a dealership in town, with Joseph and Lila's expertise. He had almost enough money saved, and set up the rest of the amount in monthly payments. He drove home very slowly and carefully, his heart banging in his chest.

Was this really what he wanted? He thought of the grief it would cause his parents. He didn't feel as if he was sinning behind the wheel of his truck, but perhaps he was. All he knew was the fact he did not want to live at his parents' home with its stupefying maze of hurts and embarrassments, navigating his way through one defeat after another.

And yet, they were his parents and his sisters, and he did love them as much as possible, which wasn't much at all. He was sorry about hurting them, he believed he was, but how could they ever realize how much they hurt him?

Shake it off, he told himself. *Get over it.*

Would he return to the old way eventually? He didn't know. He couldn't imagine going back, not as long as the old couple was alive.

He turned the wheel to the right as a car approached, still unsure of himself as it flew past, too fast for a county road. He had a glimpse of thick brown hair, eyebrows drawn in concentration, and wondered if it was the Larkin girl.

She was driving too fast.

As SUMMER'S HEAT turned into the beginning of fall, he was kept busy with painting, mowing, clearing woodland plots, and cutting dead limbs for firewood. Everywhere he went, Fred tumbled after him, yelping and crying if he couldn't keep up.

He was cutting brush by the orchard when Fred's ears perked up and he let out a funny yapping sound. He stopped, thought of Skye, but told himself he should not be harboring thoughts of her. She was way out of his league, his class, so why bother?

But he heard another dog bark and his heart leapt. Did she own a dog?

She came into view, and he broke out in a cold sweat. She did, indeed, have a dog on a leash, although he couldn't tell the breed. As she moved closer, Fred began crying in earnest, so he picked him up, told him to be quiet.

"Hey!" She threw up a hand, increased her walk to a near run, the dog straining on the leash. A large dog, but not a shepherd.

He stood, watching, holding Fred.

"Hi, Amos. Who is that cutie you're holding? Oh, my word. Let me have him."

She reached for him, her dog leaping and sniffing, held Fred to her face, and nuzzled him with her own.

"A shepherd? Really? Where did you get him?"

He took in her tawny, blond-streaked hair and pulled-down bill cap. She was close enough he could see a line of perspiration like tiny pearls on her upper lip. The day contained leftover September heat, and he knew his own shirt was soaked with the usual amount of gruesome sweat.

"Joseph and Lila bought him somewhere. They said we need a dog."

"He's a handsome little pup! You must love the company."

She searched his face, but saw the small shake of his head.

"No?"

"Not really. I'm not a dog lover."

"You will be. Hey, down, okay fella?"

She shoved down on her own dog's nose, and he promptly sat down, looking crestfallen.

Amos pointed his chin in the direction of her dog.

"What kind?"

"A labradoodle."

"Yours?"

"Yeah. He's great. I've had him since I was ten."

"Well, that's nice. This is my first time around."

"But you'll get used to him, right? They grow on you."

"I hope so."

"How old is he?"

"Uh, not sure. Seven weeks when we got him. Eleven weeks, now."

"Is he broke?"

"No. I keep the paper towel industry going, single-handedly."

She laughed, and he noticed her white teeth. She had a smattering of freckles across her nose, rounded cheeks, and a color of roses on each one. She was, in plain words, pretty. A pretty girl.

Not perfectly beautiful, but pretty in an airy, outdoorsy kind of way. Her appearance was the last thing on her mind, evidently, as he could tell she wore no makeup of any kind.

It was nice to stand close to her, to take in the details of her face. But who was he to allow himself the liberty of even this?

"Finally, you're talking. You barely said anything the two times we met."

"I didn't know what to say."

"Well, you got to meet my boyfriend."

His heart stopped beating, then resumed thickly.

"Oh. The guy at the restaurant."

"Yeah. Raul Scott. My dad's colleague's son. The one to whom I will eventually be betrothed and have the biggest bash of a wedding in the universe." She sounded anything but excited.

Amos raised his eyebrows. He could not think of anything to say, so he said nothing.

"If you're rich and powerful, everything you touch is at your command, including your daughter. He's the one my dad has chosen for me. Raul."

Amos cleared his throat. "Well, congratulations."

"I guess."

She lifted her cap, ran her fingers through heavy hair, a sheen on her freckled nose. Her eyes were pale green, shot through with brown lights, the colors of splashing water. For a moment, he felt lightheaded, tilted to the left, then to the right. He steadied himself, became very serious.

"Would you like to sit down? The grass here is pretty thick. Here. Let me put Fred down. He can play with . . . ?"

"Stewart."

He released Fred, who promptly investigated the large dog, sniffing, yipping like a bothersome child.

Amos lowered himself to the ground, wishing he wasn't so large, so overweight, so blubbery and unattractive, but here he was and there wasn't a single thing to be done about it.

She reached for a blade of grass, plucked it, and tore it to shreds. He noticed her clean hands, the trimmed nails devoid of color. Didn't English girls polish their nails with all sorts of things?

"Yeah, Raul is wealthy, super smart. Graduated from Harvard, all the honors. He's ten years my senior, works out every single day, eats nothing but salads and protein shakes. He's perfect. The catch of the decade. One little glitch. Every atom of my being resists him. They tell me love will creep up on me, and eventually I'll understand. But do you really think so?"

She was watching him intently, and he felt his own large, soft body scrunched up like a full bag of garbage, his small brown eyes like pigs' eyes, Cathy said. He was nothing, so there could be no attraction on her part. With nothing to lose, he was free to speak his mind, which was a new kind of freedom.

"I don't know anything about . . . these things." He felt the heat in his face. "I mean, I'm not much to look at, so I have no experience with, uh, with girls."

"Don't be hard on yourself like that," she said, tearing more grass into shreds and throwing them away.

"Besides, I'm Amish, or my roots are."

"So?"

"Well, if I would obey my parents, I'd come back to the fold and marry an Amish girl."

"Are you serious?"

He nodded, the guilt piling in on top of him.

"Will you, eventually?"

He shrugged. "Even if I did, I don't think an Amish girl would have me. I had a bad experience. I worked at a bulk food store and was accused of . . . of . . . you know, touching someone." He could hardly believe he was telling her this.

She looked up sharply, the bill of her cap shading the lights in her eyes. "Did you do it?"

"Of course I didn't. At that time, my self-esteem was lower than the ground. I had no idea how to stand up for myself."

"Is that why you left?"

"Not totally."

There was a pause, in which he wondered if he was dreaming. Nothing about this interaction seemed real.

"So, what's it like being Amish?"

He shook his head. "The Amish aren't all bad. I mean, there are some good things about being Amish, I guess. My family was just . . . I don't know. I didn't fit in."

"And you left because of them?"

She turned to watch the dogs. "Hey, Stewart! Easy there."

Amos laughed. "Fred's a scrappy little thing. He'll be okay."

"Do I detect a note of pride? You sure you're not a dog lover?"

She laughed, a sound like the wind chimes on his mother's front porch, only more musical.

"Sorry, didn't mean to interrupt. Why did you leave?"

"I left because I couldn't take it anymore. I'm obese, ugly. By some cruel twist of nature, my sisters are, well, they're both very good looking. My mother dotes on them. I always knew there was something wrong with me, I just didn't know what. I had a hard time in school. Dyslexic."

"You think that was a cruel twist of nature? Really? You're Amish and you don't believe God created you?"

He looked off across the fields, the cornstalks rustling in the wind.

"I know there is a God, but I guess it's hard to think He's anyone I want to know better. If He made me like this on purpose, seems kind of cruel."

For a long moment, there was no sound except the rustling of cornstalks, the thumps and rustling from the playing dogs, and the faraway drone of traffic on the main highway.

Finally, she spoke.

"Let me tell you. You're not alone. My parents are devout churchgoers, but distinctly not devout in real life. It's so messed up. My dad, the esteemed lawyer, drinks himself into a state of near oblivion every night at dinner. My mother can't stand him half the time, but we are the 'perfect' family." She flung a twig, shook her head, and got to her feet. "I don't have the slightest idea why I'm telling you this. My dad would have my hide, literally. I hate my life. But to step out of it is courting disaster, as the old saying goes."

He grunted, strained to get to his feet. "A certain desperation is what propelled me to leave, I suppose."

"I don't have that desperation yet. I mean, to stay with Raul, to do what my parents want me to, is the easy way. I'll be financially and socially secure, always have a nice house, live the 'good life.'"

"What would you want to do instead, if you could?"

"I don't know. Probably pack my things and move to Montana or Idaho, do a lot of hiking, get a job working outside. My mother would disown me, absolutely."

"I thought the English people allowed their children to be who they want to be."

"Not mine. I still have college to get through—at least two years, but maybe four or even six if I get a law degree like my dad. They have certain expectations, you know?"

She called her dog, snapped the leash to his collar, then picked up Fred, cuddled him, and handed him over.

"There you go, Freddie."

She stopped, looked at Amos, her gaze frank, evaluating.

"See you around, I guess."

He wasn't in his right mind, he thought later, but he heard himself say, "I bought a pickup. A black Chevy. Would you like to go for a ride sometime?"

She pursed her lips, narrowed her eyes.

"With Stewart and Freddie?"

"Sure. I have to tell you, though, I just passed my driver's test, so the driving might not be the best. I mean, I'm not that good at it."

She laughed. "Sounds exciting. Wednesday night at five? I have a date with Raul Friday, and probably Saturday."

"Yeah. Wednesday sounds good."

"Okay." She smiled, waved a hand, and walked away.

He squeezed poor Fred so hard he whined, then pumped his fist and would have leaped in the air if he was lighter.

He told himself there was nothing to lose. She was as good as married to Raul, so hanging out with her would just be a way to practice talking to a girl. Lord knew he desperately needed it.

As he walked back to the garage, he thought maybe there wasn't quite the divide between the two cultures that he'd thought. No parents were perfect, but some of them were real doozies. Most people weren't as good as they appeared.

Fred wriggled in his arms, so he set him down and he galloped off in his clumsy juvenile way, sprawling flat in the driveway when he veered sharply after a bird.

Amos laughed out loud, the sound frightening. When had he done that? Not for a very long time, which was very sobering indeed.

Chapter 9

Raymond sat beside Lydia, the reins loose in his large, calloused hands, the knuckle on his right forefinger already showing lumps of arthritis. He was thinking his own cheerful, contented thoughts as they moved steadily along the macadam on their way to visit his parents.

Raymond loved the month of September with its golden hue, the pumpkins ripening on the vine, the corn filled on each ear, a time of harvest soon to come. His paycheck had been a good harvest in itself and for that he was grateful as well. Life was good. He had a job he loved, coworkers who made his day, filled with conversation and camaraderie, a warm place to work in winter, a wife he loved with all his heart in spite of her tendency to be judgmental, a bit negative perhaps. But that was okay, he loved her still.

Cathy had been acting up of late, not a good influence on Lavina, but teenagers were often difficult. He prayed for them and let it all roll off his shoulders. Besides, archery season was coming, and after that, rifle season, and he was aware of the monster buck just behind the house.

He whistled low under his breath, then broke into quiet humming, thinking of what the chaps at work would say if he arrowed a ten-point buck on opening day.

His thoughts were rudely interrupted by the querulous voice of his wife.

"You're sitting on my apron."

He lifted his one buttock and she snatched it away.

"I can't reach my *schnuppie* (handkerchief) with you sitting on my apron."

He chuckled. "No, I guess not."

She blew her nose with a thunderous honk, lifted her apron, and put the handkerchief back in her pocket.

"My sinuses. I tell you. I declare we have mold in our house. You know, it's older, and setting against a hill like that, it could be damp between the walls."

"It could," he said, agreeable as always.

"We should move. I would love to have the Hutchison place everyone is talking about. You know, out on Ritter Road, there by the chicken houses. You know."

He nodded, thinking, *Here we go.*

"It's that nice rancher up that winding drive in the woods. You know where I mean. There's a shed on the property. We should go see it. Make an appointment with the realtor."

"We can."

"But the price is likely way beyond our reach."

"Could be."

"If Amos was at home giving us his wages the way other boys do, we could swing it. But not him. Oh, he has brought us so much shame."

There was no comment forthcoming, so she sniffed, hoping he might think she was crying.

"It's still so hard on me."

"Yes, I understand, Lydia. We never thought Amos, of all of our children, would be the one to leave our way of life."

Consoled by the solid agreement of her spouse, she sniffed righteously, then checked out Anna Stoltzfus's perfect grape arbor, mulched, limed, and all. Whatever with that ambitious woman, for Pete's sake. Raymond would never manage to build that kind of arbor, and as for Amos, well, he was gone. Really gone.

"Raymond, we should plant some grapes."

"We can."

"But you'd never get a nice grape arbor built. Did you see Anna's? We just passed it."

"I saw it. I was afraid you would, too."

She ribbed him with her elbow, and they both laughed. *Yes,* Raymond thought, *life is good, indeed. Enough rain to balance the sunshine, the way God intended, may God be praised.* He had a good wife beside him, and although he missed Amos, he secretly felt sure he was better off living on his own.

His own thoughts on the matter of Amos were top secret, between him and a loving Father in Heaven. The times he'd felt so bad for him, but was torn between him and his wife, the harsh decisions he often made, inwardly subjecting himself beneath her jurisdiction. . . . But what was a man to do?

He felt a kinship, a line humming with life to his son. Wherever he was, he hoped he felt the spirit of him, the longing that things might have been different. He wanted the best for him always. Whether he was English or Amish, Amos was his son, and he loved him.

He often thought about this thing of being out in the world. Yes, there were those who left the Amish, and by all appearance, were out in the world. But many Amish folks stayed in their culture, but their attitudes were aligned with the world, full of greed, only looking out for their own interests.

Who, really, was "in the world"?

Well, it wasn't for him to say. He was only a mere mortal, serving his Master here below, doing the best he knew, and for this feeling of contentment, he was deeply grateful, again.

As they turned in the drive to his parents' house, he thought of Amos, how he always enjoyed his grandfather, the gentle words he spoke, the shared humor most evident in him then. He supposed his father saw the potential in Amos, but kept his views and opinions to himself.

"*Ach* my," Lydia commented. "Mommy didn't get her cornstalks cleaned away. I should have been available when she needed me, but I'm always working."

When he stopped the horse, she was out of the buggy, her large bulk still quite agile, and Raymond felt a rush of pride. Yes, he had married a good woman, hardworking, concerned for his mother.

He gathered the reins, drew them through the ring provided for that purpose, and saw his father come down the cement walkway. Tall, his straw hat clapped on a head of white hair, his white beard like a bountiful curtain falling over his blue shirt, he had a smile on his face as he met Lydia with a hearty handshake, then walked on to Raymond.

"It's a beautiful day. So glad we're getting company."

"Yes. Lydia wanted to pay you a visit."

"*An gute frau, gel*, Raymond?" ("A good wife, right, Raymond?")

Raymond nodded vigorously, knew in his heart she was "an gute frau." Such an easy exchange between the two men, a life lived together in harmony, the appreciation of one another and their way of life the bond that held them. The ties that bind, unspoken perhaps, bringing love and trust, the peace and unity between father and son.

"Your horse worked up a good sweat," his father commented, following Raymond into the forebay of the small, tidy barn.

"Yes. He sweats easily, and the weather hasn't turned cold yet."

His father nodded, watched the horse sniff the water in the trough, then lift his head without drinking. Raymond led him to a tie stall, gave him a block of good hay.

They stood at the opened garage door, their hands shoved into deep pockets of broadfall trousers, saying nothing, contentment between them like a cozy blanket. The fields on either side of the short drive were heavy with corn, the stalks thick and rooted well, the leaves thick, each stalk containing one or two large ears, a testimony to the farmer's good management. Silo filling had begun, but these fields must have been planted late.

Cars and trucks moved slowly on the winding country road, and they heard the distant clopping of a horse-drawn buggy, the wheels grinding on the hard macadam. The sun shone overhead, creating dappled shade beneath the maple trees in the yard.

"So, Raymond, have you heard from Amos?"

"He came for a visit."

"Really? He did that? I'm glad. And it went well?"

His father's eyes shone with unshed tears, his mouth trembling with emotion.

"Well," Raymond said softly, "I would say it went okay. Lydia became upset at one point, but you know how a mother can be."

"Did he change his dress?"

"Yes. Yes he did."

His father's face fell.

The disappointment was a dagger in Raymond's gentle heart. Somehow, guilt lay heavily on his shoulders, knowing he was the father of a son who had broken the ties that bind, the first in a long string of generations reaching back to the earliest Anabaptist forefathers, a heritage honored and respected down through the ages. He had never imagined any of this and the shame of it suddenly left him reeling.

"Ya, Dat. It isn't easy. None of this has been easy. It just came on so suddenly. He never spoke much, if ever, about his feelings. I failed him, I suppose."

His father looked out across the fields of corn, then turned to his son. "Raymond, perhaps this is not the end of the story. He may yet see the error of his ways and come to repentance. Our prayers will be going to the throne of grace, believe me."

He placed a gnarled hand on Raymond's shoulder.

"And don't be too hard on yourself. I have never spoken a word of this to anyone, but our Lydia always had a way about her, just a bit, I don't know, harsh, perhaps? So if things were less than perfect with Amos, it didn't go unnoticed by us."

This unexpected kindness created a lump in Raymond's throat, and he swallowed hard, blinked back tears.

"I . . . it didn't always go the way I thought was best," he managed.

His father had said "our Lydia," which represented the acceptance of an in-law, the honor bestowed on his son's wife, which meant the world to him.

No matter what, he felt an abiding loyalty to his wife. When a man was torn between his spouse and his child, it created a puzzle, a maze of dead ends and bewildering avenues.

He would be forever grateful to his father.

In the house, he greeted his mother with a warm handshake, found the bright gaze from a lined and wrinkled face inspiring.

She was still in good health, and he found another reason to be grateful.

"*Vell*, Raymond, so glad you came for a visit."

Before he had a chance to answer, Lydia broke in.

"Yes, Mommy, if I didn't mention it, he'd never get that horse hitched to the buggy and get off down the road."

His mother let that go, saying it was time to get the coffeepot going, opening cupboard doors, banging drawers.

Raymond sank into a well-worn gray recliner, his hand going to the small table to his right, touching the stack of old German books. *Die Schrift*, *Luschtgärtlein*, *Gebet Buch*, well worn, with the tops of bookmarks in every one. Another stab of guilt. In his mind's eye, he saw his father thumb through the old books of prayer and inspiration, deeply rooted in the ways of his father before him.

He thought of his own reading material on the battery lamp stand between their recliners. *The Busy Beaver*, that heavy three- or four-hundred-page periodical arriving every week, chock full of Amish business owners' wares, spirited horses with bloodlines worth thousands of dollars, the latest off-grid inventions powered by solar or battery, women's businesses of Princess House and Pampered Chef, flower arranging and specialty baking, large colorful advertisements touting their own expertise.

It was all mind-boggling, these huge construction businesses with all the right words, needing men to help them grow. Everywhere there was prosperity, flourishing entrepreneurship, talented, hardworking

Amish men and women owning their own homes, acquiring second homes, a huge complex maze thriving in today's world according to the *ordnung* holding it all together.

There was *Game News, Outdoor Life, Reader's Digest,* and many more, some he barely had time to read. When had he last opened the *Luschtgärtlein,* the small black book whose cover title was translated in English as "A Garden of Desire"? Was there a time hundreds of years ago when a man's delight really were the old German prayers, the long gentle paragraphs of worship and praise to God alone? When Jesus Christ was their first love?

He felt a restlessness and his hands fell away, as if they had no right to touch the sacred little books. He knew within himself there was a falling away, a loosening of the desire to read the simple German prayers, the instructions of a godly life.

He heard the rattle of the popcorn popper, the two women chatting in the kitchen, heard his father's voice as it rose and fell, but his thoughts were a thousand miles away.

Perhaps it was his fault that his son had chosen an alternative path. He felt another pang of fresh remorse, wondered if his father had noticed.

"Yes, it certainly is a blessing I can still work at the spindle shop," his father was saying. "I feel as if Abner pays me much more than I deserve. He's a good boss, that man is."

He shook his head as if in bewilderment.

"Thousands and thousands of stair railings, anything you can imagine. Orders from all over the United States. I don't know where this will ever end, all this money being made among our people."

From the kitchen, Lydia's sharp reply was startling.

"I wonder where. It sure hasn't happened in our home. I work like crazy cleaning houses and there's barely enough to go around."

An uncomfortable silence hung in the room like a strange odor. Raymond shuffled his feet, cleared his throat, but did not have the heart to answer. His mother came to his rescue, cheerfully announcing the popcorn and coffee were ready.

Raymond felt a sense of well-being return as he drew up a kitchen chair, noticed the worn oilcloth on the table, the wooden Lazy Susan needing a coat of varnish, the Tupperware salt and pepper shakers long past the stage when they were pretty. Bottles of vitamins, pills, and capsules. A small glass vase containing a broken vine, one she'd put in water to grow roots. Post-it notes and a pencil.

His parents were old now, in their early eighties, still in good health, but most of all, they were content. They wanted nothing except their daily bread, a warm house, a working horse and buggy, friends, and family.

Lydia sank into a chair, helped herself to an overflowing bowl of popcorn. She thanked her mother-in-law for a cup of coffee, spooned sugar, added cream. Her mother-in-law turned to Raymond.

"Amos was home?"

"Yes, he was."

Lydia turned to his mother. "Such a shock, Mommy. Such an awful shock to see him with his hair cut so worldly. He didn't even wear his Amish pants. Jeans, with a belt. It's so terrible hard on me."

A hand to her chest, heaving a sigh, her eyebrows raised as she lowered her eyes, the picture of sorrow and humility.

"I imagine it is, Lydia," his mother said gently. "But where there's life, there's hope."

"Yes, of course. I can't see him lasting out in the world with the English, learning all those worldly ways. It'll be too much for him and he'll come back. We could certainly use a portion of his paycheck."

She sighed again, slurped her coffee.

Raymond said nothing, his thoughts going back to the small stack of German books beside the recliner. Without a doubt, the worldly ways were not with Amos alone. The world crept into their lives, brought the love of money, each man for himself, the desire for beautiful homes filled with the best of everything.

Oh, they were not exempt from the world, not at all. The only difference was the outward appearance.

On Wednesday evening, Amos dressed casually, telling himself it was only a ride in the truck. He didn't spend much time in front of the mirror, knowing the result was always the same.

Fred pattered around at his legs, getting in his path, dragging on the corner of the towel until he succeeded in removing it from the rod, chomping down on it, then rolling his furry little body all over it.

"Hey, Fred. Leave off, there," he yelled. Fred lifted his head, watched Amos intently, and promptly continued chewing the towel. Amos reached down to remove it, snapped it playfully, and laughed outright when he growled, bracing his stubby legs.

Maybe dogs weren't all trouble, he thought.

He drove carefully, felt a certain thrill in the world around him, in the surge of power beneath his foot on the accelerator, the control of his hands on the wheel. He loved it. Every moment spent driving was a delight, a feeling unlike anything he'd ever experienced.

To see the palatial home at the end of the drive was eye-opening, and immediately intimidating. A new home, two-story, red brick, annexes, and many different angles on the roof. Beautiful landscaping.

The home of a prominent lawyer, a wealthy family.

He parked in front of the four-door garage and waited. He felt like an intruder. Fred whined, put his paws on the door, his nose against the window.

His heart leapt when the front door opened and Mrs. Larkin walked through.

Her mother. He thought something might be wrong. On she came, her face set, her clothes impeccable. He rolled down the window on her side.

The eyes meeting his were cold, hard.

"If you are Amos Beiler, I'll ask you kindly to leave. Skye will not be available to ride with you this evening. And please don't try it again. Thank you."

Before he had time to collect his thoughts, let alone his voice, she turned on her heel and made her elegant way back up the flagstone walkway.

He had never felt such humiliation, an emotion he was well-acquainted with. He was so ashamed he could barely see to drive, but somehow managed to turn the truck around and head slowly down the drive, defeat his unwelcome passenger again.

Everything had been going so well, but here he was again, defeated, turned away, unwanted.

He didn't want to go home, so he turned right and drove aimlessly until he reached town, his stomach growling, his mind needing comfort.

He turned in at Burger King, carefully maneuvered his truck through the drive-thru, ordered two Whoppers and double fries, a chocolate shake, and parked at the first available spot.

He was starved, absolutely ravenous suddenly. He unwrapped the first burger, stuffed it eagerly into his mouth, followed by four or five fries, too hungry to open the annoying packets of ketchup. He barely chewed the first burger, snuffled and gobbled and sucked on the milkshake, before handing a tiny piece of the roll to Fred.

He sighed, then unwrapped the second burger.

Defeat and disappointment would always follow him, but at least there was the joy of food. Everywhere he'd been discovering more of it, places he'd have to try, intriguing names, neon signs of seafood and pizza, home cooking, Italian, Chinese.

After he'd eaten, he started up the engine, his stomach uncomfortably full, his mind telling him he was obese, had no self-control, a beast devouring his food. In his mind, he heard the voices of his mother and Cathy.

"You eat like a pig. Stop making those noises."

"Slow down, Amos, my oh. You're eating too fast. You don't even chew your food."

And he hadn't chewed. Didn't now. But there was no one to see, no one to hear, so if he wanted to enjoy his food, Fred wouldn't mind. He adjusted his stomach overlapping his too-tight leather belt, and drove along the streets, partly looking for anything of interest, and mostly not wanting to return to his empty house.

Everywhere, there were groups, couples, families, townspeople enjoying the golden hour of evening. He felt the need of friendship, a group his age, someone to confide in, to laugh with, to share his life. He didn't know anyone, had no idea how to meet anyone.

He wasn't English. He hadn't gone to high school, had never played competitive sports, had never gone to a prom or a party. He didn't drink and was frightened of alcohol and the downward spiral it might create. He knew nothing about it, really, only the small books some obscure printing shop had printed, the old stories of the dangers of substance abuse. Mothers and children fending for themselves while fathers drank away the paycheck. He sort of understood that he had an addiction to food, which was bad enough. He had no desire to wind up with an addiction to alcohol, too.

There was that gym. He slowed his truck, heard a raucous horn behind, and sped up, afraid of offending someone. But he circled the block, found a parking space beside the building, and pulled in.

Fred whined.

Amos wasn't sure if Fred would be okay by himself. He looked around, saw only a handful of cars, then reached for his dog, thought he'd ask if he was allowed in.

He avoided eye contact with passersby, didn't want to talk to anyone. Everyone smiled in Fred's direction, which made it that much harder to avoid them.

Yes, people, I'm huge and ugly, but my dog is cute. I know. The overhead lighting was blinding, brilliant, and he squinted immediately, his small eyes unable to take the intensity. His ears were attacked by the volume of thumping beats, creating a rhythm that crept into his mind, his body.

He was petrified, rooted to the doorway. He turned to leave, then changed his mind, turned back, took a few hesitant steps.

Everywhere there was motion. Men on treadmills, on bikes that stayed in place. Men lifting weights, muscles bulging from tank tops. Men with no hair, men with long hair tied in ponytails, with earrings and tattoos snaking down arms and legs.

He couldn't look at the girls. It was too shameful, the way they were dressed. He had no right to be here. This was the devil's lair.

"Hey, it's you!"

His heart leaped. He turned to flee.

"Hey, wait. Whatcha got?"

He stopped, turned, Fred's face stuck out from under his arm.

"It's Amos, right? Remember me?"

"You're Scott."

"Yep, sure am. Who's the dog?"

Amos shrugged. "Fred. Just got him."

"German shepherd?"

"Yeah."

Scott spread his arm. "Come on in. Take a look."

"I just did. I don't think this is a place for me, but thank you."

"A big guy like you? It's the perfect place. You want to live your best life physically, now's the time to start. I'd love to be your trainer. For one, I think you'd have the work ethic, with your background."

Amos looked around, the awkwardness of the situation written all over his face. He felt so much shame, his stomach churned. This place was the opposite of his entire upbringing. This was not modesty, the music was not a soft, swelling sound of Christian singing, the tattoos and long hair were a horrible breach of all he knew to be right and good.

"I can't."

He thought of exposing his soft white body, wearing only the shorts and T-shirt. Absolutely not. The glaring white lights. He'd be laughed right out of the room.

"Tell you what. Would you show up for an hour in the morning before opening? We open real early, but only a couple folks show up at five. Old guys, mostly. You can wear street clothes. It's fine, I understand, really."

He thought of the perspiration, the inability to do anything without puffing like a steam engine. He watched the men lift the weights, straining, accomplishing every goal they set for themselves.

He wanted to be like them, wanted to be fit and strong and normal. Scott saw this in his eyes.

"You know, it's your choice, Amos. If you are happy to be overweight, that's okay. It's normal for many people nowadays, and if you have the confidence to carry it off, good for you. But if I'm not wrong, I don't think you do."

Chapter 10

Amos refused to meet his eyes, felt resentment ballooning in his chest. Scott reached out for Fred, but Amos turned away, mumbled about having to get home, and left.

But the sight of that gym stuck in his mind. He worked hard as the leaves changed color, planted a few arborvitae by the backyard fence, and thought about the gym, wondered how it would feel to be strong and fit, to go through life with the confidence of a fine physique.

Nothing occurred during the nights, in spite of lying awake sometimes, listening for the sound of scraping footsteps. Joseph and Lila did not seem too concerned, and Fred afforded a form of security, even if it was a soft, cuddly, and very funny one. More and more, he found himself laughing out loud at the dog's ineffective yapping and yelping, falling over rocks and into puddles, running after squirrels and rabbits without coming even close to them, then walking away as if he was responsible for ridding the whole property of danger. Dogs were not all trouble and responsibility, even if he'd cleaned up his fair share of messes.

He missed talking to Skye. They had never exchanged phone numbers, and she wasn't on social media, so no matter how he scrolled through his phone, there was nothing.

As the weather turned colder at the end of October, he felt a certain restlessness, a longing to return home. The winter loomed before him and he found himself more often alone, thinking thoughts of his childhood, wondering about Cathy and Lavina.

He missed his father, in a way, but only if he gave in to the knowledge of his goodness, his genuine caring. He knew he'd hurt them all by leaving, but mostly his father, and he wanted to make it right as much as he possibly could.

Would his second visit home prove as disastrous as the first? He had to try, so after an early evening meal, he dressed in a navy blue button-down shirt, one an Amish man might wear, and a clean pair of black jeans and drove across the still colorful countryside to his former home. Everything appeared unchanged, still as neat and manicured as ever, the garden cleaned and tillage radishes planted.

What was this? A Re-Max sign? His parents' home was for sale. Questions raced through his mind. He parked his truck at the end of the drive, out of respect, and walked the remainder of the way to the porch.

He lifted his hand and knocked.

The door was drawn open, his sister Cathy's pretty face behind the screen door. Curiosity was the only emotion.

"Hi Cathy. Can I come in?"

"Sure."

His eyes adjusted to the dim lighting from the battery lamp, then his mother's form came from the direction of the bedroom, Lavina behind her.

"Amos! What a surprise. How'd you get here?"

His mother's face registered curiosity, but not pleasure.

"I drove. Parked my truck at the end of the driveway."

"You drove? Your own vehicle? *Ach*, Amos, how did you get your license?" She didn't wait for an answer. "You know it's wrong. God will not be mocked, did you know that? Surely your conscience will wake up soon."

Cathy told her mother to be quiet, for once. She wasn't going to help the situation yapping on like that. His mother resorted to soft sighs of sorrow, punctuated by a few dabbing motions in the vicinity of her eyes.

There was an awkward silence, in which Lavina inserted a quiet "Hi, Amos."

He smiled at her, and she smiled back, shyly, as if she was afraid he would not notice her.

"How are you, Lavina?" he asked.

"Good. I'm fifteen now. Out of vocational class."

"That's great. I got a dog," he said quietly.

Her eyes lit up.

"Where's Dad?" he asked.

"He went to the gun shop. Something about arrows," Cathy answered, glancing at her mother, who was still displaying her sorrow.

Her eyes raked over his appearance. "You haven't lost weight. I thought you'd be thinner by now, all that yard stuff."

She sniffed, told him to sit down.

He lowered himself into a kitchen chair across from his mother, getting a closer observance. He noticed the too-tight sleeves, the dress sewn shut where a row of snap buttons used to be. Was she keeping up with the latest style of dress? He thought he noticed a certain thickening of her arms and shoulders, or perhaps it was just the tight sleeves. She appeared unhappy, intensely so, but that could be blamed on himself. She must have aged, the way her eyes appeared hooded, smaller. Hadn't it only been a few months since he'd last seen her?

He waited for a few seconds, tried to feel what he knew he should be feeling, the love for a mother, a special love everyone was expected to have. He felt nothing.

"Did you have supper, Amos?"

This was from Cathy, who had taken over as spokesperson on account of his mother who was now refusing to speak, an old control tactic seemingly working well for her, the way his father always responded by snapping to attention and doing anything in his power to draw her out of "the blues."

"I ate, yes. Nancy sent leftover chicken and dumplings to my house."

"Who's Nancy? You got a girlfriend?"

Cathy lifted a hand, spread her fingers to inspect her manicure.

Pink nails? What was this? But he said nothing.

"Well, do you?" she persisted.

"No, I don't. Nancy Farmer is the housekeeper, cook, whatever, up at the big house. I live in the gatehouse."

"Cool."

Lavina smiled again, looked away.

"You should take me and Lavina to see your place," Cathy said unexpectedly.

His mother shot her a look, "Absolutely not. You're not driving with him."

"He's not *in the bann* (being shunned)," she retorted.

"I don't care. He's disobedient, does not abide by our rules, so we won't have him misleading you."

Agitated, her pouting forgotten, she leaped to her feet, almost upsetting her chair, then made her way to the sink, lifted a dishcloth, and began wiping the already clean counter, a gesture Amos was fully used to. When she became upset, which was quite frequent, she had to be doing something with her hands.

"I didn't come here to mislead anyone. I just thought I should check in, say hello."

Her answer was to turn her back without speaking.

Lavina looked directly into his eyes, raised her eyebrows. He knew she understood, would continue to understand.

"Why is there a real estate sign at the end of the drive?" he asked, to any of the three who would or could answer.

"Why do you think? Duh," Cathy said, her expression familiar, a tired patience for his stupidity.

"I know, but why? Why are you selling?" he asked.

His mother turned.

"We have first chance at a place I've always wanted. This house actually has mold in it, in the walls, and that's why we're always sick. Old houses often are that way, especially built into the side of a hill like this. Now, if you were still at home the way you should be, we'd have your wages to help make the payment. We really need you to come home."

Her words sank in like poison making its way into his bloodstream. She only wanted him for his money. She despised him. And it drove her mad that she could not control the way he thought, the way he lived, or the fact it didn't seem to bother him.

She proceeded to talk about her dream house, how she would paint the rooms, take up carpeting, how beautiful the view was. Suddenly, she pivoted to a new attack.

"Amos, you must think seriously about your future. You must. How can you marry an English girl? Think of the consequences. Think of the bad seeds you are sowing and eventually have to reap. Why wouldn't you come back within the safe confines of the Amish church?"

Almost, he spoke the truth. What was here for him? What had ever been here? In school, at home, in church—everywhere he went he was looked down on, ridiculed, made to feel like a failure.

Joseph and Lila were of the world, according to his mother, but had they ever spoken an unkind word? He had never felt anything as close to what he imaged real love was until he came into their home. He knew he had a lot of things to figure out. He had some awareness that the anger and bitterness he felt welling up in him would need to be dealt with. But it was clear to him that moving back home would be a step in the wrong direction.

"Mom, I'm trying to figure it out. You're so black and white with this. Your way is the only way. I'm not sure about anything at this point. Not even God."

"You're in a dangerous position," she began.

"Who is in a dangerous position? Us, with that real estate sign down there? Oh, Amos!" His father clapped a hand on his shoulder, his face alight. "You're here. I sure was thinking of you. Seems as if you know when I start missing you too much, don't you?"

He left his hand lingering on Amos's shoulder, like an incomplete hug. Amos smiled up at him.

"Hello, Dad. Yes, we must know when it's time for a visit. Both of us."

He almost choked on the incredible amount of love he felt for his father, which only made the guilt for hating his mother worse. No one must ever know the deep recesses of his mind and heart. It was far too shameful.

He saw the jealousy in his mother's eyes, felt the sizzle of her anger, put up the shield it would take to survive the explosion of words sure to follow. But the shield was as ineffective as ever. The words came, lacerated his heart, cracked open the wounded places from his childhood, creating even deeper pain.

She concluded her tirade by saying he would never be allowed to drive that black truck up their drive. It would stay parked by the road. Always. What were people supposed to think, driving by knowing their son was parked right by the door with no thought to the rules of excommunication and shunning?

Patiently, his father explained the fact he had never joined the church, therefore, no shunning was needed. He was free to come and go. But he backed down when her hysteria escalated. Cathy threw her hands in the air and said her mother needed help. Lavina sat hunched and afraid, the feud beyond her understanding. And Raymond folded like an accordion the way he always did, while Cathy and her mother reigned.

He told them goodbye as respectfully as he could manage. Out on the porch, he felt his father behind him. He turned, only the light through the window illuminating them both.

"Amos, I'm sorry for all the times I didn't stand up for you. Your mother is a driving force, and I often failed you. Still do."

How close he came to falling apart that night, he often thought in the coming years. His father's confession, his truth, took down every defense, chipped away at the hard reserve of strength he'd built up for survival. He didn't speak poorly of his mother, but merely stated the truth, admitted his faults, and said it all in the light of love.

He drove away that night, turned the radio up loud when a song about a father and son came on, then was caught up in so much copious weeping he had to stop the truck as his shoulders heaved with sobs. Somehow, somewhere, he'd be alright. He could feel it. He didn't know what "alright" was, he only knew whatever happened would be okay.

His father loved him.

He went for a walk a few weeks later, on a Sunday, feeling restless or in need of someone to talk to. He wasn't sure what was wrong. Fred was on a leash, gangly and uncoordinated as usual. The wind was cold in his face. Brown leaves skittered across the road, and dry yellow grass nodded in the stiff breeze.

"Hey, no, Fred. Huh-uh."

He bent to extricate an acorn out of his mouth. He was not in the mood to hear him throw up by the front door during the night. One of the worst parts of dog ownership.

Joseph and Lila had gone to church, then to the next town over to meet friends for lunch, which would take most of the afternoon.

He had given up on Skye, accepted the fact she was engaged and that her family didn't want her spending time with him. He hadn't worked up the courage to join the gym, although he thought he might come winter.

Since he had his own vehicle, he ate out three or four times a week, mostly inexpensive fast food or pizza. He could easily consume a large pizza by himself, give or take a few slices, and never ordered only one burger and fries, but two, and always with a chocolate milkshake. He felt like food was all he had at this point in life.

Back at the gatehouse, he took off his Redwing boots at the door, unhooked the leash, and heard a distant yell. Turning, he saw Skye's familiar walk, the same cap pulled low on her head as she came down the drive from the big house. As she drew nearer, he could see her windblown good looks, her cheeks rosy with the cold, her nose red with a splattering of darker freckles.

"I was hoping I'd catch you. Aren't the old folks home?" Her breath was coming in short gasps, as if she'd been running.

"Actually, they went to church, then meeting friends this afternoon."

"Okay. I left an invitation to Thanksgiving dinner between the two back doors. I guess they'll find it."

"Likely they will."

He kept looking at her, even when they stopped talking. He drank in the color of her hair and face, the green-gold-brown flecked eyes, and became speechless, the wonder of seeing her again far beyond his expectation. What if he could have a girl like her? Wouldn't you always remain happy to love and serve her?

"You have to get home?" he asked.

"Soon. Raul and his parents are taking us to Harrisburg. Some theatre. Again."

"Would you like to come in?"

"Just a peep, then I have to leave."

"Good. Okay."

She picked up Fred, who responded with whole body wriggling, yipping excitedly. She laughed, said he was getting heavy, then kicked her Muck boots off and looked around, her eyes wide.

"Oh wow, Amos. This is the cutest thing I have ever seen. And you keep it so clean. It's incredible."

"Thank you," he said very quietly. He was unused to compliments, but he'd heard English people always say thank you and understood it was good manners.

"Can I make you some coffee?"

She glanced at her phone. "It's only eleven. Sure, I'll have coffee."

He set a cup below the spout, plunked a cup in his Keurig, and brought creamer.

"You're, like, the best housekeeper ever. I had no idea."

"I love my home. I'm grateful, so I try and take care of it."

"You're wonderful. A great guy."

Suddenly, his mind was in a turmoil. He looked at his coffee cup as he stirred the creamer, watched it turn color. Finally, he looked up.

"I didn't know if I'd ever see you again. Your mother was not happy when I came by that time."

She looked up, bewildered. "What?"

"You know, that Wednesday night when we were going to go for a drive?"

"Yes?"

"When I pulled up, she ran out and told me to leave."

"She told me you'd called. Said you couldn't make it."

"She did?"

"You mean you were actually at my house?"

"I was. Well, the driveway."

She took a deep breath, looked at the stove, the microwave.

"I can't believe she lied to me. Though I guess I understand why. I have to buckle down and get serious about Raul. And I'm back in college now. Two years left. I'm just home for the weekend, but I won't be back again until Thanksgiving. I'll miss you."

"You will?"

There was silence, the metallic sound of spoons, coffee sipped. Finally, she sighed, opened her mouth to speak, thought better of it, then opened it again and said, "Amos, I don't know what it is about you, but . . ."

She swallowed, suddenly nervous.

"I think about you much more than I should. There's something so sweet and vulnerable about you. I find myself comparing you to Raul."

She lifted a hand to stop him before he spoke.

"Raul is a great guy. He's the kind of guy any girl would be lucky to marry. But the thought of riding around in your truck with the dogs brings me much more happiness than riding in his Lexus."

"But . . . look at me. I'm a mess. I'm nobody."

"You're somebody to me."

"Maybe you just want what you know you can't have. A rebellion of sorts. Against your controlling parents."

She shook her head.

"No, it isn't. I put lots of thought into it, and I came up with this. When I'm with Raul, I feel like I have to be perfect. If I marry him, I'll always have to wear perfect clothes, eat health food, live in an immaculate house. It's not who I want to be. With you, I feel . . . free. Like I can be myself, you know?"

"I do." His mouth was dry, his heart beating too rapidly, his mind telling him none of this was real. Not for him. This would never happen for him.

"Anyway, I'm too chicken to disappoint my parents. Not yet, anyway. But can I have your number, just to keep up with the old neighborhood stuff?"

"Sure. Of course."

They exchanged numbers, finished their coffee, and she rose to her feet.

"I have to go. I was only dropping off the invitation."

He gathered every ounce of courage he possessed. "Well, I must tell you, I value our friendship. You've been a bright spot in my universe," he said softly, smiling down at her.

"See, that's what I like about you so much. What other guy would say something sweet like that?"

"Thank you."

"You're welcome," she said, laughing a little.

She lingered a moment more, bending down to stroke Fred.

"I have to go. Goodbye, Amos." She scooped Fred up and kissed the top of his nose. "Goodbye, Fred."

She looked up at Amos, blinked, and was gone, the door closed gently behind her. He leaned against it, sighed deeply, realized his knees were weak. A real man with real courage would have held her hand, perhaps hugged her.

There was a sharp knock on the door, and he was sent backward. A blur of sun-streaked brown hair.

"I'll never know if I don't ask. Could I kiss you goodbye?"

He was frozen, but he felt her move into his arms. Did he put them around her, or did he keep his hands on her shoulders? He had to lower his face, but she found his mouth perfectly, and did not break away immediately. She stepped back, looked into his eyes, then placed her fingertips on his scarred face.

"Goodbye, Amos."

His voice was hoarse, thick with the emotion as he said goodbye.

"Call me. Send me texts."

"I will."

He reached for her hand, held it to his lips and kissed it, then released her with a smile.

She moved through the door, then walked backward, waving.

He went to the bathroom mirror, examined his face where she'd touched it. What if her touch would change him forever, like a fairytale? He searched again, but he truly was only Amos, now and forever, no more and no less.

But he knew then with rock solid assurance that he would go to the gym, improve his eating habits, make something of himself. He could do it. He had a few attributes in his favor, according to Skye. Cleanliness, for one.

He was, quite simply, blown away, blown sky high. "Skye" high. He would never be the same.

Thinking of his mother brought him back to reality, plummeting back to earth. Skye's family. Raul. Who was this Raul? Was it wrong for him to have allowed Skye to kiss him when she was engaged to another man? Besides, could he truly sever the ties to his Amish heritage forever? It was a serious step in the wrong direction, according to every Amish person on the face of the earth. It was the final blow to parents, the one thing they knew had taken their son forever.

Could he do this to his mother? He could. His father? He didn't know.

He paced his small house, alternatively swung between wild hope and deep despair. He wouldn't do it. She'd find another man at college, or she'd choose to make her parents happy and marry Raul.

Where did a person turn? Did God know about his life, and if He knew, did He care? Who was God? Was He real?

But by Sunday evening, he'd reached a more restful place. They were not dating, not committed at all, so he'd just have to be patient and see how things played out.

No one else knew about their meeting, their conversation, the kiss, but the thought of it was like a sweet savor to his soul, a spontaneous joy leaping from nowhere, coloring his existence with vibrant hues. He smiled, he danced across the living room, and never once did he feel unfit. Someone believed in him. The thought was a boost to his whole life, as if he'd had a terminal illness and was handed a cure, a miraculous potion of hope and healing.

Chapter 11

Winter days meant time on his hands, a certain lassitude holding court over his life, and he found himself increasingly restless. When the month of November slowly moved toward Thanksgiving, his stomach was in painful knots, knowing Skye would be back for the holiday. Joseph and Lila would be seated at their table, and he'd be truly alone. He'd left a message, texted her twice, and hadn't heard back, which left him confused and a little sad.

He sat at the kitchen island with Nancy Farmer at the stove where she was frying eggs.

"You mark my words, Amos, no good will ever come of those Larkins sending that girl off to college. Lila told me about this Raul guy. She don't want him, so why, in this day and age, ain't she allowed to make up her own mind? You mind if I fry up last night's potatoes?"

He shook his head, watched a house finch outside on the Japanese spruce, saw the lowering skies as the wind swung bare branches.

"I know none of it's my business, and I keep my mouth shut, but powerful, rich parents are used to control, control everything, and it ain't gonna work. Joseph and Lila invited for Thanksgiving dinner is just the beginning of weaseling their way into their good graces. I bet you they want to buy this place, convince Lila and Joseph to move into some kind of old folks' home."

Amos blinked, moved his coffee cup aside, as if to make more room for his answer.

"But would they sell?"

"Anyone sells anything with enough money stuck under their nose."

She took a fierce slurp of coffee, choked, wiped her mouth.

All at once Amos realized how much he loved this place, how much he loved his home, his job, the lawns and gardens a domain of his own.

He felt his stomach plummet, thought of storm clouds gathering.

"But the old folks are healthy, right? I mean for their age?"

"Nobody's healthy at eighty-five and six. I know that for a fact. Have you seen their stash of meds from the pharmacy?"

"I guess."

She served him a large plate heaped with fried potatoes, two sausage patties, and five fried eggs. As she buttered toast, she told him nothing in life was permanent, you couldn't bank on anything except death and taxes.

The kitchen door swung open, and Joseph shuffled into the room, his house slippers making no sound, his back bent in the way of the elderly. He was dressed in his usual style, a button-down shirt of the highest quality, good trousers with a belt, his pleasant face lined with good humor.

"Good morning. Nancy, my dear. And Amos. How are both of you this fine morning?" he rasped, his voice unusually hoarse.

Nancy gave him a shrewd look.

"What's with the voice?"

"Just a bit of a sore throat. I came for a cup of tea, if you'd be so kind."

He placed a hand on Amos's shoulder.

"Good morning, Joseph," he said, swallowing a mouthful first.

"A hearty breakfast for a young man, I see. How I miss the appetite I used to possess. Brad and I would put away a pile of good food in our day, when Lila would cook."

"You need to gargle that throat with warm salt water, I'm telling you. You don't want to miss the dinner at the neighbors."

Joseph completely missed the sarcasm, as he nodded.

"No, we don't want to do that. Lila and I are truly honored."

Nancy gave Amos a look of "I told you so," then raised her eyebrows. "You better stay inside then. No going out in this stuff."

She spread an arm in the direction of the window, her bare arms flapping as she did so. Amos thought of his own mountains of pale flesh, his face, neck, and arms tanned, but nothing else.

He speared the last of his toast, ran it around the remaining egg yolk, wished for a stack of pancakes with butter and syrup. But he knew he'd had enough.

Joseph inquired about Amos's plans for Thanksgiving, but he only shook his head. Going home would be nice, but he knew the holidays were spent with relatives in Lancaster or some sister settlement in adjacent valleys. He would not be welcome there. He was an outsider now, an "*ungehorsam sohn* (disobedient son)." Amos had made a break, a rift in the family, one that would never heal entirely, so it was better he stay away.

"Do your parents want you to be at their dinner?" Joseph pressed on, but kindly.

"No."

"Have you asked?"

"No."

"But perhaps you should, Amos. Making that small effort might be worth it."

"I doubt it. They spend holidays with relatives."

"Well then, I'll ask the Larkins to include you. You don't want to be alone on Thanksgiving Day."

"Please don't. I'll be okay on my own."

He felt the dreaded color rise in his face, kept his eyes averted, a hand going to his forehead to wipe imaginary particles.

"But you've met Skye and her fiancé. He's a very nice young man. I understand he's a lawyer in his own right, or will be. What an accomplishment."

Nancy let out an expulsion of air, not quite a snort.

"You think? I say it's just another rich guy getting richer. Nothing to the rest of us who are housekeepers and landscapers. Right?" She jabbed Amos's arm with a forefinger.

Amos said nothing, kept his eyes averted.

"Nancy, that was well spoken. Yes. I started from scratch myself. The working people are the backbone of America, and for that, you have my heartfelt appreciation. Both of you."

He took his cup of tea, balanced it carefully, and made his way out of the kitchen, leaving an air of goodness behind him.

"See, Amos? The man has no guile. He is as innocent as a newborn lamb. Those Larkins will be vultures, and he the dead carcass. You watch. He thinks highly of every single person around him, sees no danger in anything."

Amos did not know how to answer, so he said nothing.

"Well, you can come for Thanksgiving dinner at my house, that's what. There's Reilly, Jace, me and Tom. Might be a couple cousins. My mom, his Pap. Sure, you're welcome to come. Nothing fancy, mind you, but I do a turkey. Sweet potato casserole."

He looked at her, saw the kindness, the sincerity.

"Okay."

It would be better than sitting around, watching football by himself. He didn't understand the game very well, anyway. He had so much to learn in the English world. His television set helped, taught him how to pronounce words, how to dress, how to navigate the endless array of things and places and world news. Already, he was hooked on television series, stories that grabbed his attention and kept it. He could no longer imagine life without it.

When he watched television, he forgot his own mountainous body, his plain scarred face, the desperate feelings of loneliness, his inadequacy as a human being. He soared with eagles on nature shows, walked city streets with cops and businessmen, met beautiful women and daring athletes.

A bag of potato chips, his favorite dip, and a Diet Coke over ice made him completely happy, for a time. But then he noticed the weight gain, felt the lack of sleep, grew bored with all of it after a few months, except for an occasional show that held his interest.

On Thanksgiving, he drove the three and a half miles toward the small town of Schafer, a cluster of old houses, some kept up better than others, a Jiffy Lube, drugstore, a few restaurants and bars, a McDonald's. On the outskirts, there was a sprinkling of mobile homes with too many vehicles, but he was surprised to find that Nancy lived in an immaculate double-wide, yellow with white shutters, a green front door. The patio contained a grill, a nice table, and comfortable-looking chairs, sculpted shrubbery and a well-manicured lawn.

The number of vehicles intimidated him. Almost, he drove on, but he thought of Nancy and swung into the driveway. He got out and hesitated by his truck. If only he knew more, had more to say, was witty and well-spoken, rid of his shame and self-loathing.

The door swung open, and a short overweight man in a red shirt yelled, "Come on in."

Amos made himself walk toward the open door, towered over the short man, felt like a buffalo, thick neck, small scary eyes.

"You're Amos. Glad to meet you, man."

Amos met the beefy hand with his own, then followed him through the green door to greet Nancy. Reilly, an assortment of cousins whose names confused him, and last, her son Jace.

They nodded at each other, looked away.

The table was set with a plastic cloth, a brilliant shade of orange with a line of turkeys and cornucopias along the border. Paper plates, plasticware, napkins from Walmart, but he was comfortable with that. Much more than he'd be at the Larkins', he thought.

The house was full and bright and filled with delicious odors of food. His mouth watered. He sat down on a sagging recliner, hoped it wouldn't fold beneath his weight. Tom joined him, inquired about his work, then set off on a long and colorful journey of description about his own occupation, working as a mechanic down at Pete's garage.

"I'm not paid top wages, but I love it," he concluded.

Jace was still in school, had the eighteen-year-old's attitude, the slang, the bad language. Amos winced as swear words were exchanged so easily, no one thinking twice about the words they inserted to describe situations. Nancy's face was red with exertion, yelling about the serving dishes, the ice, lifting the turkey, everything.

There were alcoholic beverages everywhere, but he chose a Diet Coke, his favorite. There were polite smiles, a bit of hesitation, before the dinner was served. Nancy called on Tom to say the blessing.

"Really, Mom? Whatever," Jace said, actually ashamed.

"Oh, shut up, Jace. It's Thanksgiving, okay?"

This from Reilly, a younger, slimmer version of her mother, with a scarred face, short hair, and too many piercings.

Tom clasped his hands on the table, bowed his head, and mumbled a short prayer, which seemed to embarrass them all, even Nancy. Then the food began to circulate among them, rich and fragrant, one dish even better than the next. The large pan of stuffing was the best he'd ever eaten, even better than the *roascht* (chicken and stuffing casserole) his mother made.

"I wanted to have ham, too, but it's like five dollars a pound at the IGA. Too much. That'll have to wait for Christmas."

"This turkey is great, hon," Tom said. "One of the best you've ever made."

"Thanks. It's a Butterball. I won't buy a cheap turkey."

As the alcohol flowed, the voices increased in velocity as well as regularity. Amos was amazed to see Nancy downing glass after glass of wine, her face flushed and her voice louder.

He ate polite amounts of everything, praised the stuffing, and was given a rundown of the process, plus all the ingredients.

Dessert was a pumpkin pie from Walmart, a Pepperidge Farms chocolate cake, and ice cream. Coffee was discussed, but everyone declined. Amos would have enjoyed a cup, but felt embarrassed since no one else wanted one.

The cousins became quite boisterous, the parents laughing uproariously at everything. The old people frowned, but drank their whiskey neatly, sparingly. Amos had not been introduced to any of them except Jace, so he figured they hadn't particularly wanted him there.

But he was here, trying to make the best of it, catching Nancy's eye, her smile, and grateful for it. He offered to help with dishes but was turned away. Everyone, or most everyone, moved to the patio to smoke, look over vehicles, talk even louder.

Then the football began, a line of them circling the television on the sectional sofa, a sagging gray monstrosity taking up most of the living room. Amos wedged his big bulk on the end, tried to appear smaller than he was, smiled when necessary, thought he'd cheer with the rest of them, as he didn't have much of an idea what was going on anyway.

He was offered a beer, but shook his head. But when the next offer came, he accepted it, pulling up the tab and tilting the can. He found the taste repulsive, but took small sips till it was mostly gone.

The yelling increased, the swear words like hailstones. "Language!" Nancy shouted from time to time, but giggled hysterically at the smallest provocation. As the game on TV commenced, Amos realized the whole house was turning into unsupervised bedlam, the old people turning steadily more churlish as they nursed small glasses of whiskey, their eyes drooping with weariness.

He struggled out of the couch and thanked Nancy for the delicious meal, which was reciprocated with so much joy she threw her arms around his waist and hung on like an over-enthused puppy. He extricated himself politely and quietly took his leave, grateful to turn his truck and make his getaway.

He smiled to himself as he drove, thinking how he'd experienced another whole new way of life, and how this was their culture, likely handed down from one generation to the next. Alcohol was a part of their holiday, and no one thought it was wrong, not even the old people. His stomach shook as he laughed to himself, thinking of their decline into crankiness as they sipped that stuff.

He didn't judge, shrugged, and felt hungry again. He wanted to rid himself of the taste in his mouth, so he drove up to the Igloo, glad to find them open on the holiday, and ordered a large caramel sundae. He sat in his truck to eat it with a long-handled plastic spoon.It was delicious, cold and creamy with caramel and chocolate. He finished it, then ordered another, drank ice water to wash it down. Then, immediately, he felt miserable, hopelessly addicted to food. He had to find a way to stop eating so much.

Had he really been hungry for that second sundae? He felt the ice water sloshing around his cavernous stomach and hated himself. He thought of Skye with Raul and imagined driving his truck into a tree, a river, just ending it all.

Wouldn't it be easier? The winter stretched before him, the long evenings with nothing to look forward to except food and watching television. He needed a friend, someone to hang out with, but he knew no one who would do that. Skye, but she had her own life.

What had occurred between them was a farce, a wisp of fog cleared by the heat of bright reality.

Or was it?

He went home that evening with loneliness and disillusion like a heavy backpack strapped into place, filled with the ever-increasing need to develop willpower, to stop eating everything under the sun. He had to change his lifestyle, but how?

What was a hungry person to do?

Fred started at him with so much self-pity he burst out laughing, rumpled his ears, and plied him with words of endearment, resulting in a leaping, spinning dog elated to finally receive his due.

He changed into sweatpants and a T-shirt, went to the snack drawer for some chocolate, then thought better of it, and gave Fred a small amount of dry dog food.

Thanksgiving at Lydia's sister's house was well attended. Barbara was older, married to Elias King, Davie Schtef's Elias from Nine Points, a place many Amish still called "die unna Beckvay," meaning Lower Pequea. Raymond and Lydia had started from their northern Pennsylvania home at six o'clock that morning with a load of others from the community who would be visiting family as well, making the trip less expensive for everyone.

Barbara had set a table for twenty-six, the handcrafted extension table stretched to the limit with twelve leaves in place, her best linen tablecloths as white as snow and her "good" dishes brought forth and placed at regular intervals. There were plates of butter, small glass dishes of jelly, bowls of applesauce and pepper slaw.

The turkey had been dismembered and cut into pieces, mixed with bread cubes, chopped celery and onion, eggs, broth, salt and pepper, then baked in huge roasters. There was mashed potatoes, creamed celery, sweet potatoes made with brown sugar, butter, and mini marshmallows, noodles, and deviled eggs.

There were handshakes, smiles of recognition, friendly slaps on the back. Talk was plentiful, as were the children underfoot, babies crying, doors slamming, admonition from mothers.

In a corner of the laundry room, Lydia was huddled with a sister-in-law, Ruth, who had caught her unaware with sharp questions like poison-tipped arrows. Where was Amos? Why did they just let him go? How could they sleep at night, knowing he was out in the world?

Lydia did her best to explain, proving her innocence as a mother who had tried her best to reason with a son bent on disobedience, but could tell this was not well-received at all.

If one would have seen the two, they might well have thought them to be of two different orders. Ruth wore a much larger covering, with wide seams and strings tied closely under her chin, while Lydia's covering barely reached over her rather large ears, heart shaped, with a narrow seam and much thinner strings tied loosely.

Quite a bit of her hair was visible, and her cape and apron were made stylishly for her age, her dress a shade of dark beige, also a recent color pick for those who knew the latest, best style.

Ruth, on the other hand, was conservative, adhered to the *ordnung* with tenacity, and thought everyone else should be the same, seeing how they brought all these troubles on their own heads, the way they themselves always had to be in the latest style. It was much better to give yourself up to the *ordnung* and live a life of true humility, which was why she cornered Lydia in the first place.

"It is God's will, Lydia," she resumed.

Lydia nodded, two spirits warring within, the one rebellious, the other cowering in shame.

"Surely you can see your shortcomings. You have always been prone to style, had to have worldly objects in your house. *Göetza*, Lydia. Idols. We are not to have any other gods before Him. And now Amos is where he is, and it's a shame."

Lydia bowed humbly before the righteous Ruth, the minister's wife who raised her children inside the corral of her own tight convictions, who thought her way far superior to these wayward mothers who bore a resemblance to their own teenage daughters, all slipping off the track of the obedient, playing fast and loose with God Himself.

"We did the best we could, Ruth. Seriously. He was always withdrawn, a difficult child. I couldn't reach him."

"No wonder. He wasn't good enough for you. He never came up to your expectations."

That irked. The truth hurt, hit the bull's-eye, and Lydia saw red. She was injured, yes, but furious as well, so she mumbled something about helping with the dinner and slipped away.

The nerve of her.

When heads were bowed in silent prayer for an extra-long time—it was Thanksgiving, after all—there was a glitch in the pure prayer of love and gratitude as the two sisters duked it out in spirit. Let her raise her brood of sanctimonious do-gooders, going around judging those lesser than herself, see where it got her.

And Ruth thanked God she had always taken the *ordnung* seriously, hoped Lydia would repent and take Amos's sins on herself. Raymond didn't have much to do with it, poor henpecked man.

And so these two drank their spiritual whiskey and grew steadily crabbier.

Lydia was secretly pleased when Ruth had barely enough mashed potatoes, thought she was a real tightwad. She ate *roascht* and celery and asked how many potatoes she'd peeled, irked when Ruth made sheep's eyes and said the potatoes had been grown wet, so they didn't take much milk and butter, decreasing the amount. Rachel and Becky agreed, heads nodding as they pushed *roascht* onto their spoons with their forks.

Talk turned to potato growing, what kind, when to dig them, what type of fertilizer was best.

"Which is better, cow or chicken manure?" Lydia asked, eating her *roascht* the right way, using only her fork.

"Oh, I think horse is hard to beat."

"Lime. Every garden needs loads of it."

"I think sulphur."

"Never heard of it."

"Hybrix, that's what. You should have seen my radishes."

And so forth.

Gardens were taken seriously. To harvest pounds of vegetables and put them up was a true and noble calling, a testimony to a housewife's good management and hard work. Shelves were lined with rows of jars with colorful pickles, red beets, peaches, applesauce, tomato products, all of it producing a sense of accomplishment, a deep inner pride in the ability to provide wholesome food from a well-kept garden.

Dessert was served. There was chocolate cake with a thin layer of vanilla icing, cornstarch pudding with a center of chocolate pudding, mince and pumpkin pie with fruit salad consisting mostly of peaches and pears, home-canned. The absence of Cool Whip was keenly felt by Lydia. What was cornstarch pudding without Cool Whip?

She should be ashamed of herself, serving that pudding from the nineteenth century.

Over steaming sudsy water, they talked of ordinary, mundane day-to-day lives, their work, husbands and children, accidents, home remedies, the price of eggs. But Lydia had taken a cup of coffee and retreated to the living room to sit with Raymond, receiving his look of adoration, which helped to heal her wounded ego. When Ruth saw what passed between them, she thought perhaps she'd been a bit harsh. Lydia placed a hand on Raymond's arm, laying it on as thick as she could for Ruth's benefit.

The conversation turned to the drive to move West, one Amish settlement springing up in Montana, another in Wyoming, all hardy pioneers who were paving the way for others. The East was filling up, the newlyweds couldn't afford the price of land, of small homes.

"Well, they wouldn't have to have the best," Becky commented.

"I'll say. When we got married, we rented that moldy trailer for five years. We saved fifteen thousand dollars," Elam remarked, his heavy black beard wagging.

"And bought the Johnson place for less than two hundred grand," he went on, clasping his long thin hands around his crossed knee.

"That wouldn't be possible now. More like four hundred," Raymond said quietly, then looked around to make sure no one disagreed.

"True. I guess there's sound logic to moving West."

"The distance. Think of the distance."

"And the cold. They said Yoni's had thirty-five degrees below zero."

"That's ridiculous."

"Here, here. Who creates the weather? We won't get blasphemous here."

Good-natured smiles, a few chuckles. A mother reached out to grab the arm of a passing toddler, clap her on her lap and wipe at a runny nose, the child twisting its body away from restraining arms.

And Lydia sat solidly beside Raymond, thinking many thoughts of martyrdom. She watched the clock and looked forward to the driver's arrival.

Her recliner and the *Reader's Digest* seemed like a safe haven after the dressing down from that sister of hers.

CHAPTER 12

INCREASINGLY, AMOS'S WEIGHT BOTHERED HIM, THE WAY HE HEAVED himself into his truck, felt the tilt when he flopped in his seat. He needed to address this problem, once and for all, but it was hard to know where to begin.

He searched online, found an onslaught of weight loss solutions, all with golden stories of success, hundreds of pounds lost, health revitalized.

By Christmas, he'd gained another ten pounds after discovering the joys of Moose Tracks ice cream, often finishing a half gallon container in one evening.

The winter was mild, with occasional snow squalls, temperatures in the low forties, so he asked Joseph if he could work on the windfalls by the garden gate in the backyard, a job that would keep him occupied for a few weeks. Lila was especially delighted, saying she'd love to have that area as an azalea and hosta showplace, complete with a brick walkway, a water fountain, and cement birdbaths. She drew a plan for him, and he was alarmed to see the translucence of her skin, the tremor in her thin fingers. Joseph coughed and coughed, but waved a hand away when questioned.

While he worked with a chainsaw and axe, he thought of Skye. He had to be honest with himself that the embrace, that kiss, was a one-time thing. Maybe just a moment of confusion for her. No one like her would truly be attracted to him in the real world, would they?

The alternative was hope, and that always ended in defeat for him. It was easier to put it behind him.

The chainsaw growled through fallen trees and his heavy boots kicked the cut branches aside. Fred sniffed, ran from one spot to another, chased imaginary animals.

The sun had been warm on his back, but he felt the cold on his face. He stopped the chainsaw and looked around. Storm clouds moved across the face of the sun, partially obscuring it, leaving a white, fuzzy orb in the middle of a pewter-colored sky. He recognized snow, and a tingle of happiness claimed him.

He'd always loved a snowstorm, sledding on the hill behind the house. He'd shoot down the front yard and across the garden to the slick driveway which served to increase his speed. By the time he reached the bottom he felt weightless. He'd been flying.

Cathy told him the only reason he went so fast was the amount of weight he possessed, that and he always had the best sled.

He didn't care what she said—whether she breathed unspoken insults or not, he had flown with incredible speed, kept his sled stable, guided it like a pro.

He stopped his chainsaw, set it down, and stretched his back, then turned to look at the house in the dull light of heavy clouds. From this angle, it was even more beautiful, the sunroom jutting from the back, the stone foundation blending into well-kept shrubbery. He loved this house, this property, and some buyer down the road from now would be very happy, for sure.

He hoped Nancy wasn't right about the Larkins' scheming. But money spoke volumes, it was true.

All he could ever hope for was a house like Tom and Nancy's, which would be good enough for him. A truck, a mortgage, some furniture, a nice lawn, perhaps a few trees, and he would be grateful forever.

He swiped the back of a hand across his forehead, removed his cap, and ran his fingers through his hair. He felt alive, energized with the thrill of cleaning up this ignored patch of ground.

He looked forward to learning how to lay a brick walkway, how to design his own garden layout, with Lila's help. A new sense of purpose ran through his veins.

He looked up and caught sight of Skye, walking her dog on a leash. At first, he thought she was alone, but then realized the form of a man striding beside her, his arm around her waist.

Raul.

He wanted to melt away like snow in spring sun, disappear completely, but the dull thud of his heart reminded him he was perfectly alive and capable of handling another disappointment. He knew she was meant to be with this man, so it was the right thing for her. But still he wept within himself, if only for a moment.

"Hey!"

She'd caught sight of him. He waved, a hand lifted weakly.

She was half-running, her dog leaping on its leash, pulling on the sleeve of the man behind her. Breathless, windblown, the tawny head of hair he found so attractive, all green, gold eyes and dancing freckles.

"Hi! Amos, this is Paul. Paul, as in P for pickle. Not Raul."

His chest caved with a lack of breathing, but he managed a smile.

"Good to meet you."

He nodded.

"Paul is finishing up his biology degree at my school, then he's heading to Harvard for grad school."

Amos saw thick dark hair, a tanned face, square jaw, and squinted brown eyes. Textbook handsome. God had been really generous when He created him. A sour acid flowed in his veins. All he could manage was another nod.

Skye beseeched him with her eyes.

"Aren't you happy for me? I finally broke free of Raul. And Paul here even managed to impress my parents!"

She laughed, laid her head on Paul's shoulder. He drew her close.

Amos scraped the toe of his foot along a pile of shavings, then lifted his face to look at her. He hadn't thought he would ever find the courage to speak, but he found his voice and said thickly, "Well. Isn't that something? I certainly hope he means more to you than I did."

"Oh, Amos, don't say that. I needed a friend, and I do like you."

He said nothing.

An uncomfortable silence hung like the thick gray clouds between them. Fred bounced up and sniffed noses with Stewart, then took off running crazily, Stewart tugging on his leash.

She watched after him, her pretty mouth set in a thin line.

"Can't you be happy for me?"

"No."

Paul looked down at Skye and raised his eyebrows. They both burst out laughing. On a scale of one to ten, the cruelty was over a hundred. He turned and walked away, blindly.

Later, he retrieved the chainsaw and axe, wiped the blades, and stored them on the shelf, his anger cooling as he worked. So, this was what caring about someone did to you. He would never do it again, never. But then, he should have known better. He was no match for her, and he'd allowed his ego to be tricked.

It was just another defeat, another downturn on the road of life. Would it ever change for him? Maybe someday. Maybe not.

He went on an eating binge of bratwurst with sauteed pepper and onion on white rolls, macaroni and cheese, and Moose Tracks for dessert.

He slept on the recliner in front of the TV, woke up with a roaring gut and screaming thirst, followed by intense loathing of his lack of willpower.

He thought of the gym every day, lifted a log above his head, stood with his feet apart and flexed his muscles. If only he could be alone, where no one could see him, he'd do it.

He began watching fitness shows, but quickly got sick of perfectly toned and tanned bodies, none of the participants half as big as he.

He called Scott, asked what time the gym opened. Scott told him to come on down, they'd discuss it. Which he did. He was taken to Scott's office, given a schedule, told the best time to arrive and leave without meeting more than one, maybe two people.

He wound up telling Scott more than he thought possible. His life, his upbringing, the all-consuming appetite, everything. Then he felt ashamed, wondered why he'd done it.

Scott sat back, his massive arms crossed, his blue eyes containing something he couldn't place. It was as if they had the power to draw him out, as if he needed to hear his story.

"I'll tell you what, Amos. I'll be here the first few times. To get you started."

Amos shook his head, "No."

"Why?"

"I don't want anyone. I'll figure it out."

"But you need someone to guide you through the repetitions, the mix of cardio and weights."

"No. I'll get a book."

"OK, I have one for you." He reached for the bookshelf and pulled off a paperback book.

Amos thanked him brusquely, then moved through the door, the whole conversation rankling. What power did this guy have?

It was disconcerting, spilling his life story, feeling heard for the first time in his life.

Was it losing Skye that finally tipped his resistance over the edge? Well, he never had her, actually. He was so stupid, foolishly thinking he might have a girl like her.

He had to do this for himself, Scott told him.

Cathy texted him on Christmas Eve, asking him to come home. She'd asked for his number when he'd last been home, but he hadn't realized she had a cell phone. He did go, pulling up on Christmas morning. He parked his truck beside the real estate sign, which was still stuck in the ground, and trudged up the hill to the house, opened the door, and called out.

"Come on in, Amos," his mother answered, meeting him in the living room.

"How are you, Mom?"

"Oh, I'm doing okay. So, you're home for Christmas. Cathy said she was going to text you."

"She did. Where is she?"

"Sleeping. She was at a party last night."

"On Christmas Eve?"

"Yes. Ephraim and Sadie went to New York, so Susan had some friends over."

He shook his head. "Mom . . ."

"Don't start, Amos. You are far more disobedient than her. She doesn't behave, but at least she goes to the Amish church."

Amos sighed, stayed quiet. It was, after all, Christmas Day, and no matter what he believed, Christmas was special, and he did not want to ruin it for the family. He greeted his father, testing the waters to see if he was accepted and loved, and was not disappointed. A strange sob of overwhelming gladness had to be stifled, but his eyes shone.

"How's it going, Amos?"

"Good. Real good, Dat."

"What are you doing, now that it's winter?"

"Not that much. I'm working at sawing up fallen trees."

The door to the upstairs slammed, and Cathy slouched into the kitchen, her hair disheveled, her face red with swollen eyes. She went straight to the refrigerator for a glass of ice-cold water, drank it down thirstily before rasping a greeting. She cleared her throat, tried again.

"Hey, Amos."

"Hello, Cathy."

She blinked, rubbed the sleep from her eyes, then went to the stove to pour herself a cup of coffee.

"Man, I feel like something the cat dragged in."

She fell into a kitchen chair, coughed, a hand to her chest. Her mother hovered, questioning without uttering a word.

"Now Cathy, we need to talk."

Cathy waved an insolent hand. "Get away from me. Don't start this early in the morning. It's Christmas, so Fa-la-la-la-la. Can I help it if we celebrated last night?"

Shocked, Amos sat open-mouthed.

He watched as their mother turned away, saying nothing. She opened the oven door and slid out a roaster, lifted the lid, and inserted a fork in a tender ham. She replaced the lid and the roaster, closed the oven door, and turned, a hand on her hip.

"Cathy, you will not speak to me like that. I don't care if it's Christmas or not. I have had enough. You go clean yourself up and get dressed immediately, and I mean every word."

Cathy shrugged, went to talk to her father, and when Raymond came to the kitchen, Amos could tell he was displeased.

"Shouldn't you go a little easy, Lydia?"

"No. She makes me so angry lately."

"She's having a hard time."

"Oh, really. Well, you aren't discipling these children, so someone has to step up and take responsibility. I mean it, Raymond."

And Amos thought, *home sweet home.*

Raymond sat in a chair by the window, turned his head to watch the birds at the feeder, his shoulders slumped. Amos looked at his father, wondered what he was thinking.

Cathy flounced upstairs, a trail of martyrdom behind her, leaving the room in cold discomfort. His mother banged lids, scraped pans, and said nothing.

Awkwardly, Amos sat on a chair opposite his father. Slowly, he turned to Amos, his eyes liquid with unshed tears, his mouth soft with emotion.

"Did you see that redheaded? Most of the birds at the feeder have been fewer in number this year, but that's a real plus, seeing him."

"No, I didn't see him."

"Well, he was there."

A long pause, where neither of them really knew what to say, their faces set in painful anxiety as the seconds tripped on. Amos desperately wanted to talk about Cathy, about his disappointment with Skye, the Thanksgiving dinner at Nancy's house, so many things. But his tongue was tied in his mouth, knowing he was no longer in their world and that his opinion and experiences didn't matter.

He opened his mouth, then closed it again. Finally, he asked if they had any prospective buyers for the house.

"We've had a couple, yes. The one couple is serious. They're working on a bank loan."

From the kitchen came his mother's strident voice.

"We will get the Johnson place as soon as these people's loan is approved. I can hardly wait. I have so many plans. You're a landscaper now, Amos. You could come help us, tell us what to do."

"Really, Mom? You would want that?"

"Well, you're not excommunicated. You never joined the church."

"I didn't mean that. I meant, you really want my opinion?"

His mother eyed him without expression, that flat blank stare, giving him no hope of approval.

"As I've told you many times, you are disobedient to your parents, breaking an important commandment God gave to Moses, and handed down to every generation since. The least you can do is help us out in our time of need. I imagine you know a thing or two about shrubbery and trees by now."

Amos felt the old sense of unfairness welling up. So many hot words stuck in his throat, glued to his tongue. What about Cathy? Was she honoring her parents carrying on like that, doing things her parents would never believe. Was it enough just to dress in Amish clothes? He turned his head to watch a blue jay greedily gobbling unsalted peanuts.

To regain solid footing, he turned the conversation to birds and the weather, his father's occupation, the visit to Nine Points, all friendly conversation laced with normalcy.

Christmas dinner was served on his mother's good Christmas plates, the triumph of her forays into thrift stores. She'd been ecstatic to find Lenox Christmas plates with wine glasses to match.

Amos remembered her return from Rochester, unpacking them from the Goodwill bag, her face wreathed in smiles, exulting in the fact they'd be able to set a magazine-worthy Christmas table after she found the perfect tablecloth at TJ Maxx. And greenery, perhaps cloth napkins with rings.

She'd chattered on as she slid them out from the newspaper wrapping, then washed them in hot sudsy water.

"Yes! We Amish women who love beautiful things have to find it in our homes, our yard and garden, since we can't wear fashionable clothing like worldly women."

Amos had reached for another handful of corn chips, asked if there was a difference.

"Of course there is, Amos. We're still plain on the outside."

Amos had crunched the corn chips between his teeth and said nothing, knowing he was only a thirteen-year-old boy.

Now, he viewed the table and smiled. It was golden reindeer and ornaments this year, with faux pine and spruce, a Jello mold in red, green, and white, name plates, and the same cloth napkins in gold rings. It was very tasteful, very not Amish. But he could see how it all delighted her heart as she served ham and her special potatoes made with ranch dressing, cheddar cheese, and a thick layer of buttery corn flake crumbs on top.

His mouth watered.

"Sit, Amos, make yourself at home. Cathy. Where's Cathy?" his father asked.

"Upstairs. Call the girls."

When they were seated, they bowed their heads in silent prayer, the traditional way. Amos never prayed, but thought of Joseph praying out loud, clasping one of Lila's hands, and one of Amos's, always thanking for the food, blessings to those around them, and for Amos. At first, this made him uncomfortable, but in time, he became accustomed to it, felt it flavored his day.

Amos lifted his head, took large portions of every passing dish, drank iced tea copiously, then helped himself to seconds.

Cathy and Lavina picked at their food, cast sidelong glances.

"So, Amos, do you cook for yourself?"

"Sometimes."

"Where do you eat if you don't?"

"The big house. Sometimes I eat out."

His mother frowned. "You know, I'd like to see where you live, but I'm afraid if we went to visit, you'd take it as an approval, and we don't want that. You still belong here."

Amos said nothing.

Cathy sat back in her chair, eying him through half-closed eyelids. "You are bigger than ever, Amos. Surely you don't have a girlfriend."

"No."

"Aren't you planning on getting married? Like, ever?"

He shrugged, lowered his eyes, and picked at a crumb on his plate.

"Don't you think about losing weight?"

"I do. I'm thinking of joining a gym. A guy I know owns one."

"Now Amos, that's no place for you. Half-clothed people working out. It's all the way of the world."

His father stared at him. A frown created vertical lines between his eyes. "Don't you work hard enough keeping those grounds in shape?"

"Not in winter."

Cathy tossed her head. "Just stop eating so much."

"Yeah," Lavina tossed in, cementing Amos's suspicion that Cathy was molding her into a younger version of herself.

"It's not easy."

"Course not. Addictions never are," she countered.

And Amos sat, a mound of flesh topped with an unattractive face, the skin crosshatched with scars and fissures, like sand after a heavy rain. He felt every inch of his imperfections, reached for another slice of ham, and folded it between a dinner roll before stuffing it hungrily into his mouth.

"You weren't hungry for that," Cathy said, but not unkindly.

"I know. Just . . ."

He shrugged.

He had not gone shopping, had no gifts for his family, and they had none for him. His mother explained quickly that as long as he was living the life of the *ungehorsam* (disobedient), there would be no gift, as it would be an approval of his lifestyle, which they did not want.

They definitely did not give him their blessing, driving that truck and having an English haircut, abandoning the Amish way. This was not how he was raised, this was not God's will.

So he sat quietly, watching the girls unwrap gorgeously wrapped gifts done up in ribbon and greenery, squeal and hug their mother over dress fabric, baubles, prints for bedroom walls, tennis rackets, and white Nike sneakers.

"Tennis?" he inquired, not understanding.

"Lots of girls in our group play," Cathy explained, airily.

"In long skirts?"

"We make shorter ones to play," Lavina added.

"I see."

"You're making fun of us. Well, at least we're still Amish."

He raised his eyebrows and said nothing.

He left that day with the puzzle of his life more incomplete than ever. Was the only disobedience that counted that of leaving the Amish way of life? Did it really not matter that Cathy and Lavina rode in cars, spoke with disrespect, and probably even drank alcohol and smoked with their friends?

Generations before had allowed this time of sowing the proverbial wild oats. The carousing, even drinking and smoking, late nights in cars. Or had they?

He believed there were some Amish people who were stalwart, obedient, pure in heart, loved the brethren, raised their children to love Christ in their youth. Amos had plenty of cousins he considered the salt of the earth, real Christians who followed sincere convictions.

He thought of his father, like soft butter, molded easily to anyone's convictions. Usually his wife's. If his father wanted to keep his marriage on an even keel, sail smoothly on waters as smooth as glass, he could never have a real conviction of his own, and in the slim chance he discovered one, he would never be able to voice it.

Chapter 13

Joseph and Lila had planned a special evening with Amos the day after Christmas, so he dressed carefully, spending more time in front of the bathroom mirror. He no longer shrank from his ruined face, but accepted the scars as part of who he was. His brown hair was cut professionally, the shadow of a beard he liked.

Wearing dark, solid colors helped to minimize his bulk, he learned from online clothing sites for large people, so when he shrugged his leather coat over his shoulders, he felt almost OK about himself. Besides, the old couple never looked at him with judgement or ridicule, but pure and honorable acceptance. He felt safe with them in a way he'd never experienced with his own parents.

He was welcomed warmly, both of them holding his hands as they went to the living room lit brightly with golden lights on the immense tree Amos had helped decorate. There were dozens of Christmas figures, small ropes of lights wound through endless ropes of greenery, another, smaller tree in the dining room and kitchen.

They loved Christmas, they told him, but had to cut back on the decorations because of their advancing years. There was a time when the whole place was a Christmas show, where folks would drive by slowly to see all the lights.

Joseph read the Christmas story in Luke, one Amos had heard over and over in German and Pennsylvania Dutch. He had listened to his mother read from the Bible Story book, the glossy blue Arthur Maxwell set most Amish people had in their homes. He remembered vivid depictions of richly dressed people from those days as well as poor shepherds, the angels hovering in the night sky.

But he had never heard anyone read it with such tenderness, such intimacy and love, the words spoken in soft tones knocking gently on the door of Amos's disbelief and bitterness.

Maybe God was there for people like Joseph and Lila, good people who loved everyone.

Sometimes, if he allowed himself to feel it, he hated his mother, resented his father's weakness, dreamed of telling Cathy exactly how he felt, wanted to smack Lavina for her smug copying of Cathy. He resented them all, never wanted to go back.

These thoughts intruded on the purity of Joseph's words, stopped the building of any spiritual trust or love he had felt in the beginning of the story. Unaware of Lila's eyes on his face, his features changed from happiness to doubt, then slid into some remembered injury to another, until finally he wasn't listening at all.

Joseph closed the Bible, laid it gently on the end table beside the brocade arm of the couch, folded his hands and said joyfully, "Yes, yes! What a story. After all these years, the significance just keeps sinking in more."

Lila's eyes shone as she slipped a hand beneath his elbow, laid her white head on his shoulder.

Amos swallowed, felt like an outsider to so much love. Would his life be different if his parents were like this? He didn't know.

"Amos. I have never asked you this. What is your relationship with God like?" Joseph asked seriously.

A kind of panic overtook him. He felt the sweat break through the surface of his hairline. He shifted his weight uncomfortably, cleared his throat, and ran a hand over his face, horrified to find the palm of his hand slick with sweat.

"Uh, well, I don't know. I . . . uh, you know. The Amish don't really word it that way. I mean, you know. I don't know how to answer that question."

For a long moment, Joseph eyed him intently, the old blue eyes so alight with interest they seemed to blaze.

"Do you read your Bible, my boy?" he asked finally.

"No, I'm sorry."

"Don't apologize. All in good time."

He clapped his hands. "Now we need to celebrate the birth of our Lord and Savior, Jesus Christ, sent to Earth to die for our sins. The greatest gift the world will ever know."

With an effort, he got to his feet, went to the heavy old-fashioned stereo set, and reached for a record. He adjusted the needle and soon the swelling of joyous music filled the room. Amos recognized the words of a Christmas hymn they sang in school, and quick tears formed in the corners of his eyes.

Lila presented him with two small boxes, in gold paper with heavy white ribbon, an attached card.

"For you, dear son," she said softly, a hand on his arm.

His fingers were clumsy, but the old couple waited patiently till he lifted a beautiful wristwatch from white tissue paper.

"Thank you," he said, very quietly, choking on the words.

"You are so welcome. I hope you enjoy it for many years."

He adjusted the band on his wrist, enjoying the feel of it. He pushed away the sound of his mother's voice in his head telling him wristwatches were forbidden.

"And now the other box," Lila trilled, visibly excited to see him open the gifts.

He struggled in the same way, but eventually found himself staring at a picture. A photograph of the front yard, the tractor with him beside it, clipping shrubs. The frame was exquisite.

"Really? Why did you frame a picture of me?" he asked, but was smiling broadly.

"You will appreciate it one day, even more than you do now. We take so much pleasure in your work, as you seem to do as well, and for this we appreciate you in a way you will never know."

Words like honey with the healing properties of an elixir. He blushed, plucked at a loose thread on the knee of his jeans.

"Thank you," he said shyly, having no idea how endearing his words were to the old couple.

They had glasses of wine, some odd little cakes, crustless sandwiches of which he could easily have eaten the entire plate, tiny pretzels with small slices of smelly cheese, mushrooms, cherry tomatoes, endive and black olives, all of which he found unappealing, but he daintily consumed some of each thing.

The food was of no consequence, however. Not on this special evening, filled with so much love and acceptance. As the music swirled around them, the taste of the wine on his tongue, he felt transported to another world, one in which his shortcomings didn't define him for the first time in his life.

He closed his eyes, imagined himself thin, handsome, skilled in conversation, able to tell good jokes.

As he left, he was enveloped in warm hugs, appreciation surrounding him by the warm words they spoke repeatedly.

But as soon as he'd left for the gatehouse, he told himself they didn't know who he really was, would likely never know, and when they found out, he'd soon be replaced. He was a young man without blessing, a disobedient son who threw away a precious heritage handed down by the godly forefathers. A disappointment to his parents, the whole band of religious relatives he'd known.

How would all this come to an end? Surely he'd come to a tragic end, the way all those did who didn't obey God and their parents.

He shivered in the cold night air, his dark thoughts a form of truth all their own.

With no one to turn to, no one to accept his defeat, he pushed it all away in the box where he kept everything else he did not want to examine too deeply. Skye was there. And Scott. His sisters. His cousins who were thin and agile, popular, handsome young men who were likely preparing to join the church and be married to nice young Amish girls very soon.

He inserted a key in the lock, let himself in to the house, ruffled Fred's ears, then set about fixing a huge bowl of Wheaties. He ate potato chips as he sugared the cereal heavily, poured milk from a gallon jug, then tilted it and drank from it directly.

There was no one to see, no one to care how or what he ate or drank, so he did what came naturally, easing his hunger with inordinate amounts of food, the one thing satisfying to his heart, his body and soul, comforting a place deep within.

He received a phone call from Scott, urging him to think about the New Year, the perfect time to start at the gym. He promised he'd be there, but the end of January came and he still hadn't shown up.

Winter days were hard, the loneliness pressing down from leaden skies, the brown landscape resembling his life. No color or joy.

Nancy asked him to help her strip wallpaper in the kitchen, so he checked with Lila, who said of course he could help. He opened the back door to the sight of Nancy seated at the small kitchen table, her head in her hands, weeping quietly, as if the pain was too much to bear.

He hesitated, but she raised her blotched face, waved a hand to tell him to come on in.

"Don't mind me," she said thickly, then honked into a wad of paper towels, crumpled them, and threw them across the table. She got to her feet, went to the paper towel holder and tore off a section, wiped her eyes, and turned to the refrigerator door for a Pepsi.

"Sorry," he mumbled. "Don't mean to intrude."

"No need to apologize. You're supposed to help with the wallpaper, right?"

He nodded, saw the swollen eyes.

"Well, sit down. Coffee? Pepsi?"

"Coffee. I'll get it."

"Sit."

She brought a box of club crackers, peanut butter and jelly. He'd eaten, but started spreading a cracker.

"I need a shoulder to cry on, Amos. You know Jace? My boy?" Amos nodded.

"He's on drugs. Heroin. Selling it, too. I just found out. I tried to tell myself he's just losing weight, nervous about losing his job, twitchy, weird, but deep down, a mother knows by the company her children keep, and believe me, he brought home some losers. You know how I found out?"

Amos stopped spreading peanut butter, shook his head.

"The cops brought him home. Found him passed out at the laundromat, of all places. Was in possession, so it was off to jail. Do I have money for his bail? Of course not. And plus, his Pap is going to kick him out."

Amos shoved a cracker into his mouth, chewed, listened quietly.

"That's not the worst. His girlfriend is on it, too. Plus, he's going to be a daddy. In jail."

She began a series of choking sobs.

Amos felt a heaviness in his chest, a physical pain for the crying housekeeper who would never hurt a flea, who did not deserve this, to his way of thinking.

"I never thought I would ever see anything like this. He was a good boy, a decent kid in school. He simply got in with the wrong crowd. How? How did it come to this?"

Amos didn't know, had no solution, so he shook his head, but his thoughts spun. Here was poor Nancy, her son in serious trouble, a disobedience, in her culture. Here was he, disobedient to his own culture, bringing heartache to those he loved. Or used to love.

A great guilt snapped into his face, like an activated air bag in a wrecked vehicle. The disappointment to his parents ran parallel to what Jace had done, even if it was done in a much more conservative way.

To Nancy and Jace, driving a car and dressing English was not a sin, it was a way of life. But substance abuse and children born out of wedlock was not what most parents wanted for their children.

Where did it all start, and how would it stop? How did the sins of the fathers play into the whole equation?

He didn't know, so he let it go, punched the guilt away. Everything would work out in the end, he supposed.

He looked at Nancy.

"How long will he be incarcerated?"

"I dunno. He's gonna have to stay. We don't have any money."

"Perhaps it's a good thing, being in jail. Like, he could quit the drugs if he can't get more, right?"

"Are you kidding me? You have no idea. There are always connections."

Amos realized he knew very little of the real world, he'd lived such a sheltered life. He felt silly, out of place.

Nancy Farmer, mother of a heroin dealer. Raymond and Lydia Beiler, parents of an obese, disobedient son. An English one, driving a truck. Nothing Amish about it.

So where did the parallels begin, and where did they end? Whose fault was it all?

"Let's get going, Amos."

Halfheartedly, he wiped crumbs from the table, closed the plastic sleeve on the crackers, buying time. He needed to talk to someone but had no idea how to get started.

"Uh, Nancy?" he mumbled.

"Yeah?"

"You think . . . I mean, you . . . ah, nothing."

He couldn't create a decent question, so what was the use trying? Perhaps he was okay the way he was, although he was aware of needing something.

Intent on the weight of troubles on her back, Nancy was only half-listening, so he got to his feet and followed her to the hallway and back wall of the kitchen with a spray bottle and scraper. They worked together in silence, neither one in a state of mind to support the other, although Amos opened his mouth a few times, meaning to confide in his own guilt, before thinking better of it.

But he thought how the wheel moved on, conservative or otherwise, how the sins of the parents were visited on their children, over and over and over, although he understood very little of how it all worked.

And after that, Nancy began to talk.

Her mother and father came from upstate New York, close to the Canadian border. Life was cold and mean. Hard winters, lean times. Everyone drank alcohol to keep from going crazy, at least when there was money to buy it. They all drank. She always had.

And now look where Jace was. Well, it wasn't her fault. It was the United States government and their crazy rules, cracking down on stupid stuff and letting the serious stuff go. It's why her parents moved to Prince Edward Island. For the fishing, and free health care.

When Jace got out of jail, he'd have to do the right thing, get a real job, support his girlfriend. Likely he wouldn't be able to, with having a record now. That's what happened. She'd end up a single mother getting WIC, food stamps. How was she going to get by without financial support if he couldn't get a job?

"I can't keep that baby. I have to work. Tom doesn't make enough, slouching around that garage. It's just one big mess, is what it is, and I'm not kidding you."

She scraped faster, her words spilling from her mouth, her worries swirling around his ears.

But Amos was smart enough to realize she really did blame other people, or groups of people, for all of her troubles. None were her problem, at least not directly. Jace was a victim and so was she.

He could not quite fathom how breaking the law made you a victim if you chose quite deliberately to do drugs, or became a father at a very young age. Was he a victim of his own making?

As he scraped wallpaper and listened to Nancy's theories, he began to sort through the puzzle pieces of the world, compare them with his own, unknowingly attaching bits and pieces of Scripture to certain happenings. With his thoughts occupied, the day flew by, and before he knew it he was back in his small house, cozy and warm.

His phone beeped.

Skye Larkin. Hope sprang in his chest.

"How are you? Thinking about you."

A great joy rose in him. She thought of him.

Quickly, he texted back. "Doing great. Miss you."

He hit send without thinking.

All evening there was no response, although he checked his phone every five or ten minutes. In the morning, he read: "Sorry. Went out with Paul. I'm in love."

After that, he knew she would not be back, ever. He needed to sever those wild, crazy hopes, get over it. He was a friend to her, and absolutely nothing else. Yet he longed for one more glimpse of her, the healthy aura, the thick windblown hair. His heart felt calloused by lost loves, disappointment, and raw, bloody defeat, as if he'd been dealt blow after blow after blow.

When did one become a victim? He felt as if he was treated wrongly by his mother and sister, by his coworkers at the bulk food store, and now by his best girl, Skye.

The worst, though, was in his early school years, when he was like a walrus among seals, a turtle among leaping frogs, always much too big and cumbersome, a face like a bulldog.

In February, when Nancy's troubles and gray days coupled to put him in an unsteady frame of mind, he went to talk to Scott, who said he'd meet him at four o'clock in the morning at the gym, but Amos couldn't quite force himself to go. Three mornings later, he went to the gym for the first time, blinking in the harsh white lights at 4:18 on his watch.

Scott had no idea he was there. The only person there was Scott's helper, a middle-aged man with a bald head and huge moustache named Ralph.

Amos was wearing sweatpants and a T-shirt. He walked around the room, examining equipment, taking his time, before deciding on a brisk walk on the treadmill. Grasping the side rail, he turned it on, figured he could start a fast walk, and almost fell flat on his stomach. Terrified, he jumped off, hurting his shin in the process.

If Ralph had observed this, he made no move to be of assistance, so Amos felt fortunate to get away with that first misstep. Maybe he shouldn't even try. Not everyone was cut out for the gym.

He decided to use the bike, which went much better. Perched on the seat, rotating the pedals, leaning forward like a racer gave him the advantage of feeling safe, in control, so he kept going.

But he felt an ache in the calves of his legs, a tired defeat in his thighs. He was doing fifteen miles an hour, which was something, wasn't it? His chest heaved. He could hear his heart in his ears. Sweat popped out everywhere, but he kept going. His breathing came in short hard puffs. The room spun.

He climbed off, afraid of a heart attack. He felt initiated into the world of working out. A gym rat. Wiping the perspiration, he felt great, alive, powerful. If he could pedal a bike that long, and at that speed, he was in pretty good shape.

Ralph came out of the office to ask how it was going. "Pretty good. Did the bike for ten whole minutes. Felt the burn." Amos grinned, reaching down to rub the back of his leg.

Ralph said that was great. Did he want to try a few weights? Amos shook his head.

"Not today. I feel as if I've had a real workout."

Ralph watched him go, smiled, and shook his head. Figured nine out of ten, he'd stop at Wendy's for two breakfast sandwiches, which was exactly what Amos did. One sausage and one bacon.

But he knew he was on to something good. When had he ever breathed like that for an extended period of time? When had he ever felt better about himself?

Never.

He told Nancy as they applied white paint to the clean walls, and she congratulated him, genuinely, which was more than generous of her, the way she was bogged down with all the cares in her life.

She told him about eating better, choosing protein over empty carbs, drinking plenty of water.

Getting out of bed at three-thirty in the morning took discipline, so he started going to bed earlier, until one night when he woke up to the dreaded scraping sound. Cold chills went down his back and his whole body froze, visualizing the hooded figure in the back yard.

Slowly, he got out of bed, crept to the window, lifted the slat of the blind and dropped it immediately. Fear like lightning.

Almost against the window, a dark hood was bent sideways on his way to his trash bin. Fred lifted his head, ears pricked, then laid back on his paws. Slowly Amos pried the slats apart.

The hooded figure was lifting the lid of the trash bin, his shoulders moving as he lifted one garbage bag, then another.

Suddenly, without warning, Fred exploded, rising to his feet in a lighting quick move, hoarse barks tearing from his throat.

The man dropped the lid and ran swiftly, Fred going crazy at the back door.

"Hush, Fred, down. Down now. Let him go."

So that was all the night visitor wanted. The trash bin. Was he a scavenger, or was he actually hungry? A man or a youth? Dangerous or merely desperate?

It took him a long time to get back to sleep, and he skipped going to the gym. His shins ached anyway, so a day of rest would be welcome. He fried eggs, ate four slices of toast, then went to the big house to find Joseph.

"So he's hungry. Likely a poor soul," Joseph remarked, as he sipped his morning coffee. "Keep an eye out, and perhaps we can win a new friend."

"Cold and hungry." Lila nodded. "The poor man. Good for Fred. See, he's already worth his money."

Nancy said the old couple wasn't thinking straight, that guy was up to no good. You couldn't trust anyone these days, and certainly not some crackpot in a hooded sweatshirt. She suggested Amos might as well keep a gun handy.

On his walk home that evening, he sniffed the moist cold air and it reminded him of spring. A budding forsythia, tulips and daffodils pushing through the snow. A time of renewal and a time of gearing up for his real work.

He found hope welling in his chest. Real hope of a brighter, better future, whatever it might be. He'd begun to see a certain starlight far away in the dark of a night sky.

Chapter 14

Raymond, Lydia, Cathy, and Lavina took up residence at the Johnson place in early spring. Dismayed at the amount of money it took for the closing costs, taxes due, and other unforeseen costs, they had to borrow ten thousand dollars from a wealthy brother in Lancaster, who grudgingly wrote them a check, with firm demands of payback to the tune of two hundred dollars a month. If this stipulation wasn't met, interest would be charged.

He signed his letter, "*Aus lieve* (with love), David," which irritated Lydia to no end, saying how could he have any "lieve," asking for that money back like that. He was so rich he'd never miss it, and besides, he didn't know what "lieve" was.

Raymond said, "Now, now, Lydia, he helped us out, but we do need to pay him back. We'll use the income tax return."

That fired her up like a steam engine. She wailed about how she was going to use that money to remodel and landscape. So Raymond said alright, he'd ask to work overtime.

"If only Amos was home, his wages would soon have it paid," she lamented.

Lydia soon discovered she did not love the Johnson place without the money to renovate. For one, the trees took all the nutrients from the grass beneath, and there were large bare spots that became a muddy smear every time it rained. She often thought of her lush grass on the hillside, the sun and rain and fertilizer a wonderful thing.

Her kitchen was in the back, with dark oak cabinets, which were not in style, but for now there was no money to replace them.

Raymond was given eight hours a week overtime, boosting his paycheck considerably, so that the two hundred a month could be paid back in the required time. Lydia took on two more housecleaning jobs, developed an excruciating case of bursitis in her right shoulder, and blamed it on stress from the required two hundred dollars. She sat in her old recliner with a soft pack of ice and the ibuprofen bottle beside her, seriously threatening the girls with being grounded if they didn't get those dishes washed.

She hated the carpeting in the living room, hated the color of her old recliners, but knew there was no money for new ones. She admitted to herself—but certainly not to anyone else—she wished they'd never bought this place.

Cathy began to date another young man from Lancaster, one whose siblings had all left the church and lived as English people, which brought a shiver of fear to Lydia, parachuting from her lofty position with Cathy so fast she couldn't catch her breath on the way down. She pleaded and cried, begged her not to date him, but Cathy was obstinate. She flung her shoulders around and tossed her head, said he was cute and funny and drove an amazing truck. He was a roofer and made tons of money, and there was no way on earth she was ever going to live the way her parents did.

Her mother squeaked a limp sentence about prayer and the will of God, and Cathy informed her she had prayed and read a whole chapter in Corinthians thirteen about love, so she had nothing to worry about. It was God's will, she was convinced of it.

"But what about the siblings? How can a whole family go English?" she whined.

"The parents stayed Amish, Mom."

A long sigh from her mother, a dab of the white Kleenex.

"Cathy, you can't do what Amos did. It would be the death of me. My nerves couldn't take it. I'd have a mental breakdown."

"Mom, that's manipulation of the worst kind. Stop it or I'm telling Dad."

And so on.

Lavina planned a trip to Florida, but was strictly forbidden to go. Troubles mounted when the old sewage system backed up when April rain came in torrents. Raymond found the clogged pipe, fortunately, and worked all night with a kindhearted neighbor to fix the problem, while Lydia lay awake stiff with anxiety and wondered if it had been God's will they bought this place at all. What a pack of troubles had befallen them, really.

And Lavina went ahead with her Florida plans for fall.

AMOS WAS HAPPIER than he'd ever been, with the sun on his shoulders, workouts at the gym, his white flabby arms and legs a bit more toned than before. He felt unbelievably energized, his whole outlook improved, whistling as he raked soggy leaves and twigs, mowed and cut edges, brought a bouquet of daffodils for Lila and one for Nancy. He spread lime and sulphur, ordered a pile of bark mulch, pruned and trimmed. Soft breezes teased the budding branches and waved the forsythia and lilacs.

He thought of his parents, but had not heard a word since Christmas, which might be for the best. He wondered if they'd moved yet, was curious to see where they lived.

His workouts became more intense, Scott often egging him on or working out with him. Competition grew as weeks passed.

He still refused to work out with anyone else, shy to the point of being a recluse, and so the early morning ritual continued. Lifting weights was a surprise for him, quickly learning he could lift more than he'd thought possible, and that was all the encouragement he needed.

He smiled now, and laughed out loud, drove his truck with the windows down, his elbow looped over the left door, his music turned up loudly. But he still ate alarming amounts of food. Foods high in calories, laden with fats and sugars, eating fast the way he always had, consuming way more than he should.

Scott repeatedly pushed good nutrition, which Amos listened to with a small smile, a flash of recognition from his small brown eyes, but never a true acceptance.

He found his jeans loose, his T-shirts flapping, and became ecstatic. He worked in the sun, acquired a deeper color, the acne scars evening out somewhat.

Yet he dealt with a pressing loneliness, a sense of lost identity. He had no idea who he really was at this point in his life. Was he truly an English person? Did driving a car and dressing English make you one of them? Or would he always be Amish, deep down in his heart and soul?

He had no friends outside of work. There was Scott, but he was beginning to get on his nerves, preaching all the time. He had Bible verses on the wall, a Bible on his desk, asking if he knew Jesus. Had Amos accepted him personally as his Lord and Savior?

He knew who God was. And His son Jesus. He had known about them since he was little, listening to the Amish preachers every two weeks. He sat on benches, held the thick black *Ausbund* (hymnal), and sang along with the lull of the plainsong, that slow rhythm of song originating in a Swiss prison back in the 1700s.

Of course he knew about God, probably better than Scott did. He was Amish, after all. Or had been. He was blessed, a direct descendant of the forefathers, the revered pilgrims who'd gone ahead and opened the way for all the Amish, a clean path of righteousness if you kept the *ordnung* and lived a devout and humble life.

But Scott kept asking the same disturbing question.

But do you know Christ? Have you accepted Jesus?

"Probably," Amos said. "I don't know."

And Scott looked at him for a very long time without saying anything, which bothered him a lot.

Scott's blue eyes were like Joseph's. They seemed to see right through to his soul, and no one was supposed to do that. He became uncomfortable around Scott, wished he'd leave him alone.

Scott got the message, said he was sorry to pressure him, and stayed true to his word, which gave Amos a few weeks of peace and quiet, but his mind continued to work. He had maintained a vague sense that leaving his Amish home also meant leaving God behind, if He existed. But now both Joseph and Scott seemed to be calling him to God, or their version of Him. Was it really the same God of the Amish church?

Perhaps he should never have left his parents. The thought gave him a sense of uneasiness, as if the frightful consequences for his rebellion would rain down on his head at any moment.

He told himself he'd return one day, after Cathy was out of the house and he had proven to himself he was capable of more than his mother thought. Someone with the ability to hold a job, to be financially responsible, to improve his health and appearance, to think on his own without attaching himself to someone else's view. For now, he would have to realize he was on a journey. He couldn't expect his new identity to come together fully in a week, a month, a year.

Yes, his mother had often failed him, his father limp and swaying to any winds of adversary, his sisters unkind, condescending. But could he blame the path he had chosen on his family? Was blame even necessary?

And still loneliness dogged his days, a relentless adversary. He knew the need for friends, male companionship, but had no idea how to go about making friends. He was so outsized, so unattractive, coupled with a lack of personality. What man his age would want to talk to him?

But he loved the early mornings now, the sharp scent of wet earth and forsythia, of lilac and dandelion when he got into his truck to go to the gym. He often felt a sense of gratefulness, a fullness in the region of his heart, but he had no idea what to do with it, exactly.

His time at the gym increased, his workouts becoming more difficult as time went on. Scott was there on most mornings, quietly inserting opinions, instructing him without Amos even fully being aware of it.

He was lifting weights, straining, grunting, shaking his head as he let the weights fall, saying that was it, no more.

He stood, wiped rivers of perspiration, felt deeply ashamed. Scott handed him a soft towel, a bottle of water, slapped his shoulder.

"Yeah, man," he said excitedly.

"What?" Amos asked, puzzled.

"Good going there. You keep that up and you'll see change."

Amos grinned. "You serious?"

"Of course I am. You're lifting much better, getting it right."

Amos lowered his head, kicked self-consciously at a barbell.

"I don't know about that."

Scott smiled, sat on a padded bench used for bench pressing.

"You know, Amos, you're settled in. The gym got into your blood, right?"

Amos nodded.

"Which is good. You're changing on the inside and soon you'll see the results on the outside. What I'd love for you to do, is come to church with us. Have Sunday dinner. We could go to a nice place so Kim doesn't have to cook."

Amos looked up, suspicion narrowing his eyes.

"Kim? She your wife?"

"Yes. My soulmate. My whole world."

"Wow."

"What? What's that supposed to mean?"

"I don't know. Guess I'm not used to people talking about their spouses that way."

"Have you met a girl? Ever been in love?"

Amos hesitated, then shook his head.

"Never?"

"Well, I guess sort of. There was this neighbor girl."

"Was?"

"Yeah. She went to college, met someone. She was just nice to me, took pity, I guess."

"You know, Amos, you really have zero confidence," Scott said, not unkindly.

Amos bit his lower lip, cleared his throat before turning to toy with cables on the bench.

"I have no reason to be confident. I'm morbidly obese and have a face like cottage cheese."

"Oh, come on."

"Seriously. Some quirk of God or fate or whatever robbed me of good looks. My parents are fairly attractive, my sisters both good looking, popular. I'm the family clown."

Scott eyed him levelly for a long moment.

"God created you, Amos. He formed you in your mother's womb. He loves you more than you'll ever comprehend. He has a special purpose for you. Knows exactly what will happen to you in the future. He created your facial features for a purpose, and you know it's a good purpose because He is good. I promise you He wants what's best for you. But you won't really feel that until you accept Jesus Christ as your Savior. After you give your life to Him."

"I told you to cut out the preaching. I'm from an Amish home, raised in the church and know right from wrong. So just . . ." He drew his fingertips horizontally across his throat for emphasis.

"Knowing right from wrong isn't what it's about. I mean, that's part of it, but . . ."

Angered, Amos walked away, gathered his jacket, and left. Scott watched after him but didn't try to stop him.

In his truck, a fierce rebellion seized him, an aversion to good-looking, sculptured, confident Scott who thought everyone had to think the way he did. What did he know about anything spiritual, running that gym with all the half-clothed individuals catering to their egos?

It was wrong, to his own way of thinking. He came from the Amish who would never think any of that was okay, so who was Scott to instruct him in the way to Jesus?

He ate copiously at the early morning diner, ordering the biggest breakfast on the menu, with hotcakes on the side. Drenched in syrup and butter, he washed it all down with coffee, left a sizable tip, and prepared to pay his bill.

Out of the corner of his eye, he caught sight of two dark figures, then turned away before Emanuel Beiler and Joe Zook could recognize him.

He winced when he found them standing at his table.

"Amos. Raymond's Amos."

Slowly, he gave in, turned, and looked up at them.

"Hello."

"How are you, Amos?" Joe Zook spoke quietly, not unkindly.

"I'm doing okay. And you?"

"Alright. It's good to see you. I hardly recognized you with the haircut, the beard."

Ashamed, Amos said nothing.

"So, when are you coming back to the fold? Our prayers for you continue. You won't be able to find peace out here in the world."

Emanuel Beiler grasped his shoulder. "We miss you in church."

Amos nodded, picked up his knife, laid it down again.

"You're putting your parents through so much. 'Honor thy father and mother so the days may be long in which you live.' You are living in sin, Amos, and it's hard on your parents. Especially your poor mother. She sits in church and cries so much. For you."

Amos nodded again, would not raise his eyes.

"Think on these things, Amos. Don't wait too long to come back, have your sins forgiven."

They moved on, and Amos took a deep cleansing breath, all of his energy draining out. The day stretched before him, devoid of life, of color or joy. He was terribly confused, his head pounding with anxiety. Yes, he knew he was a sinner. Of course he was, dressed in English clothes, different haircut, driving a truck, drawing the veil of sorrow over his family. Suffocating them with the path he had chosen.

He barely remembered paying, barely knew he was driving home, guilt as thick as molasses choking him. Yes, he was guilty of all they had said. He did not honor his parents. Was no honor to them.

But why should he? They had never honored him. And he had always been a dishonor, even as a young child. His mother had always felt ashamed of him, long before he left home.

He felt the incoming tide of fear and rebellion, guilt and shame crashing over him in a powerful wave. What was the use trying? He was doomed to live out his life as a failure, a lost black sheep knowing only defeat.

This turmoil continued as he worked that day. Pushing the pressure washer out of the shed, he tripped on the blade of a shovel, lost his balance, and fell hard on the cement floor. He got to his feet, rubbed his shoulder, and bent to check the gas supply before replacing the cap. He gave the usual yank on the cord, then another, before trying a third time. Still nothing.

He looked up to see Joseph coming slowly from the big house, tapping his cane on the brick walkway, his back bent even more since the day Amos met him. He was wearing his old green sweater with patched elbows, his usual brown everyday trousers, a white fedora on his head. He stopped to grasp a branch of lilacs, inhale deeply, then watch a flock of juncos before moving on.

In the time Amos had been here, he'd never seen him angry or upset, no matter the circumstances. His life was an open testament of every good thing a human could possibly possess, him and Lila both.

He felt more love from both of them than he'd felt in a lifetime from his parents or sisters, but had never understood what the old couple had, other than age and experience. If there had ever been unfairness in life, it had come through the untimely death of their only son, leaving them childless for the remainder of their days.

And still they loved.

"Good morning, son," Joseph called out. "Beautiful day!"

"Sure is," Amos answered. "And as soon as I get this thing started, it will be even better."

Joseph leaned on his cane, chuckled.

"So, what are we pressure washing today?" he asked.

"The walkways and the screened-in porch at the back of the house."

"Good thinking. Yes. Perfect. Lila was just saying how she'd like to get some of her overgrown houseplants out of the living room. She would like for you to repot her fig tree, if you can work that in sometime this week. If not, it's perfectly alright."

"I can do that. No problem."

He kept yanking on the starter cord, pressing the choke button repeatedly.

"Have you checked the spark plug?" Joseph asked.

He found the problem to be just that, and grinned at Joseph as he cleaned it, reassembled the part, and started the engine.

Joseph held up a hand.

"There. Good work. Now, I meant to ask if you're still going to the exercise place. When I'm sleepless, I find myself pacing restlessly, and saw you leave at a few minutes before four o'clock."

"Yeah. I go five mornings a week now."

"And you find it helpful?"

"I do. It's funny how that works. Instead of being tired, I'm energized for the day."

"Good, good. You're doing a great job, energy or not. Lila and I are so relieved to be rid of the pressing responsibility of this vast amount of upkeep. We should retire to a home for the aged, but it would take the life out of us both."

Amos nodded.

"We love it here. It's our heaven on earth. God has been good to us, and I worship Him with a grateful heart. Did you see the climbing tea roses?"

"You mean along the screened-in porch?"

"Yes. Ah, but they're the essence of heaven. A reminder of God's love to all of us. Now when you go back there to do the pressure washing, be sure to stop and smell them. They're not like modern day roses, but from a plant that's been there for generations. Wonderful scent."

"I'll stop."

"You do that. Now, have you eaten? Nancy is making waffles."

"I ate at the diner."

"Then I won't keep you. I'll tell Lila about the back porch. It will make her very happy."

Always, when Joseph left, he felt a warm glow, a sense of renewal like warm breeze on a cold day. Or stepping into a warm room after being out in the cold. He supposed it was his age, an old man filled with love and wisdom, one who loved God in spite of having gone through hardship.

The power washer chugged loudly, in the way of all gas engines, revving up as he applied the spray, slowing down when he stopped.

He loved to pressure wash the old house, to keep it spotless, as if it showed its best color after being thoroughly scrubbed. It was still a part of his life he was immensely grateful for, the beauty of this fine old property, and his appreciation of it.

Perhaps it was a trait handed down from his mother, this grasp of beauty around him. His mother had always found a way to incorporate beauty into a simple environment with very little money. Yard sales, thrift shops, a quart of paint, and she created a look found in her favorite magazine.

She'd always been happy when working, whistling low under her breath, a soft hum of contentment. The front porch of the old white house built on the side of the hill had been transformed into an eye-catching place of beauty, with black porch rockers matching the shutters, pink and white geraniums growing profusely on sunny corners, with great, cascading ferns in shady spots.

He'd secretly been proud of her, but was always too shy to say anything. Now, he found himself visualizing this porch and brick walkway, the things he could accomplish if given a chance.

Which would never be his, a poor laborer for the wealthy, but it was fun to dream.

He saw that the floor of the screened-in porch needed a coat of paint, so he decided to use a mop and soapy water to save the existing floor, then talk to Joseph about pressure washing later. He never wanted to be bold, or make unwanted suggestions, always afraid of being intrusive.

He opened the back door quietly, went to the laundry room for the plastic bucket, began to fill it at the sink, reached below for Mr. Clean and a mophead. He whistled low under his breath, the turmoil of his day forgotten, the physical exercise lifting the dark clouds.

His phone rang.

He fished it out of his pocket, checked the caller, and frowned when his sister's name came up.

He sighed, said, "Hey, Cathy."

"Hey."

"What's up?"

"Just wondered if you'd come help out over here."

"With what?"

"Oh, Mom's having a meltdown, or another one. Honestly, Amos, I'm sick of her yelling. We're in the new house and she hates this carpeting, took up a corner and found pine flooring, so now she's going nuts. Dad doesn't want to do anything yet, says we'd have to rent a sander, and we don't have the money. She's determined to sand it manually, like, on hands and knees with sandpaper. You have to come help. We're all going crazy."

"That bad, huh?"

"Stop talking like English people and get over here. ASAP."

"I have to talk to my boss first. It won't be today and I'm not sure about tomorrow. Won't she want to do it herself, anyway?"

"You mean Mom?"

"Who else?"

"She's a mess. She took on two more houses and can hardly do all of the cleaning, never mind refinishing an old floor."

"Mm-hm."

"Well, just get over here as soon as you can. You're going to have to help Dad pull the carpet up, then we have to remove the staples around the edges, all that before sanding. I'm not planning on breaking my back and neither is Lavina."

"Alright. I'll call you when it suits."

"I'll text you the address. Don't forget us."

"I won't."

There was a soft click and Cathy was gone. He lifted the mop and bucket, sighed audibly, did not want to go. It sounded like the place was more of a battleground than ever, with everyone bowing to his mother's needs. One thing was accomplished, followed by another, then another.

But it was his family, and he was called to honor them.

Chapter 15

He went back to work on the porch, his thoughts going to his family. "Dysfunctional" crossed his mind, but he brushed it away, ashamed. Who was he to judge an Amish person? They were doing the best they knew how. He wondered what his father's views were on carpeting versus pine flooring, but knew his mother would overpower him regardless.

His thoughts swerved aside to having a wife of his own someday, a dream that now seemed even farther away. He couldn't help thinking of Skye Larkin at times, but mostly it ended in self-loathing, ashamed of the way he'd allowed himself to fall for her.

She'd been nice to him, and that was something, he told himself repeatedly. He still wished he could see her, talk to her, find out about this Paul, if nothing else. But knew it was best to let her go.

Whether he admitted it or not, he wasn't sure about marrying a girl without a plain background anyway. Did English girls wash dishes and do laundry, keep a house clean and all of that?

The big question was if they would appreciate his background. It was too complicated. But he hoped and dreamed of having a wife, someone to love and care for. Didn't everyone?

The back door opened, and Lila's mop of thin white hair appeared, her frail body wrapped in a heavy robe. She lifted a smiling face.

"Why, good morning to you, dear boy," she breathed.

"Good morning, Lila."

"Oh my, but you make me happy. Joseph just told me. But that plant doesn't have to be repotted now. Just whenever. I know you're busy. I'm just so pleased with having this porch done so early in the season. Thank you so much."

"You're welcome."

"Come in for lunch and I'll have Nancy make you a waffle."

"Okay."

The door closed behind her, leaving a smile on his face. Waffles sounded great, having worked off that early breakfast. He hitched his jeans up, drew his belt in another notch. He hated belts.

He thought often of how much more comfortable suspenders were, but he'd get used to these English clothes eventually. He grinned, inserted a hand below the belt, knew they were actually no longer a good fit. He began to whistle a well-known tune, then picked up his mop and cleaned furiously.

He ate two fluffy waffles with chicken gravy, a side of coleslaw, and drank a quart of iced tea, listening halfheartedly to Nancy's harangue against the local laws, the whole system flawed and out of control. The United States was going down, there was no doubt.

This always left Amos reeling, as if he'd been knocked sideways and needed to find his bearings again. Was it really true what she said, or was a person meant to take his dues if he broke the law? He had always thought if you did wrong you paid your dues eventually and it was no one's fault but your own, or was that an old-fashioned way of thinking? Nancy kept up the tirade as he ate, sniffs and fist banging at the close of the most emphatic opinions.

After lunch, he felt sleepy. He found a warm spot on the south side of the garden shed, drew a lawn chair over, sat back, and closed his eyes to the gentle sun. He mulled over his day, smiled as he found it all very interesting, this observation of characters inserted into his life. He frowned about Scott's repeated preaching, felt genuine anger at Emanuel Beiler. Joe Zook, too. They had no idea what he needed or didn't need. Neither did Scott. He'd figure this all out on his own, thank you very much.

He had a notion to forget about his family and the carpeting crisis. If his father didn't stand up to her then it was his problem. But obligation raised its face. He was the son, after all, and it was the least he could do, for all the disobedience.

He drifted off, his face to the sun, and woke with his nose and forehead on fire. He touched his face tentatively, shrugged, and got back to work.

The pressure washer motor whined and water sprayed as he finished walkways, then turned to find he was being observed. He stopped the engine, wiped his hands on his jeans, and stepped toward a black minivan. The door opened and a young Amish girl stepped out, casting an uncertain glance in his direction.

"Hi."

"Hello. Can I help you with something?"

"I don't know. Is this the home of, let me see, Joseph Brown?"

"Yes, it is."

"They had an ad in today's paper for someone to clean house, and I talked to him on the phone. He said they'll be home."

"Sure. Just go up those wide front steps. Ring the doorbell."

He did not recognize her at all. He watched her take the front steps two at a time, thought she must be really strong for her size.

Pleasantly plump, he thought, grinning a bit, then felt foolish.

No one should notice things like that, although he had to admit, he did. He went back to his pressure washing, but kept an eye on the front door. He wanted to ask who she was.

He shut off the motor when she emerged, walked toward her. "Excuse me, but can I ask . . ."

She stopped, raised an eyebrow. He noticed darkly tanned skin, eyes like a bluebell on a cloudy day, with brown hair streaked in blonde. Her lips were full, her cheeks rounded, and when she smiled her two front teeth protruded very slightly, which only added to her charm. She was short, he guessed a few inches above five foot, and by no means thin.

"Who are you?"

He held up a hand when she opened her mouth.

"I mean, that sounds weird, but I'm from the Amish. And I don't remember you at all."

"Hmm. You don't look Amish."

"Well, I'm not anymore."

"We, our family, just moved here."

"That explains it."

"Who're you?"

"Raymond Beiler's Amos."

"Cathy and Lavina's brother?"

"That's me."

"Huh . . ."

He felt the embarrassing blush, lowered his face, kicked at a fallen twig.

"Do you ever come to the Saturday night parties?"

"No."

"Why not?"

He shrugged. "I don't know. Not really my thing."

"How do you know if you never come?"

She raised the eyebrow again, smiled her crooked tooth smile, which he found to be the most adorable thing.

He had to know. "Did you get the job?"

"Yeah. I can't start until the end of May. My sister's due to have a baby, so . . . duty calls."

Amos nodded. "I didn't ask your name."

"Anna. Anna Riehl."

"Good to meet you, Anna."

She raised the eyebrow, smiled, and was gone. Pink dress, black bib apron, tennis shoes. Her white heart-shaped covering. She was as cute as a button—it was an old phrase, but it truly fit her.

His day was turning out to be very interesting indeed.

He enjoyed an evening of solitude, except for Fred, who followed him around everywhere he went. He grilled a steak, upended the hot sauce bottle over it, made a spinach and tomato salad, and took it out to the back patio, where a few rays of spring sun found its way through pine branches. He shared a few bits of steak with Fred, who sat perfectly still, his round eyes never leaving his plate, then snatched up the tiny morsels and instantly returned to his watchful post.

It was a mellow, perfumed evening, the aromas and sights of the golden hour creating a soft, sighing need, a longing for something he could not name.

All in good time, he reasoned.

Scott would say he needed Jesus, but he still wasn't sure God was even real. Too many questions and not enough answers.

One thing he was sure of: your childhood defined you. The manner in which you were raised, the people around you who created your culture, your way of life handed down through the generations. He was a product of the culture he was raised in, and he didn't much like the results.

Hm. But that Anna was cute, though. Well, she'd find a nice Amish boy. He had no intention of being Amish ever again. But what was the alternative? He never felt at home anywhere else, either. Perhaps he should go to church with Scott sometime, just to see.

If this Anna knew Cathy and Lavina, it meant she was with the group of youth who ran a little wild and enjoyed more liberating activities like bowling or going to movies, riding around in cars. To be honest, he was scared of even thinking about them. He'd never been accepted in the more conservative group, where the youth basically did what was expected of them. He could only imagine how he'd be treated by the more liberal youth.

He drank the last of his ice water and went to clean up.

Joseph had given him a Bible, a small black leatherbound one, with "Amos Beiler, dear son," inscribed on the inside. He'd always felt silly, seeing the perfect calligraphy, felt ashamed of the "dear son." He certainly would never take the place of their Brad. It felt almost wrong to accept their affection.

He opened the Bible slowly, let the soft tissue-like pages fall, then read a few passages in Galatians. Nothing made any sense. He wasn't sure any of these writers knew what they were talking about. It seemed like they were going around and around in circles, as if they were trying to find their way out of a maze. He closed the Bible, placed it on the stand by his recliner, and sighed. He crossed his hands over his stomach and stretched his legs in front of him.

It was pleasant to think of Anna, so he allowed himself the indulgence of remembering her face, the way the sun shone on her hair. But he assured himself nothing could ever come of it. It was disgraceful how he fell instantly for any girl who merely spoke to him.

He fell asleep with a smile on his face and woke up with the memory of pleasant things.

A MONTH LATER he'd managed to lose another fifteen pounds, the workouts at the gym getting more and more intense. He'd thrown himself into weightlifting and cardio and learned to love the way he could forget about everything else while he was pushing his body to its limits.

He drove to his parents' new house during an April downpour, wipers moving furiously across the windshield, clouds of mist from hissing tires all but obscuring his view. His neck was stiff, his nerves in knots when he arrived, only to find an air of conflict the minute he entered.

"How are you, Mom?" His innocent greeting was received like a magnet receives needles and pins. His mother glared at him, then seemed to change tactics and began complaining, describing her sorry state of affairs, dabbing theatrically at her eyes.

Raymond had said no to refinishing the floor.

"Amos, could you loan us a couple thousand to have this floor done?"

And that was just the beginning.

He listened quietly, nodding, but he could find no sympathy for her self-imposed suffering. His father had gone to a meeting, something about a support group for a troubled marriage.

"But Amos, he said we could live with this carpeting until the ten thousand is paid, which is another four years. Four years of that miserable, filthy carpet. I mean it, Amos, I can't do it. Just give us a few thousand. I know you have it."

He did have it, but he had no intention of going against his father's wishes, and he told her so, as kindly as possible, sending her into a fit of weeping. She gave him a wounded look before stamping off into her bedroom.

He went to find Cathy, who shrugged and started to vent her own string of complaints about the state of their family. Then, suddenly, she stopped and looked at him standing in the doorway. "My word, Amos, what is happening to you? You don't even look like yourself."

"I've been working out."

"Wow." She stood stunned for a moment, then went on to tell him the news from her group of youth.

Almost, he'd felt like a real brother, leaning over Cathy's shoulder to see pictures of the new boyfriend.

"Don't you ever think of girls?" she asked.

"Of course. I just haven't met anyone."

Cathy considered this, then said seriously, "Are you sure you want to marry an English girl?"

"Why do you say that?"

"They're brought up so differently."

For a long moment, Amos said nothing, then decided to speak his mind.

"Cathy, there are lots of marriages that are a lot better than our parents'. And I mean, in the English world. I hope you see that. The way we were brought up, we never got to see a real, loving, unselfish relationship. I don't think either one of us know the first thing about a good marriage."

"But we're Amish. *Real* Christians," Cathy shot back.

"We are flawed human beings like everyone else. Cathy, look around you. Look at Mom and Dad. Is that the kind of marriage you want?"

"See, Amos, you're so English, you're already against us."

She flounced off down the stairs to find her mother seated at the kitchen table, eyes swollen and red from weeping.

She went to the refrigerator to find something, or to bide her time, then closed it again. Amos joined them in the kitchen.

"Mom, look at Amos. Did you notice his weight?" Cathy asked.

"I see. Are you dieting?"

"No. Well, not really. Working out at the gym. Next step is changing my eating habits. I guess I have a little. It's tough."

"You do look different. Your face is so tanned," she said, between sniffs. Then, "Amos, please. Dat won't mind."

"Mom, I'm sorry. I won't do it. I can't go against Dat. Can't you find it in your heart to accept the carpeting for a while?"

"Just go, Amos. I'm tired now."

So he let himself out the door and into the balmy evening, noticing the scent of pine and leaves budding on trees. He thought how he could spread grass seed over the bare spots beneath the trees, but he had no intention of returning anytime soon.

She had wanted the Johnson place so badly, and Raymond had done everything in his power to make it possible. Now there was everything wrong with it. Carpeting was only the beginning. The kitchen cabinets smelled musty, the commode didn't flush properly, the basement needed a dehumidifier.

Amos drove away vowing to live his life on his own terms.

He told Scott about the visit, and he listened with patience, asking questions here and there. Scott realized that Amos had lived with his mother's discontentment all his life. He suggested gently that perhaps Amos had sometimes felt like the musty kitchen cabinets needing to be replaced. Or the carpeting.

And so Amos sat, his elbows on his knees, not meeting Scott's eyes as he talked. He noticed the sky red in the east, the sun rising unexpectedly. He'd talked for two hours, or close to it. People were coming in to start their morning routine.

"You need counseling, Amos. Ultimately, you need Jesus in your heart, but your story also needs to be untangled by a professional. Would you go if I helped you find someone?"

"Counseling? You mean where crazy people go?"

"Where smart people go. Everyone has issues. Only smart people know they need help dealing with them."

"Where'd you pull that from?"

"Sarcasm isn't helpful here."

"Sorry."

"I'll have a few numbers for you tomorrow, okay?"

Amos nodded. They were only numbers. He didn't have to call.

ANNA ARRIVED THE third week in May, on a Tuesday morning when he was planting purple petunias, foxtail, and white alyssum in blue ceramic urns, Lila hovering, directing.

"Oh, it's Anna," she said breathlessly. "Where's Joseph? Well, I'll meet her, direct her to her first room."

She hurried off, and Amos quickly realized she might fall in her nervous flutter. He hurried after her and asked her to be careful. She took his arm, steadied herself.

Amos watched Anna mount the stairs, her face open and honest, smiling that smile, greeting Lila graciously, saying hello to Amos.

"Yes, my dear, come this way. I'll show you to the first room, which is the guest bedroom upstairs. In the attic. We have three stories here, my girl."

"But should you go up two flights?" Anna asked.

"I certainly should. And I'll be back down as well. That's what a handrail is for."

Anna looked at Amos and up went the eyebrow.

"Amos will move the furniture and remove storm windows for you. Joseph planned to do it, but he forgets his age. Have you two met before, by any chance?"

"When she came for her interview," Amos answered.

Slowly they made their way up the stairs, hovering over Lila, then reached the top of the second set of steps without mishap.

They surveyed the two large guest rooms, noticed the storage in the dormers leading to the roof. There was heavy oak furniture, massive in its size, cumbersome drapes to be vacuumed and put back on heavy rods.

Lila went back down and Amos helped carry everything up two flights of stairs, showed Anna the porcelain clawfoot tub where she could refill the bucket if necessary. He moved furniture, glad for every weight he'd lifted at the gym.

"She's a little bitty thing," Anna observed.

"She's still pretty capable though," he answered.

Anna said there was no way this job would take her all day.

"She's very picky. Likes her stuff done right, so take your time. Money doesn't seem to be a problem here."

"I can tell."

He helped her take down the heavy curtains, which took longer than either of them anticipated. Then he raised cranky old windows, removed storm windows and screens, stacked them neatly against a wall. He didn't want to leave, so he asked if there was anything she needed done before he went back to work.

She was polishing a mirror and spoke to him without turning.

"She didn't say anything about bedding. Should we remove it?"

"I'll ask."

When he returned, he told her to leave it, no one ever slept up here. He added that Nancy was preparing coffee break in the kitchen and they were supposed to join them.

"Who's Nancy?" she called back from a trip to the clawfoot tub.

"The housekeeper. She cooks, does laundry, general cleaning."

"What do you do?"

"I live here. In the gatehouse."

"That little house at the end of the drive? It's cute."

"Yeah."

"Why'd you leave home?"

"It's a long story."

"I bet. Let's go. I'm hungry."

He found himself feeling shy and awkward, the old inadequacy returning. He felt every acne scar, every cumbersome movement, knew that he put too much cream cheese on his toasted bagel.

Anna had confidence to spare, perched on a barstool, stirring a sizable dollop of creamer in tea. She didn't like coffee, just black tea laced with plenty of milk or cream. She chatted with Nancy as if she'd known her all her life, discussing recipes and furniture polish and the size of the old house, while Amos chewed methodically and wrestled with soul-sapping defeat.

He was a bump on a log, a swelling protrusion on an otherwise healthy appendage. He heard himself slurp and swallow repulsively, while she laughed and drank her tea, enjoying her food.

No one noticed him, so he finished his coffee and left.

"Hey, where you going?" Nancy called.

"I have work to do," he said brusquely, shouldering his way out the door.

She was Amish anyhow, he reasoned, and he wasn't. She was far too confident, would walk all over him if they got married, and he'd be a poor puppet like his father. He decided he didn't need her, didn't even like her.

But he found it hard to concentrate on his work. Anna was adorable, in a short, round, energetic way. Kind and polite to Lila, a real worker, ambitious with her happy outlook. But she talked so easily to Nancy, while he sat on the sidelines feeling steadily worse, which was the last thing he needed.

Here he was, immediately attracted to anyone who would treat him with everyday, ordinary friendliness.

Loser. Dumb. Stupid.

His phone rang and he saw that it was Lila.

"Yep."

"Would you please help Anna with some of the boxes on the top closet shelves? She's not quite tall enough. You will need a small ladder. Thank you, Amos."

He put his phone away, checked the third-story windows, then made his way to the garage for a ladder. He carried it the whole way up the two flights of stairs, barely winded.

Anna was on her hands and knees, cleaning behind the immense armoire with the gold hardware. She got to her feet in one swift move. "These," she said, pointing to a shelf stacked with cardboard boxes. He nodded, set up the ladder, and got them down, one by one. The tops were coated with dust, the shelves beneath showing the exact imprint.

"Thanks," she said. Then, "Seriously, what is this old couple going to do with this gigantic house full of old stuff? Their kids will have a job to do someday."

"They don't have children."

"Seriously?"

"Their one son died."

A look of sympathy passed over her features, and there was a moment of silence between them.

"Well, back to work," she said, more subdued now. "Don't worry about the ladder, just leave it. Lila wants to go through most of these boxes."

He did not want to leave, he realized. He needed to ask about her family, listen to her voice a bit longer when they were alone.

"So," he began. "Anything else?"

She was bent over, wringing a cloth above a plastic bucket filled with sudsy hot water. Around her, a shaft of light through the dormer window picked up the dust, brightening the faded wood floor, the faded green wallpaper and the dark trim.

The room was dull, old-fashioned, had likely stayed the same for a hundred years, and he wondered if it would stay this way for another century. The old four-poster bed was made of cherry wood, the quilt appearing to be stitched by hand. For a few seconds, he pictured this aging forlorn room, slowly growing feeble, like the owners, and what would become of it?

The bright spot in the shaft of light, this young girl named Anna, would follow him for a long time. She had an aura of happiness, a genuine humor about life and the people around her. He felt as if he could absorb some of it, if he was fortunate enough to be in her presence a while longer.

"Um, let me see. I know the minute you go down the stairs, I'll need you again."

And then she looked directly into his eyes and smiled with a genuine parting of her mouth, the white teeth like pearls, protruding ever so slightly, her eyes crinkling and sparkling.

"I like having you around," she said, the words like colorful bubbles rising in the air.

"You do?"

"Of course. I love people. They're so interesting. You know what I thought when I saw you the first time?"

Amos shook his head, the power of speech gone.

"I thought you appeared to, I don't know, have gone through a lot? It's in your eyes."

Amos could not look at her, so he nudged a cardboard box with his foot, coughed, walked to the dormer to look out the window.

She began wiping the armoire, slowly, methodically.

He turned. "It's embarrassing, my story."

"Why?"

"I don't know. It just is."

"You want to hear mine?"

"You mean, now?"

"No. We both have work to do."

"Right. But yes, I'd like to hear your story sometime."

He turned to make his way to the stairs.

She watched after him, and smiled to herself.

Chapter 16

He went to the gym, putting all his concentration into lifting two hundred pounds, then two hundred fifty. He ran on the treadmill till perspiration ran down his back, soaked the front of his T-shirt. He felt the jiggling of his fat, loathed his own body, hated his red, swollen eyes in the face with cottage cheese skin.

His heart beat heavily, his breath came in hard, painful gasps, but he lumbered on. Two miles, three. He ran on, away from cloying defeat and shattered dreams. The brightness of Anna, the untrustworthiness of Skye. Deceit and pain. Things would never change.

His thighs screamed for mercy, his ankles throbbed.

He became aware of a figure watching him, then slowed and stopped. Scott handed him a towel, silently. Amos plucked at his T-shirt, felt the sweat, felt disgusting. He was a pig, he told himself. A fat, unattractive human being who had no right to be in a gym.

"How far?" Scott asked, inserting a straw into a protein shake, handing it to him.

"Not quite four," he puffed, wiping his face, his neck.

He said nothing, but held up a fist. Amos grinned, bumped it with his own.

"How's the weight?"

"Forty-two pounds down."

"Serious?"

"Yeah. Last time I checked."

"God's on your side, Amos. You're doing it, with His help," Scott said, smiling into his eyes.

"God has nothing to do with it, Scott."

"God has everything to do with it. You think it was just an accident that you wound up at this gym? He loves you so much."

"He's got a strange way of showing it."

"Sometimes that's true. Here's the number for the counselor."

"I didn't agree to counseling."

"True. But put it your phone, anyway."

Amos sighed, put the number in his phone, refused to meet Scott's gaze. Nosy, too pushy. He wanted to tell him to back off, leave him alone, but he didn't.

"You should finally come check out my church this Sunday."

"No thanks."

"Okay. But you'll consider it?"

"Maybe."

"How was your week?"

"It was okay. Actually, I met this Amish girl, Anna. She was hired to do the housekeeping at the big house. I helped her move furniture, take down storm windows, that kinda thing."

He watched Scott's face warily, felt the unwanted blush spread across his own face.

"And?" Scott prompted.

Amos swiped the towel around his neck, clearly flustered.

He took a long sip of the protein shake.

"I don't know. She's cute. Short, funny. She's, like, happy. You know, bright."

"Uh huh? And?"

"She said she wants to hear my story."

"And you invited her to your house? You're taking her to dinner?" Scott asked.

"No, no. Of course not."

"But how will she ever hear it?"

"She doesn't need to. She's like my mom, I think. Calls all the shots. Ambitious. She'd walk all over me."

For a long moment, Scott said nothing, trying to process what he was hearing, while Amos paced, his mouth turned into a frown of unhappiness. Scott saw the need, felt the Spirit working in his heart, reached out to Amos and put a hand on his shoulder.

Amos sprang away from his touch.

"Don't do that, okay? I'm soaked. I'm vile, sweating like a pig."

"Sorry."

"Look. I gotta go. Time for me to leave."

He almost ran out the door and to the safety of his truck. Away from the danger named Scott.

He found it easier now, driving past the diner, Wendy's, McDonald's. The protein shake took away some of the insistent urge to eat, at least until he could get home. Once home, he cooked six eggs with hot sauce, salt and pepper, then went to find Joseph. Fred went galloping off into the trees, did his business, and trotted proudly after him.

Clouds covered the sun, but there would be no rain before late afternoon, according to the weather station. He wondered how he'd ever lived without a phone or television, both endless sources of entertainment and knowledge. He didn't care what his parents said, the devices he owned were the best thing that ever happened to him. They never failed to deliver what he wanted or needed, unlike most human beings he encountered.

He heard the distinct sound of a Carolina wren, watched as it flitted into a niche above the garage door. He could faintly see the outline of a few twigs, a wisp of hay, and knew it was raising a brood of little ones. He smiled to himself, thinking he did believe in creation, how God had started the whole world with a spoken word. Everywhere you looked, there were things to see and wonder, amazement at an unfurling leaf, the flash of an oriole. He'd have to fill Lila's oriole feeder, invading Nancy's kitchen for grape jelly.

He found Joseph dressed, getting his car keys, Lila pulling on a light sweater.

"Good morning, son," he called.

"Good morning, Joseph. How are you, Lila?" he answered.

"We are perfect, exactly the way God intended eighty-some-year-olds," she answered gaily.

Joseph chuckled, "Off to the doctor's office this morning. Blood work."

"Every old person's excuse to eat breakfast at Perkins," Lila said, winking at Amos, just a bit flippantly.

Amos laughed. "Eat a pancake for me. Is it alright if I mow the orchard before it rains? I have weed eating to do as well."

Joseph straightened, poked his cane in his direction.

"You're the boss, my boy. The old place has never looked better, and I trust you one hundred percent."

Lila beamed, placed a hand on his arm.

"We appreciate you so much. God led you straight to us and that is no joke."

"Thank you," Amos managed, but quick tears and a lump in his throat garbled his speech. He helped Lila down the stairs, then waved them off, watching the expensive vehicle wind its way slowly down the tree-lined drive.

He filled the mower with gasoline, checked the oil, then heaved himself onto the seat. Perhaps there wasn't quite as much to heave as before, but there was still far too much of him. His stomach rumbled. He thought of pancakes soaked in butter and syrup.

The mower sputtered to life, and he was off to the orchard, Fred lolloping along, his pink tongue swinging from his opened mouth. Amos watched as he darted into the thicket by the small creek, then lost track of him as he began mowing the heavy grass between trees.

Lost in thought, he became aware of the sharp scent of dandelion, chickweed, tufts of bromegrass chopped beneath the whirling blades of the mower, the neatly cut swatch behind him. The sun on his back, the bounce of the mower, and he felt a sense of accomplishment, the kind words from the old couple adding a certain savor to his day.

Did they really mean it, though? He was just doing his duty, and he didn't do the job better than anyone else. Probably not as good as many landscapers would have done.

To be honest, he loved his job, took pride in being able to restore this old place to its former glory. Better, even. He'd planted, replaced, trimmed, reseeded grass, fertilized and sprayed, learned so much. Could he start his own landscaping business someday?

Dreams. Dreams always evaporated like bubbles, blew away on an ill wind and burst into nothing. No one would hire him, an oversized person with one truck and a rusty mower, no knowledge to speak of.

Better to stay with Joseph and Lila.

But they would not live forever.

He felt the sickening bump, gave a small sound of dismay, stopped the mower, and was off in one quick move. A cry like the cry of a small child, and he saw the reddish-brown coat of a fawn. A baby deer, bleating helplessly, mangled and bleeding, its liquid brown eyes pleading.

Horror gripped him. Nausea rose in his throat. He knelt, tried to touch the poor, helpless baby, but only increased its pain and agitation. He got to his feet, a dozen thoughts crashing in his head, seeking a solution.

He'd get on the mower, drive to the garage, get the twenty-two, the air gun he used to shoot starlings. He had to help this suffering animal, somehow, put it out of its misery.

How did one go about killing a beautiful animal? He felt worse than he'd ever felt as he drove as fast as possible back to the garage, leaped off the mower, and went inside.

"Hey!"

His heart in his mouth, he retraced his steps to find Anna, wide-eyed.

"Boy, am I glad to see you. Joseph and Lila left instructions for me, but I have no idea where to find a stepladder or how to operate the washer."

She took a look at his face. "What's wrong with you?"

He told her, terribly ashamed, felt every inch the loser he was. Someone with more sense would have seen the fawn.

"Let me go with you. I want to see how badly it's hurt."

"There's no room on here."

"Then I'll walk."

She motioned, waving an arm. "Go, I'll follow."

He hesitated, imagining his fat back bouncing on the mower, but told himself he didn't care, had no business harboring dreams.

When he reached the fawn, he stopped the mower, waited till Anna walked up, her color heightened, breathing hard. She bent over, saw the injuries, and shook her head.

"Look," she whispered. Slowly, she pointed, then gently rolled the tiny animal, revealing a puddle of blood, a gaping wound with exposed entrails. As they watched, the fawn laid down its neck and head, breathed deeply, and was very still, the beautiful brown eyes set, never to see its mother again, or life in the surrounding fields and woods.

Amos was tongue-tied. A shadow raced over his features, leaving him with a dread so deep it was like a leap into darkness, an endless abyss of shame and fear. This was all his fault, ending the life of an innocent animal, bringing death and grief to one of God's creatures.

"I'm sorry," he muttered finally.

He looked down at Anna, horrified to find her weeping softly. He'd done that, too. Caused this beautiful girl untold sorrow.

He turned, walked away, putting distance between him and the havoc he'd created, desperate to get out of her sight. She would loathe him, wouldn't be able to stand the sight of him. He'd failed miserably, like he always did. He could hear his mother yelling at him, reminding him of who he was. "Don't do that, Amos. Don't you know better, Amos?"

"Hey!"

He kept walking.

"Where are you going? We need to bury the poor thing."

He was aware of her quick footsteps, her breathing.

"Why are you walking away?"

He whirled around, put out two palms to keep her away.

"Stop yelling at me, Anna. Stop it. I don't want to hear your scolding. I know I'm dumb, stupid, but I couldn't help it. Get away from me."

He was breathing hard, and his eyes showed so much agitation she felt a moment of terror. But being who she was, she swept the fear away as efficiently as possible and got down to business, which was telling him exactly what she thought of him, which wasn't much at the moment.

"Okay, fine. Be a coward. Be whatever you want. But I'll bury it by myself. Don't yell at me, either."

She pushed past him, leaving him feeling deeply ashamed, adding to the misery and defeat. He just stood there and waited like an idiot.

When she returned with a shovel, he told her the coyotes and foxes would make short work of a good meal, which only fanned the fire of her anger, her mouth in a straight, pinched line, with no words escaping as she plunged the shovel into the soft earth by the thicket.

Amos watched her determination, then attempted to take the shovel. She relented, and he went to work. Together they lifted the poor little fawn, as light as a kitten, and folded its limbs carefully into the hole.

Anna was weeping silently.

Every shovelful was like a kick in the stomach. When the little grave was filled, he turned, wiped his forehead with the back of his hand, and stood awkwardly. He had no idea what he was supposed to say or do.

Anna sniffed, looked up at him, and asked for a handkerchief, a paper towel or Kleenex, whatever he had. He didn't have anything, so he shrugged, spread his hands palms up. She calmly reached up and tore off a maple leaf, soundly blew her nose, and pitched it.

"Why did you get so mad?" she asked.

He shrugged.

"Whatever," she said, and tossed her head. "I didn't take you for that kind of guy."

He shrugged, drove the lawn mower back to the garage, letting her walk. He found the stepladder, carried it to the house, then waited on the patio until he saw her walk back from the orchard. He took it inside, heard the door open and close, then footsteps.

"Where do you want this?" he called.

"Laundry room. And can you help me get this washer started?"

When he'd done so, she asked, unexpectedly, "You want something to drink?"

"Yeah, I guess a lemonade."

"Sure, I'll get it."

She returned carrying two glasses clinking with ice.

He was too embarrassed to look at her, but heard her slide onto a patio chair, swallow.

"So, what made you so mad?" she asked again.

He took a deep breath, "To tell you the truth, I don't know."

"You said you were stupid, or something to that effect."

She placed her elbows on the table, put her chin in her hands, and he felt watched. Observed far too closely.

"I'm not good at analyzing feelings," he said curtly.

"Is that right? Interesting."

Silence hung between them. He watched a hummingbird hovering above a clematis bud, then move away in a flash.

"I mean, you didn't have to get so huffy. I didn't say you . . . any of it was your fault. Accidents happen."

She finished her lemonade, set the glass on the tabletop. He took in the contours of her face, the small, straight nose, the fullness of her healthy cheeks, but would not meet her eyes. He was actually afraid of her appraising gaze, which was cowardly. He knew that, too.

"Well, accidents were a big deal at . . . when I was a boy."

"What do you mean?"

She lifted the glass, shifting the ice, then crunched a piece between her teeth.

He looked out across the lawn.

"Don't make me say stuff I don't want to say."

"Why not?"

He shrugged.

To talk about his past was like flinging himself over the lip of a precipice, with no hope or promise of a safe landing, only the wrenching exposure of free-falling, terror creating a deathly spiral of the unknown. He had to abandon the safety of keeping it all inside, that tether to being hidden in a dark place where no one would ever know, enabling him to turn a normal face to the world.

He did not have the courage to let go.

How many times had he cried by himself? How many times had he truly believed himself to be an oddity, mentally unstable, a body like a mound of bread dough, rising, rising?

Two hundred pounds, two hundred fifty, then three hundred.

"You're zoning out," she said quietly.

He sighed, bit his lip.

"Why do you even talk to me? Why don't you just go clean your rooms and let me alone?"

"Because I'm curious about you."

He began to speak, changed his mind. Too hard.

"What were you going to say?" she asked, tilting her glass for more ice.

"Nothing."

"Yes you were."

"Look, why don't you just bug off? Really. You're Amish, I'm English. Nothing can come of this."

"You're not English."

"I left the church."

"You never joined."

"No, but I was raised Amish. My parents and sisters are still."

"So, you have no plans of returning?"

"Probably not."

She gave him a hard look.

"Why?"

"I don't really know why. Maybe because of bad memories. I had a miserable childhood. My mother never really accepted me, the way

I looked. Still look. I was huge, really big and overweight, with, well, this face."

"What's wrong with your face?" Anna asked, crunching down on ice.

"I have two beautiful sisters. Really pretty. Can you imagine someone as ugly as me growing up in the same home as them?"

Her brows lowered, and she pursed her lips.

"Who told you that you're ugly? You want my honest opinion? You're just as attractive as they are, in a rugged way."

Amos lowered his gaze to his empty glass, trying to absorb her words, to believe them for himself, a handrail for the first tentative step toward the light.

"You know, lots of homely children grow into their looks as they get older. I don't think you're bad looking at all. And don't you think I could have carried my own stepladder and got that washer figured out?"

Chapter 17

Anna was born in the middle of seven children, efficiently dividing the family in half: three boys older, three girls younger.

She lived on the south side of Rochester in a section of the Amish community called "South Dale," meaning they had church services when the north district did not. Having lived in northern Pennsylvania for only a few years, she hadn't known Cathy and Lavina had a brother and was amazed to find him English, with no plans of going back, which really irked her.

Three of her brothers had married and two of them excommunicated a few years later, deciding Amish rules made no sense and had nothing to do with salvation. Dragging reluctant wives in their wake, they attended the church of their choice, while Anna watched her parents' private sorrow, bravely leaning into the stiff winds of adversity.

Courageous. Her parents were true warriors to lay down self, accept the adult choices their sons had made, and love them in spite of their concern. Shunning was practiced mildly, to stay in tune with church *ordnung*, but the boys and their fledgling families were always welcome, always greeted with love.

They had been raised as liberals, every one of them, and on the rare occasion discipline was exercised, it was usually by the mother, met with disapproval from the father. When they began their years of "*rumschpringa*" the boys all owned a vehicle after the age of eighteen. Mischief was winked at, and sowing wild oats was considered the way of it. Beer cans in the dumpster, English clothes in the piles of laundry, cigarettes smoked on the back patio.

They were "youngie."

When ministers came to see her parents about repeated disobedience, there was always an accompanying measure of rebellion, the parents speaking of the bishop's strict ways. What sense did all these rules make? None, that's what.

And cellphones appeared, cars parked behind the barn, things tolerated and accepted. But as older teens, the boys "settled down," were baptized and married in the Amish church. But then two of them pivoted again, rejecting their Amish community entirely.

And Anna was in the middle, forming her own intelligent opinions, endowed with a natural propensity to voice her thoughts. She loved life, a happy individual often cheering up her downhearted parents with humorous remarks, reminding them frequently of their own inability to abide by the laws of the church, her three younger sisters chiming in.

School-aged children skipped through a happy home and seldom stayed sad when the family hit a discordant note, but Anna was different. She learned quickly, and was so aware of the fact she was fancier than her classmates, a leader in style when she was sixteen. She knew her mother was not as plain as many others, which didn't seem to bother her one way or another. She formed her own version of life among the Amish and didn't care much what other people thought.

Their home was rather astounding, a new two-story house made of fieldstone and shake siding in different shades of brown and beige, a macadam driveway and a barn, shop combination palatial enough for most folk's houses. Her father was a roofer, "Riehl Roofing for a Real Job Done," and enormously successful.

Anna had never known an existence without available funds, but often questioned her Amish way of life, living in a house far superior to those of their "worldly" neighbors, who were content to live in their double-wides.

She questioned everything, her quick mind missing nothing.

"So, who's worldly here, Dat? The Arendts are content with a lot less than we are. What sense does it make, driving a horse and buggy, living in this mansion? Huh?"

Eyes twinkling, only half-serious, and her father took no offense, but laughingly told her the ancestors had a strong German work ethic, had the best farms in Germany and Switzerland back in the sixteen-hundreds. This was true, Anna agreed, but were they wealthy landowners back then? Back in the day when Amish people were truly Amish.

"You have a bright mind, young lady, and are quick to use it. However, there is a place for women in our culture, and you have to understand that someday." He said it with good humor, but she understood that she should stop pushing him.

Her mother was a workaholic, a complete whirling dervish around the place. She kept their home absolutely spotless, the lawn and garden groomed to her own specifications, a landscaper taking care of costly shrubs and trees. Laundry was done to perfection, the whites glaringly so, the solar-powered Speed Queen chugging away the dirt and grime. The sewing machine hummed along swiftly, turning out brilliant colors of fabric into dresses made in the latest style, bib aprons and capes and aprons all done in black.

She was a wonder, talented in every duty, thriving on hard work and a tight schedule, never driving her horse and carriage, always calling a driver to accomplish whatever she set out to do in less time, no matter about the money.

At church she often fell asleep quickly, her head nodding as if it had a will of its own. It was just the way Alan sie Rachel was, the women said, justifying a dear friend. She had trouble sleeping at night, couldn't help it, poor dear.

It was in this environment that Anna grew and thrived, attending church sporadically, never pressured into going if she had been out late in the evening before.

When she met Amos, she was intrigued. Here was a man with more character in his pockmarked face than any fifty-year-old. He was not handsome, in a conventional way, but possessed a certain rugged look, one she found attractive.

She'd had her share of admirers, a few dates with pale young men who failed to spark her interest, their white hands on steering wheels reminding her of submerged starfish. Amos had a depth to him that captivated her imagination.

He was slightly terrified of her and would never ask her out, so she'd have to accomplish this feat in an underhanded way.

She took on more hours at the Browns, just to be near Amos. And at the end of the month, he promised to pick her up and bring her back to his house to make something on the grill. She had told him many times she'd like to do that, but he'd pushed it off, saying he was busy, or her parents wouldn't approve, or his house needed cleaned or he was tired.

Finally, one Friday evening, when the onset of summer was just around the corner, he said okay. Seven o'clock—but this was not a date, just a coworker dinner. She laughed until her face was red and not terribly attractive, either, but he laughed and asked what was wrong with that.

"You should be in politics, doing one thing and calling it another," she finished, wiping her eyes.

"You're making fun of me," he said.

She asked if she should dress English or Amish. He told her to do whatever suited her best, then went out and bought a new shirt in a size smaller, the whole time repeating to himself that it was not a date.

He had not forgotten Skye Larkin and the kiss. Not just yet.

He washed his truck, vacuumed the interior, polished the dash, showered and shaved, donned his new shirt. When she arrived, she was dressed in a somber navy blue. His heart raced at sight of her, the absolute charm of the white heart-shaped covering, the black sandals.

"Good evening, kind sir," she trilled, hopping into his car before he had a chance to be gallant and hold the door for her.

"I can hardly wait to see your house. Did you tell Joseph and Lila?"

"Of course not."

"Well, you could have."

"Sure. It's just having a coworker over for dinner."

"But it's not a date?"

"No."

She moved about his house, touching, exclaiming, saying it was adorable, and did he ever appreciate what he had? He stood in the kitchen doorway, an elbow propped on the trim, grinned and nodded at everything she said, which was a lot.

When the tour was over, she told him she felt a bit awkward now, being alone with him and not working.

"I'll get you a bucket and rag. You can wipe the floor if you want."

She smiled up at him. "I would do it for you."

His eye twinkled, and he told her to hold on, he'd get the bucket. She punched his arm, and he grabbed her hand, held it a few seconds longer than necessary.

They both smiled more than usual, couldn't quite be quiet or sober, putting steaks on the grill, popping macaroni and cheese in the oven, tossing a salad. He mixed green tea with lemonade, set it all on the table on the porch. He talked about his time at the gym and slowly learning to eat healthier, his weight finally to the point where he felt better about himself, the difficulty in going that first time.

"I mean, for someone like me, you can't imagine the embarrassment. Scott, the owner, was a big help."

She nodded and a silence fell, not uncomfortably. Amos told her Scott invited him to church, repeatedly.

She cut into her steak, said it was perfect, then asked if he was going to go.

"I don't know. I don't know what to expect. I'm afraid they're into that worship music, all the arm raising and swaying, getting all carried away. I'm not into that kind of thing."

"What are you into?"

"Nothing. I don't understand God or religion. He never did much for me."

She looked up from her steak, eyes keen as a ferret's.

"You want me to write you a chapter about martyrdom?"

"What's that supposed to mean?"

"Poor me. Poor pitiful me. God forgot me."

He blinked. "Sarcasm is highly unattractive."

"So?" She shrugged. "I have zero tolerance for self-pity."

"Maybe you would think differently if you heard by story."

"Feel free."

So he started to tell her. He kept talking after the mosquitoes chased them inside, and as he made coffee, served apple pie from the Mennonite bakery. Scoops of vanilla ice cream.

She listened intently.

He found himself starting to tear up, finally, a release of pent-up emotion. Ashamed, he turned his back, then got up and walked away.

"But Amos, are you sure that's how it was? Your family? They're real Amish, aren't they?"

"Yeah, the best. Keep the *ordnung* real well, as far as I know."

She shook her head. "Wow, I had no idea. They're . . . I mean, I know it's your parents and sisters, but they're so unkind."

"It's my home. Can you see why I left?"

He wiped his eyes, sat down again.

"You don't believe the Amish have anything to offer?" she asked in a very small voice.

"Not really, no. Not for now, anyway."

She was quiet, playing with the apple pie, pushing it around with her fork.

"What about me?" she asked softly.

"It wouldn't work. I'm damaged goods. And I'm not going back to that life. Look at Joseph and Lila. Never Amish a day of their life, and yet they shine with real love. Real kindness. Over and over, I tell myself, tomorrow all of this will be gone, none of it is real, and still it goes on and on. I don't deserve a quarter of what they give me."

"It's called grace," Anna said excitedly.

"What?"

"What you just said. That's the same grace we receive the day we accept Christ as our Savior."

"Now you sound like Scott."

"But it's true. Jesus is real, Amos, and so is grace."

"For everyone?"

"'Whoever believes on Him shall be saved.' Amos, listen to Scott. He knows what he's talking about. Go to church, see what you think, okay? You know Jesus can take all those hurts in your heart and heal you completely. He can do that."

"Are you even really Amish? I've never once heard an Amish person talk like that."

"Of course I am. But we—our family, perhaps—we think a bit outside the box. We don't fit Christians into categories. Either you believe or you don't, no matter which church you go to."

Far into the night, they talked. He was reluctant to let her go, and she did not want to leave, but when the clock struck one, she said her coach might turn to a pumpkin if he didn't take her home.

He turned to her, then, and thanked her with all he had in him, telling her she was the best thing that ever happened to him, although he hoped she realized there were many roadblocks to a real relationship. He simply wasn't qualified.

She smiled, and he caught her humor when she said they were still young, the world stretched before them.

"You know, Anna, I really did enjoy this evening."

"Good."

"Maybe next time we can go out to dinner at some nice place, or whatever you want to do."

Was this voice coming from him?

For an agonizing moment she said nothing, toyed with her apron, obviously trying to come to a decision. His heart fell, but quickly recovered after he told himself he was fine with refusal. Disappointment as usual.

"You know," she said finally, "you may think there's something wrong with me, but I don't take this lightly. I need time to pray about it, see where the Lord leads. There are so many marriage problems among our people, so many unhappy couples bound to each other for life."

Amos instantly felt the warning signs, the white flag of defeat.

"My parents love each other," he said defensively.

Up went the eyebrow. She shook her head.

"After what you told me?"

"Well, call it what you want. But my dad does everything he can for my mother. I think, in her own way, she appreciates it."

She opened her mouth, closed it again.

"Be honest, okay?" he said, surprised at his boldness. "Is this just your way of putting off your real answer?"

"Of course not. I don't have an answer yet. I need time to pray. I need to seek the face of the One who loves me."

She stood in the yellow lamplight, her tanned face with the beauty of her unusual eyes, her mouth in a line of seriousness, her white covering like a halo. He would never be good enough for her. Never.

He held the door and she moved ahead. She barely reached his shoulder, but was substantially built. Strong, capable. He was painfully aware of her, so near, and yet miles away.

It was in that thought his spirit reached out unknowingly, and he felt the words, rather than heard them.

"Let it be, Lord, let it be."

Cathy's boss at market told her they wouldn't need her for the remainder of the year. She was working at the bakery, the largest stand at Richmont Dutch Market, baking whoopie pies and cakes all day long. She asked for an explanation, but no real reason was given, leaving her walking the uncomfortable tightrope between self-doubt and anger.

Her mother would be furious, this much she knew, so she decided to tell her immediately, without cushioning the blow. She flounced into the kitchen and threw herself into a chair, her pretty face pinched with displeasure.

"Hello Cathy," her mother trilled. "How was your day?"

"I was fired."

"You what?" Her voice rose an octave.

"They fired me."

"Why?"

"Who knows? He wouldn't say. That's illegal, isn't it?"

"We're Amish, Cathy. We don't use lawyers or go to court, so it doesn't matter." She wrung her hands, then set to aggressively wiping the clean counter. "I'm just glad Abram Lapp isn't from this area, so people don't have to know. I can go to church and hold my head up at least."

"Knock yourself out, Mom. Do you know how many girls from our church district work in that market?"

"I never thought of that. Fired, though. Is that what he said?"

"I don't know what he said. Just that he wouldn't need me."

"It couldn't come at a worse time. There's the nasty carpet still. And I was going to plant new shrubbery with my share of your paycheck. Now what?"

Her question ended in an anxious wail, having her heart set on the arborvitae at the local nursery. And a cement birdbath for the garden, something she'd wanted for too long.

"I'm keeping my last few paychecks, Mom."

"Whatever for?"

"Stuff."

Her mother knew it was a waste of breath to dissuade her, so she opened the back door and let herself out, back to her work in the garden, the place she had planned on all kinds of plants, birdhouses, but most of all, a wonderful, very expensive birdbath. You could buy them with a solar attachment, with a small fountain creating bubbling water, perfect for drawing in songbirds. Her heart sank as she stood at the edge of the new garden. So many possibilities, such a lack of available funds.

If only Lavina would agree to a better-paying job. But no, she, of all people, worked as a maid. A real *maud*, going from place to place helping young mothers with canning, housecleaning, or being there when a newborn joined the family.

Lavina was sixteen years old, adding new dimensions to a life containing many questions and few answers. She had always been in

Cathy's shadow, taking on some of her views, a lot of her liberal ways of dressing, choosing to spend her weekends in cars with youth who did not appear to be from Amish homes. She always had a sense there was something deeper, better, but had no clue how to find it.

She fell into the position of being a *maud* when their neighbor's six-year-old was taken to the emergency room with a burst appendix, leaving the children alone. They'd asked for Cathy, who refused to go, so Lavina went, of course. She found a one-year-old, a three-year-old, and two school-aged children, all boys with dark hair and eyes the same brown hue, tanned faces, and sweet smiles, their sunny dispositions winning her heart.

The house was new, with nice furniture and home décor, clean and bright. She stayed all day, fed and cuddled and laughed and played, washed windows and swept floors, made Mickey Mouse pancakes. She felt as if she found some purpose in her time there. She told Sara Ruth if she ever needed a *maud*, to let her know. Word of her availability spread like wildfire, with so many young mothers with a new baby every other year, or barn chores, or simply needing an extra pair of hands for housecleaning in the spring or fall.

Years ago, having a *maud* was very commonplace. Teenage girls would be sent by their parents wherever the need arose, staying a week at a time, sleeping in guest rooms, up at the crack of dawn to help with the milking, cooking, cleaning, washing, yard and garden work for the grand total of sixty dollars a week, which was handed over to their parents before getting themselves ready for the short weekend. Then back to work early Monday morning.

There was no use complaining, no use getting the blues when you arrived. The parents had spoken, so you went, for better or for worse.

But in modern-day Amish circles, Lavina was a rarity, as more girls chose to work at the market or elsewhere for more pay and fewer hours. As time went on, she was sought after continually, her calendar marked full with names of Amish households.

She was tall, willowy, a graceful girl with big brown eyes and streaked dirty blond hair, a certain wistfulness in her expression, as if she stood on a threshold without quite knowing what to expect.

She paid attention to life in the other Amish homes she visited and realized more and more that her parents were not the norm. Most homes did not feature a mother who whined incessantly and a father who avoided conflict like the plague.

At Elam Stoltzfus's she found a conservative way of life, a middle-aged couple who milked a herd of Holsteins, lived in a farmhouse built of brick in 1879, with two sets of double chimneys and no front porch, loose windows, and only one replaced door. Lizzie had just given birth to her twelfth child, the tenth daughter. Her oldest was a boy of fourteen and a half. Lizzie was short, loud, and round as a barrel, her stocky legs carrying her along as hardy and tough as a tugboat, managing those twelve children like a drill sergeant.

Lavina felt the laughter bubble within her the first hour she stepped in that house, the stentorian cry from the couch in the living room snapping her to attention. Children were everywhere, almost all unkempt daughters in various stages of performing household chores. Little girls on a bench washing, rinsing, and drying dishes, another one clearing the table, yet another one appearing shyly with a wire basket containing brown eggs.

Lizzie had a firm grip on the rudder of homemaking, childbearing, and its bothersome aftermath, the postpartum period of "taking care." She hated "taking care." If she felt good, she saw no sense sitting in her recliner watching weeds grow, tomatoes rot, dust collect, or laundry go unwashed. Scolded profusely by her Amish midwife who stuck to the old ways of taking care for six whole weeks, she struck a deal and waited for three weeks to fire up the gas engine on the wringer washer. She had a *maud* now, Raymond Beiler's Lavina.

And Lavina learned there were still folks using a gas-powered engine to do laundry. Her own mother used an electric washer, an automatic Speed Queen. For Lavina, there was something dear, something solid and grounding in bringing that gas engine to life, lifting the first pile of sorted laundry—the baby blankets and sleepers, the tiny onesies—putting them through the wringer, watching them spill into clean rinse water, hanging them on the line in the brilliant light of a summer day, fat bees droning past, laden with pollen, barn cats stretched out by the sandbox, watching her with yellow eyes.

Lizzie made the meals—quick, simple food, but hot and seasoned well, with store-bought bread and Welch's grape jelly. All these children kept her stepping, and who had time to play with bread dough? Not her. Sourdough was the thing these days, which brought an impatient snort from the efficient Lizzie, saying she was raised on white bought bread and hamburger gravy and there was nothing wrong with her health.

For breakfast, she served fried eggs, sausages, stewed crackers, and oatmeal. It stuck to Elam's ribs until lunchtime when he ambled in and sat down to Campbell's tomato soup and a ham sandwich. Lizzie laughed at Lavina's surprise when she spied the pantry shelves lined with every flavor of store-bought soups, ramen noodles, and other low-nutrient foods.

"I don't have time to obsess about health food," she said unapologetically.

Lavina was amazed at the easy exchange of love, the quiet flow of talk, the unity and strength of opened Bibles and a child's prayer. Spates of song, happiness, and contentment were taken for granted, something never failing to amaze Lavina.

Elam said they should have a front porch to sit on, to watch the rain on summer days, but Lizzie waved a hand downward, said, "Puh, who has time to sit on a porch? Once these children re grown, half of them gone, then we'll get a porch to sit on." A few of the girls reminded her they might stay, never get married, which meant she'd never get to sit on her porch. That sent her into gales of belly laughs.

It was the easy way Lizzie addressed life, the ebb and flow of accepting circumstances, shrugging shoulders, and digging in, no matter what had to be done. If the need arose, the piles of laundry stayed on the *kesslehaus* floor and the oldest daughter helped Elam in the fields.

Raking hay, throwing hay bales, baling corn fodder, were things Lizzie deemed more important than her own housework.

Lavina tried not to compare her own mother with Lizzie. They were two very different women. Flaws and all, her mother was still her mother, so she might as well accept her as she was.

Mark Miller had a ten-year-old Down's syndrome boy with a sunny disposition. He thrived in a circle of love and acceptance from his siblings, the parents beaming approval from the sidelines. For reasons beyond her understanding, this always brought sadness, thinking of Amos. He, too, had been different, but had to struggle every step of the way, growing up without the proper foundation so naturally built in most families.

He had not been attractive as a child, truthfully. He was prone to overeating, disgusting table manners, his beady, greedy eyes, snatching at food with sausage fingers. At a young age, Lavina saw the loathing in her mother's eyes, the pity in her father's. She wondered why her father did nothing to stop the ridicule.

She had felt protective of Amos, at one time. She wanted him to stay, but was often embarrassed in church or at her social gatherings. He had so many unsavory habits, scratching himself, blowing his nose and examining the contents before pocketing the results. He always had bad breath, his hygiene haphazard at best, his eating habits revolting.

Ach Amos, she thought from time to time. *Ach my.*

And he had no motivation or ambition to speak of. He lumbered from job to job, without talent, putting in hours and expecting nothing. He simply seemed to be born with so much less, so few qualifications in any area.

But Cathy had swooped her up and swirled her away with her group of friends and Lavina learned early on there were many pleasures in life. Excitement. Places to go, things to see, weekends blooming like an exotic flower, pulsing with light and beauty, fading quickly. The times she did attend church services she was half-awake and caught very little of the sermon, whispering and joking with her friend Priscilla when they knelt for the long German prayer, terribly relieved when the three hours on hard benches was behind her.

Sometimes she felt an emotion akin to rage against her father, the way he refused to take Amos's part, even when she saw the raw pity in his eyes. Was it her mother's power over him, or was he a coward, hiding behind his books and magazines on the recliner? He might love their mother, but wasn't courage worth something, too?

In the homes where she worked, when Father spoke, everyone sat up and took notice. But most of the fathers could be fun, too. They played baseball, laughed and roughhoused, read stories, knelt for the evening prayer, took genuine delight in their families.

Lavina came to see her father's lack of involvement as a form of selfishness, staying in his wife's favor regardless of circumstances.

Too much thinking, too many hours spent trying to figure out what their family's biggest downfall really was, and she began feeling depressed, unable to sleep well at night. The smallest thought of Amos brought stinging anxiety. Dry-mouthed, with a racing heart, her energy waned.

All of this remained hidden, although Cathy noticed how she stopped caring about boys. Young men were batted away with a sweeping arm, eyelids lowered halfway, a look of distaste, like milk gone sour.

Cathy tried, would bring up the subject repeatedly. This one was cute, that one kept noticing her. What was wrong with another one?

Her mother noticed too, and asked Cathy why Lavina wasn't eating at the supper table. Cathy, on her phone, looked up without comprehension, shrugged, and went back to her phone, while Lavina was upstairs reading a book from the library, listening clearly to her mother's concern.

She wasn't eating much these days, consumed with anxious thoughts of Amos, out in the world, away from the family. If he married an English girl, whose fault would it be? He could easily have a wreck, be killed. Would his soul go to Heaven?

She took a deep breath, steadied herself, but could not control her raging thoughts. She knew she needed to talk to someone, but who was available? No one knew her family was less than perfect. Amos had chosen to leave, broken his parents' heart, and everyone saw that as his problem.

So while Cathy lived in a bubble of false security, Lavina struggled on the sidelines, weighing the pros and cons of family life, the cards always stacked against them.

She decided to go see Amos. He had not visited in some time, and if anyone could understand, he would.

She picked up her phone, her thumbs moving swiftly.

Chapter 18

In the weeks Anna left him with her indecision, he threw himself into lengthy workouts, now lifting over three hundred pounds, running six miles on the treadmill, then going back to crunches and curls, exhausting himself.

It was good, the adrenaline flowing, perspiration flowing, a thumping heart all a part of his routine. He was addicted to the rush of endorphins, the feeling of serotonin, his body beginning to make visible changes.

He preferred a protein shake to a chocolate milkshake now, ate his fish steamed with lemon juice beside a pile of sauteed vegetables. He still enjoyed a Double Whopper from Burger King, but only on occasion.

On September twenty-second, he weighed two hundred and fifty-two pounds. He no longer wore any of the jeans he'd bought when he left the Amish, or any of his old clothes for that matter. The mirror was kinder now, more forgiving. It was the first time in his life he did not turn away in disgust.

The leaves on the trees were slowly turning, but the days were still warm, the nights pleasant. He kept his windows open and depended on Fred to hear strange noises, although he no longer feared the sliding feet of the harmless intruder. He thought of Anna often, tried to deal with this time of waiting, not knowing, as best he could.

He was on the zero-turn mower when a white van slowly traveled up the drive, rolling to a stop in front of the garage. The front door revealed his sister Lavina, and his heart leaped with happiness at the sight of her. Reaching down, he stopped the mower, slid off and onto his feet, waving. Lavina was speaking to the driver, so he waited, then moved to greet her.

She stood alone, thin and bewildered, blinking as if she'd stepped into light from a dark place.

"Lavina!"

All the gladness in his heart was in his voice.

"Amos, seriously," she said, breathless.

"What?"

"You're . . . you look so different. I hardly knew who you were. Your face, your hair, your . . . everything. What is going on?"

She was smiling, but was clearly amazed.

"I'm working out harder than ever. It's sort of an addiction."

"In a good way?"

"Of course."

He stepped up and placed an arm around her shoulders. "Come on, Lavina, I'll introduce you to Joseph and Lila."

She turned frightened eyes. "No, please, Amos. I can't."

"Why? Is something wrong?"

"It's just . . . I don't know. If it's okay, maybe when I leave."

Amos shrugged. "Okay."

They walked down the drive, his arm around her shoulder, which did not repulse her at all, the way it might have before. He would never have attempted a physical touch back then.

He opened the door, ushered her in. Fred rose from his spot by the couch, stretched and yawned, then set up a friendly waving of his tail.

"A dog? Really? You have a dog?"

"Fred. He's pretty much always at my side, except when I'm at the gym."

She was on the floor, with Fred licking her cheek, obviously pleased to meet her. She laughed, rubbed his face, told Amos how lucky he was.

"I always wanted one," she said.

"But it's weird how I didn't. I protested when Joseph suggested it. I didn't want him at all, and now I can't imagine life without him."

"Mom would never allow a dog."

"No."

It was as if a line of uncomfortable energy connected the two of them, both aware of having a fractured home but not willing to admit this to each other. Silence stretched between them until Amos snapped it by saying, "Sit down. I'll get you something to drink. Diet Coke, Diet Sprite, Gatorade, or zero-calorie lemonade."

Lavina gave a short laugh. "Boy, you're stocked."

He filled two glasses with ice while she commented on his cute house, sticking her head in the bathroom door, then the bedroom.

"You make your bed?"

"Of course!"

They both laughed. He took a sip of his Diet Coke. She followed. Silence hung between them. He found his eyes taking in the details of her face, the angular contours, dark circles beneath her eyes, her neck too long and much too thin.

"You're thin, Lavina."

She nodded. "I know."

"You okay?"

"Not really."

"What's going on?"

She looked away, then took a deep breath. He watched her wrap her arms around her waist, lean forward, then lean back, her gaze to the ceiling.

"I work as a *maud*, Amos."

"Yeah?"

He waited, but there was no answer. He could tell she was battling inner feelings. Finally she sighed, took a sip of her drink, and began to tell Amos about her questions, her fear, her conclusions about her father, and last, the battle with depression and mounting anxiety.

"Cathy was fired from the bakery, and Mom is absolutely fit to be tied. It's two hundred dollars a weekend for her, and now it's gone. You know Cathy won't go back. She'll never set foot in that market again."

She paused, looking at Amos quizzically. "Amos, you're almost handsome," she blurted out.

"'Almost' is key." But he was grinning widely.

"Oh, Amos. I wish Mom could see."

A shadow crossed his face. "It wouldn't make a difference."

"It could."

He shook his head.

"Lavina, you need to talk to someone who can help you sort things out. I know if you turn to Mom, she'll have handfuls of herbal pills and literature to go with it. I'm here for you, really I am. But I'm still figuring things out, too. I can give you the name of a counselor if you want. Believe me, I have struggled more than you will ever want to know."

"Have you seen the counselor? Is he English?"

"No, I haven't been yet. And yes, I'm sure he's English. Scott gave me the number."

"English counselors are not for Amish people. They mislead you."

Irritation coursed through his veins. He stayed quiet, counted to ten.

"That's probably not true. Scott is a Christian, a real one. I don't know where I'd be without him."

Lavina's eyes were dark with suspicion.

"We're Amish, Amos. You are, too, in spite of thinking otherwise."

"What's the difference, really?"

"Well, we're plain. We're better to God because we dress the way He wants us to."

"Do you really think God works like that, Lavina?"

Lavina was clearly upset. She stated her case, allowing Amos to see the great void in which they had been raised. He didn't understand religion or spirituality well, either, but this was unbelievable. He tried, but realized they had come to an impasse, she knowing very little and he not really understanding what he did know.

What were they? Orphans? Stray kittens struck down by disease? Lavina looked awful, really, wringing her hands, her voice high and tight with the knot of worry and fear in her stomach, the same thing he'd felt so many times in the past.

"I don't know what to do."

"Ask mom about seeing a doctor."

"I can't. I don't know how. She won't spend the money."

"What about Dat?"

She shook her head.

Finally, she said she'd just go back to work, try to put all of it behind her. "It's in my head, Amos. I have to stop thinking of myself."

"No, I disagree. Depression is real, and it's treatable. Think about it, and stay in touch with me."

She nodded, then told him her biggest fear was him being out in the world and not being able to get to Heaven when he died. Shamefaced, groping blindly for unaccustomed words, she let her shoulders drop in defeat, spread her hands palms up, and said, "I don't know, Amos. I'm just repeating what I've heard over the years."

He gave a short, hard laugh, bitter with remembrance.

"Don't worry about me. I know I'm not in a good place, but going back won't fix anything. Yes, it would please the Amish community. Mom and Dat would be beside themselves with joy, but would that really fix anything inside of me? Deep down, there's all this trash, piles of old hurts and anger against Amish people who treated me unfairly. I don't know what to do with all that."

"I'm as blind as you are, Amos. I don't know how to overcome these awful doubts and fears either."

"Could Dat help? You know, he apologized for not being there for me. It meant a lot, actually."

"He did? Wow. But no, he's never there."

"What do you mean?"

"Amos, you have no idea. Things are worse, and Dat's solution is just to keep his distance, stay away as much as possible."

They realized they both had no solution, so agreed to drop the subject and move on. They went to meet Lily and Joseph, Fred at their side.

"This is really beautiful here, Amos. What a beautiful old house. You must really love your work."

"I do love it. Sometimes I can't imagine why I got so lucky."

"You deserve it."

"I do?"

She nodded.

Joseph and Lila were in the sitting room, the afternoon sun slanting through the heavy drapes they'd drawn to the side, softening the dark shades on the patterned rug, creating a golden light in which their white hair made them seem ethereal. They both rose unsteadily to their feet, politely extending blue-veined hands gnarled with arthritis, their touch as soft and velvety as talcum powder.

"I was hoping you found a girlfriend, Amos," Joseph quipped, his eyes crinkling and sparkling.

"Oh now," Lila said. "What about our Anna?" She placed a hand on his arm.

Amos felt the dreaded blush, turned away from Lavina.

"Would you like some tea?"

"No, no thank you. My driver is coming in a few minutes," Lavina said quickly.

They chatted a few more minutes and left with Lavina hissing questions the minute they were out of earshot.

"What was that about, Amos?"

"What?"

"You know. About Anna. Who is she?"

"It's a girl who does spring and fall cleaning. She's very nice, but mostly we just work together."

"Is she Amish?"

"Yes, she is. But really different. Not Amish the way we are."

"What's that supposed to mean?"

"I don't know. Forget it."

And no matter how hard she tried, Amos clammed up, refusing to budge until the white van made an appearance, coming slowly up the drive.

"Lavina, come again sometime, okay? Whenever you need someone to talk to, just call a driver. Or I'll come get you."

"Mom won't approve of it."

"She doesn't approve of a lot of things."

There was no answer from Lavina, but a quick wave, an uncertain look.

"Can I give you a hug?" she asked.

"Of course."

Supper was ready at home, a good home-cooked meal of mashed potatoes and ham, fresh corn, and late tomatoes. Raymond praised his wife's cooking, but when there was no reply, he glanced furtively at her closed expression.

Cathy shoved a mouthful of ham sideways and cracked loudly, "Oh, come on, Mom. Pouting is only making the situation worse."

She shot her daughter a derisive look, then continued eating. Silence hung like a black veil of hurt and resentment, but no one seemed to notice, the evening sun slanting through the doorway, creating blocks of yellow light on the linoleum. A cardinal called to its mate, was answered immediately. A branch raked against the side of the house.

The dishes were washed in the same silence, the girls going to their rooms and Raymond outside to work with the chainsaw on a pile of downed trees, while Lydia went to the pantry for a large chunk of chocolate cake in a dish. She spooned canned peaches over it and ate the whole delicious concoction standing by the sink, satisfying the disappointment about Cathy's job.

She'd find a way to buy the shrubbery. She'd have a yard sale, put less money on her secret credit card. Kelly might give her a bonus.

Raymond whistled as he worked, thankful he didn't have to know what she was pouting about this time. She'd get over it if he stayed on her good side. She always did. He should say something to Cathy about her lack of respect, but the thought filled him with dread. She'd look down on him, hate him even, then where would he be? You had to keep the love, and he did love both his daughters. And Lydia. He loved Lydia best of all, he only wished she could be different, be more content. He knew he had little to offer.

Some men were more talented than he, running successful businesses, managing employees. Sure, they dealt with stress and headaches, but it meant money in the bank. They could own their vacation homes, their rental houses, their own palatial houses; he wanted no part of it, in spite of Lydia's unhappiness.

He'd often wondered if he should try his hand at creating a business of his own, lay down his own life to serve his wife, but found an aversion to this, a shiver running up his spine to think how he would be going against his own convictions.

"Having food and raiment, therewith to be content." How often had he clung to the words of Jesus, but would never tell his wife. He knew silence was always best.

Amos finished mowing, his thoughts churning now. Obviously, Lavina was not emotionally healthy, but who was he to advise her? There was a point in time when he was worse than her, by far, and now he was slowly healing, little bits and pieces of gratitude finding its way into his heart. Or was it his soul or spirit? He wasn't sure what the difference was.

He wished Anna would contact him, but if he was painfully honest, it would probably go the way of Skye Larkin. She'd not want to hurt his feelings, and later, he'd find out she'd moved on.

He was still young. He had time. But when he thought of Anna, he hoped with all his being she was sincere. She definitely understood things about God that he didn't. But he wasn't going to get all worked up about it, this religion stuff. He'd be thankful, work hard, improve himself, and hope for the best.

He heard his name being called. Turning, he saw Lila waving from the front porch. He waved back, then hurried toward the house when he saw the urgency. Something was wrong.

He walked fast, then ran when he saw her move swiftly across the porch and through the door.

He hoped it wasn't Joseph.

Yanking the door open, he felt his breath leaving his body in short hard gasps, dismayed to see Lila wringing her hands, her face as frail and white as tissue paper.

"Come," was all she could manage.

He was lying at the bottom of the stairs, groaning audibly, a hand waving feebly. But he was conscious, his eyes squeezed shut as he endured the pain.

Amos bent over him, calling his name, but there was no answer.

Quickly, Amos reached for his phone, put in the number, spoke hurriedly.

"Joseph, there's a medic on its way. Can you make it till they arrive? Lila, maybe a small pillow would help."

Bending down, he stroked the old man's shoulders, brushed back a few stray hairs, as soft and white as feathers.

"You'll be okay. Thanks, Lila." He gently inserted the pillow beneath the old man's head, then stood helplessly, Lila nearby, her eyes red with weeping softly.

He turned to her. "Nancy's gone home?"

"Yes, she has."

She lifted rheumy eyes, imploring him, "Will he survive this?"

"Yes, I believe he will. Was he going up the stairs?"

"I don't know."

Joseph was taken to the large medical center in Williamston, the largest town close to them. It was a seven-story building made of glass and brick, with a parking garage nearby. Amos found he was intimidated by this glass behemoth, the parking garage a modern-day miracle. Lila rode in the ambulance and Amos followed more slowly in his truck, soon remembering he had no experience with city driving or parking.

He found the emergency room, talked to a receptionist, and waited. He scrolled through his phone, the way most everyone else did, and time seemed suspended. Half an hour disappeared, and then another forty minutes. It occurred to him how many human beings across the planet went through life like this, zoned in on another world in which there was endless entertainment, knowledge, and world news, to name only a few of the things available.

Strictly forbidden among the Amish, viewed as evil by the majority, the small devices still found their way into many Amish homes, usually by the more liberal youth who then kept them after joining the church and getting married.

However, there were still plenty of the conservative Amish who shunned all forms of cell phones, kept their phone shanties with a landline, and took their messages on voicemail, keeping the old tradition of having nothing handy. Lengthy telephone conversations were viewed as unnecessary, especially among the women who tended to gossip, repeating slanderous news.

Even with a phone in a cold phone shanty, gossip often found its way from ear to ear, sisters or cousins or friends setting a time to call or be called via voicemail, enabling the grapevine to stay alive and well, women discussing events or whose offspring was disobedient in school or among the youth, sharing juicy bits of news to astound the other. Or, sometimes, words of encouragement as each one found they were facing an uphill battle in life. When conversations became lengthy, the cold, damp air would remind them it was time to go to the house.

"Amos Beiler?"

He looked up, nodded.

"Come on back."

He followed the aide, a tall, buxom woman shuffling along in huge white Crocs, her top imprinted with a dizzying print in brilliant colors, her hair a deep purplish red.

"They're taking him in to surgery, but I'll bring you to where his wife is waiting."

"Thank you."

He followed her into an elevator and up to the third floor, then to a waiting area with huge glass windows, the evening sun illuminating the parking lot below.

Lila was grateful to see him, her eyes beseeching as he sat beside her and took her hand. He was worried her age and frailty would be put to the test. Before the nurse left, he asked for a blanket. He spread it across her lap, then asked if she needed anything to eat or drink.

She placed a hand on his arm, but shook her head, then bowed her shoulders, closed her eyes, her lips moving in prayer.

Amos watched, wondering. He became uncomfortable, noticing the length of time elapsing, and still she talked to God.

Did He hear her?

He looked away, cringing when he saw she was being observed.

She opened her eyes, gave him a wan smile, but her blue eyes were alive with the joy prayer had brought her. Amos wished he had this comfort, this place to go when things beyond his control turned up.

"Now then, Amos. I believe Joseph will be alright. He has a fractured hip, you know. The bane of old people when they fall."

"He broke his hip?"

"He did. But he'll be fine. It's amazing they were able to get him into surgery so quickly. Now, I would like to have a cup of good hot tea if you would be so kind."

He would. He would do anything for this old couple.

Going to the nurse's station, he made his request and waited till a young nurse brought him a Styrofoam cup with a lid, her eyes friendly as she handed it to him.

"There you go. Sugar? Milk?"

"I'll take both. Thank you."

"You're welcome."

She turned away, but not before he saw a certain look in her eye, the slight notice of him, a feeling of approval or something. Bewildered, he walked back to Lila, wondering. He was used to being viewed as invisible, slightly repulsive, a non-person who had to apologize for his existence. Asking for a cup of tea would have been almost impossible with his infected acne on his face, small eyes buried in folds of diseased flesh, a body speaking of excess and bad habits.

Had he changed so much?

Lila accepted the tea gratefully, waved away the sugar and milk. He sat beside her, noticing the tremor in her hands, the thin wrists birdlike.

"Amos, what would we do without you? You're our special guardian. Like an angel to us."

"If it wasn't me, someone else would have answered the ad in the paper. Likely someone even better."

She smiled and shook her head.

Across from them, a young couple sat apart, lost in their own separate misery, the woman uncomfortably overweight, her T-shirt exposing rolls of untamed flesh, the thin jacket doing little to conceal it. Her face was lined with worry, her eyes vacant as she stared out the window.

He was thin, with long stingy hair and an unkempt beard, his gray bill cap pulled low over brooding eyes. Amos glanced quickly, looked away, wanting to avoid conversation with more strangers.

But Lila caught the young woman's eye and asked how she was doing, mentioning it surely was a beautiful evening out there.

Amos froze, mortified.

"We're okay," she answered curtly.

"Someone you love in surgery?" she inquired sweetly.

Almost, Amos put a hand on her arm to stop this unnecessary exchange, afraid of being put down, silenced by this unhappy couple. He glanced at Lila, whose fading blue eyes were alight with interest.

"Our son."

The man shuffled his feet uncomfortably, and Amos noticed his shoes, old worn-out sneakers with frayed strings untied. Bits of mud and gravel residue clung to the soiled soles. A great pity welled up in Amos, recognizing the discomfort, the feeling of being odd, drawing eyes directly to the source.

He met the man's eyes, a quick smile. They both looked away. Then back again, trusting.

"Nice evening," Amos said, then instantly berated himself. Dumb remark.

"Yeah," from across the room.

Lila was now in a conversation with the overweight woman who was already dabbing at overflowing eyes, her face splotched with purple. She moved across the room, her tea tucked beside her, leaned forward, and placed a thin hand on the woman's arm.

To his surprise and discomfort, the man left his seat and sat beside Amos, opened his mouth, and began to talk.

"Eleven years old. Brain tumor. Fell down at school. We thought he was dead."

Cold dark eyes, brooding beneath the bill of his cap.

"I'm sorry," Amos offered, feeling empty and inadequate.

The man shook his head bitterly, swore low under his breath.

"Ain't fair. None of this is right. He's just a kid, and a pretty good one, too. And you know what the doctor said? He said there's a chance he won't wake up from this surgery. 'A chance.' It's all just chance, isn't it? And I've been unlucky my whole life. 'Chance' is never on my side."

Amos could offer nothing, afraid of saying the wrong thing.

Chapter 19

In the weeks following Joseph's hospital stay, Amos often thought of the man in the waiting room—the worn sneakers, the sense of futility and despair. Why hadn't he said anything? Realizing he didn't know what to say only made him feel worse. Why did God allow eleven-year-olds to develop a growth, allow it to adhere to a healthy young brain, to steal a youthful life? Or was it really just chance, like the man had said?

Bitterness welled in him, leaving a sour, acrid taste in his mouth. He too had had his share of bad luck. His Amish upbringing should have been marked by loving parents, a firm foundation in truth, contentment and a sense of belonging. Some Amish kids got that, he knew. But instead, he'd stumbled through ridicule and unfairness, a lack of caring, love and approval always somewhere beyond his reach. The only words he remembered from church were those that struck fear through his heart—talk of the world coming to an end, an austere God on his throne pointing an accusing finger directly at him.

He had nothing with which to encourage the man with the worn-out sneakers who stated his truth bluntly, without faith.

Yet he couldn't quite accept that everything was just chance, either. There had to be something more, didn't there? He realized it was time to begin searching, time to figure things out. He made a silent vow to God, or whoever. He was going to figure some of this out, all by himself, by watching people around him and deciding for himself what was right and what was wrong.

He became Joseph's caregiver, slipping into the role of getting him out of bed, into the bathroom, back on his chair. Strong and patient, he had no idea how seamlessly he maneuvered the frail old man from one resting place to another.

As the winds of October scattered leaves, he cleaned the garage, mowed grass, oiled and stored equipment, his phone constantly buzzing as Lila asked him to help with Joseph.

He was strangely happy, inexplicably content, ministering to Joseph's needs bringing an emotion he had never experienced. Nancy was there, and Lila, but Joseph needed Amos most. The third week after surgery, he was walking with only a cane, the walker pushed against the wall. Lila and Nancy clapped and cheered, egging him on, until he waved his cane and grinned with pure enjoyment.

Nancy changed the sheets on his hospital bed, tugging and folding, her wide back bending, sheets snapping as they were put efficiently into place. She brought fresh water with ice, a small dish of cantaloupe and honeydew melon, a few lozenges for his throat, a cup of tea for Lila.

Amos watched Lila's sweet old face, the tears welling in the faded blue eyes, and knew what was forthcoming.

"Oh, my dear, what would we do without you? The day our door was opened to you, Nancy, the angels from heaven ushered you straight in."

Nancy huffed. "Now, Lila, if I wouldn't be here, someone else would, I ain't that much."

"Of course you are. Joseph and I would have to sell this property, live out the rest of our lives in a retirement home, if you and Amos had never come to our door. God directed you straight to it, that's what."

Embarrassed a bit, slightly flustered, Nancy told Amos there was a chocolate croissant in the kitchen if he wanted it.

Amos smiled, lifted his eyebrows.

"Oh now, don't give me that. You can't live on vegetables and steamed fish and you know it."

"I'll get Joseph settled first."

He knew all the right moves, allowing him to settle on the edge of the bed, a hand behind his back, another behind his knees, patiently and so gently sliding him back into bed. Then he arranged the pillows, drew the soft blanket over his thin legs, brought the bedside table on wheels. He handed him a fork for his fruit and filled the glass with ice water.

Joseph looked up at Amos, his old eyes alive with the usual spark, a wide grin spreading across his face.

"You missed your calling, young man. Yes. Completely missed it."

Amos grinned back. "Who would do the yard, old man?"

Joseph threw his head back and cackled delightedly.

"Old man, indeed. You wait till this hip heals up. I'll show you who's old."

Amos laughed with him and was struck by the thought of Joseph being like a father, or maybe a grandfather, someone he'd known all his life. In the time he'd been here, he had never been reproached, belittled, made to feel inferior. He'd only been encouraged, uplifted, and praised.

Ah, Joseph. Was there ever a saint on earth like him? And he drove a car, had electricity, and watched television—all things of the world, all forbidden, according to Amos's upbringing. Joseph was a "man of the world." And yet, he possessed a joy and strength he'd never seen in his own father, a devout man who was accepted as an upstanding member of the Amish church.

ANNA ARRIVED AGAIN to do the seasonal deep cleaning. He drank in the sight of her in the early morning sunlight, dressed in the brown of an acorn, a black bib apron and heart-shaped white covering, a pair of tan Skechers on her feet.

His mother's voice came to him. "I don't know where her mother is, dressed like that." She was not here, but he still heard her voice, the constant dissatisfaction, the need to criticize and belittle others. He felt an ache in his chest, the need to rise above this.

He was on the porch, the wide, beautiful porch he loved, blower in hand. He faced her, watched as she came up the steps, all bright joy and energy, the blond streaks in her brown hair riveting.

"Hey there, Amos Beiler," she called out, laughing in the free way of hers.

"Good morning, Anna."

"It's a lovely one. What's new?"

"Well, I've been busy. Learning new things. I'm doing more care-giving these days."

"Great. That's wonderful. You're actually caring for the old man?"

"He had a hip operation, so I've been helping while he recovers. The lifting, moving him around."

She stood a few feet away from him, and he realized again how short she was. Did she reach his shoulder? With her face uplifted, he could not take his eyes away, but allowed his own to convey the happiness he felt at the sight of her. It was a moment of being transcended from the porch to a place he had never been, a new dimension of himself, a daring to go where his heart led.

She looked away, and the spell was broken.

Immediately, he felt the old loathing of himself, the hulking lump, the face crosshatched with disease, pig eyes.

His face closed, his shoulders tensed. He turned away, the blower roaring to life, sending dust, twigs, and leaves ahead of him.

He thought he heard a distant sound, but kept the leaf blower going, until he felt a solid thump on his forearm, and looked over to find an irate young woman glaring up at him.

"Stop that thing."

He did, in disbelief.

"I wasn't done talking to you."

"Sorry."

"I'm *nāva-sitz*ing (serving as an honored wedding guest) on November first. I'm allowed to invite two people. Would you come to my friend's wedding if I invited you?

He looked away across the lawn to the backdrop of trees, the colors like a box of crayons, vivid, impossibly colorful.

"Amish?"

"Of course. I said '*nāva-sitz*ing.' English people have bridal parties."

"Probably not. I'd feel weird. I'm English. I don't own a suit."

"You could purchase a *mutza*, a vest and a pair of trousers. You know that. Come on. You'd be invited as a *nāva-sitz* buddy, so you'd get an important seat at the table in the evening. Plus, you could pick a girl to take to the table in the afternoon. Wouldn't that be fun, being Amish again?"

"I'll think about it."

"Great." She held up a hand, palm out. He high-fived, quickly stepped away.

He would never allow himself the luxury of that long look again. Forbidden territory, for someone like him.

He used the blower to clean the porch, lost in thought.

The only memories of Amish weddings were a few cousins, one church wedding, all a blur of impossibility, negative feelings piled like an unsurmountable mountain of garbage, a landfill of misery.

He was never assigned a girl to spend the evening with, that old tradition of the bride and groom pairing the youth to eat the wedding meal together and share a hymn book to sing after. He was painfully aware that no one would have wanted to be paired with him, so the bride and groom simply left him out. He wasn't the only one, since there were more boys than girls, but it still hurt. Twice the size of normal young men, a face like an ogre, he'd shuffled self-consciously to the table with the other young men who had no companion. He'd kept his face lowered, choked down food through a throat gone dry, hating everyone.

And then there'd be the syrupy exchange between Cathy and his mother the following evening. They'd talked excitedly about which young man had asked for her hand, which one asked to go to the evening table. A special honor. Not two, but three had asked. Radiant, she tossed her shoulders and laughed uproariously at her own jokes, said she'd created quite a stir for the bride.

To be asked to attend an Amish wedding was like scraping an old infected wound with the edge of a serrated knife. Beyond painful.

His phone buzzed.

He read Anna's text. "Can you bring a stepladder?"

He walked slowly to the shed, taking in the new cleanliness, the total organization, a true sense of having done something right. He loved this place, loved everything about it, the repair work, the painting and cleaning, mowing and weeding. Someday, he would have to leave, but he didn't have to face that now.

He lifted the aluminum ladder and carried it to the second floor, peering into rooms till he found her by the scent of cleaner.

"You took your good old time," she quipped. "I need to get these drapes down."

"I can do it for you."

She tilted her face, considered. "You know how much I dislike these crazy heavy drapes? Why would anyone bother with them?"

"Lila's old. Every window used to have them."

"Yeah, but imagine this house with fresh paint and better window treatments. The first thing I'd do would be . . ." She paused, lowering her voice. "Paint this awful trim work and these dark doors."

Amos said nothing. He thought of Joseph and Lila, how their pride might be hurt if they heard Anna, but he didn't know what to say.

"What? Say something," she said quickly.

He was climbing the ladder, so he busied himself getting the drapes down, wished she wouldn't watch. He felt as big as an elephant, a wobbling walrus, saw the dirt on his shoes, felt his T-shirt ride up, the heat suffusing his face in a painful blush.

"Oh, I don't know. I think they like this dark trim. It's what they're used to."

"Sure. Of course. Just thinking out loud. It doesn't hurt to dream. You know it makes time go faster when you think about things while you're working."

Amos climbed down with the loosened drapes, moved to the next window, and repeated the procedure without comment. He had been surprised at his own quick defense of the old couple. This was their house, their drapes and trim work, and who was she to critique any of it?

She recognized this, being perceptive of his emotion, and told him she didn't mean to be rude.

He softened. "You're not. It's just that they're so proud of this old house, and they've cared for it so well. Maybe it's strange, but helping them tend to it feels like . . . like kind of an honor."

She watched his face, pondered his words, thought of the devotion, which was really something for a young man. Sometimes he was so open with his expressions and his words, and other times he just shut himself off, like drawing shutters over a window, putting an abrupt end to any ordinary exchange. Mysterious, really.

ANNA'S PARENTS HAD lived their whole lives in the Lancaster area, but found themselves increasingly hemmed in by encroaching construction, exploding real estate taxes, and the seemingly endless rush of life around them. They visited many outlying sister churches, but finally settled in Northern Pennsylvania with the river, the lush valley surrounded by mountains, and the price of land completely reasonable. Anna and her sister Barbie had been less than impressed, having joined the group of youth in Lancaster, but they were both adventurous, wanted to please their parents, and agreed to make the most of their move.

Not that any of it had been easy. To live in a secluded area, with no neighbors, no sound of traffic, and the dark mountains looming ominously at night had been their undoing those first months.

Her father, a short, compact man of fifty, struggled to start a roofing business, often becoming preoccupied with the stress of remodeling the rather old house they'd purchased. Her mother was a real courageous soul, a stalwart, buxom woman with an optimistic outlook and a love of nature, so she adjusted to the move immediately, purchasing a good pair of binoculars and a *Petersen's Bird Book*, learning about types of birds and their habits. She painted and planted, directed carpenters, and ended up with a lovely home in the woods at the base of the mountain, thanks to the efficiency of her husband and Stoltzfus Builders.

The home was a normal one, containing all the activity of family life, but was steeped in love and shone with grace and mercy toward those around them, and to each other. Morning devotions, scriptures taught throughout the day, and respect to God and the elders of the church formed a rock solid foundation for the children, although the *ordnung* was not kept to the letter. They felt no shame in winking at the little things, the way Allen and Rachel had both been raised themselves.

So, Anna was allowed to ride in Amos's truck, allowed to spend an evening with him, but with the clear understanding there would be no serious relationship with him as long as he did not consider himself Amish. Anna confided in Barbie, describing Amos as someone who had a problem with his family, had obviously been mistreated, but had never retaliated in the way so many rebellious Amish had. He didn't party at all. Never drank or smoked. He really had no friends, except the old couple and a few gym rats, obviously Christians trying to get him to go to church with them.

"Different," Barbie said. "He's different."

Anna described the aura of sadness, the mysterious quietness of him, but Barbie never heard a physical description nor was shown a picture of him.

"Well, is he good looking?" she ventured finally.

Anna considered the question, then said he wasn't textbook handsome, but there was something about him, something she couldn't place. He fascinated her, was what it was.

"He says he was hideous, growing up. His parents and sisters were ashamed of him. He weighed over two hundred pounds in school, was the butt of everyone's jokes."

"Do you know how damaging that can be?"

"I know. And I think the reason he left was largely on account of mistreatment, although I think his own family was the worst."

"Seriously? I'd love to meet him."

"He'd never."

"He wouldn't come here?"

"No."

Barbie shook her head, wondered if Anna was getting herself into something proving to be foolhardy in the end. She had never seen her sister as serious, as preoccupied, as she was now, the usual sunny disposition clouded over. She sensed a certain portent. Very seldom did these situations turn out well, especially involving a troubled young man who had rebelled against his upbringing and now found solace in the love of English people.

Anna brought the subject to her parents, who discussed it openly with her, which eased her mind considerably. They listened with an open mind, brought a sensible verdict to the table, that of giving it time.

"A guy like him, who didn't find love and acceptance among our people, is vulnerable to just about anything," her father said quietly.

"I mean, in a way, it sounds like he's doing an amazing job of it," added her mother. "He sounds quite responsible, really. But he still doesn't want to return to his roots?"

"No. Not at all."

"So why do you even consider him?"

"I don't know why. He's nice, fun to hang out with. There's just something about him . . ."

"But he's not Amish."

She shrugged, pouted a bit.

"We would be terribly hurt if you left the Amish, Anna," her mother said, her round eyes shining.

"Why? Why is it such a catastrophic deal if someone leaves our church? Other churches don't excommunicate or shun if you decide to switch. You're saying if he doesn't return to the Amish, I can't see him, right?"

"One question at a time. The big deal is we're steeped in tradition, hold the standards of our *ordnung* very high. It matters to us how we dress, how we live, and value an old-fashioned way of life. When children leave, parents feel as if all they've taught their children is thrown rebelliously in their face. We shelter our children from the ways of the world, which has many liberal practices we don't accept."

"But what about the home Amos comes from? What good did being sheltered from the world do him if his own home wasn't a safe place? Oh, I don't know. My mind is all clogged up."

Anna gripped each side of her face, her elbows on the table, clearly upset.

"A day at a time, Anna," said her father. "I know you're searching for answers, and you can see what that old couple has done for Amos. All believers rejoice in hearing about other believers, and it sounds like Joseph and Lila are genuine Christians who are filled with the love of Christ. It's not our job to look down on them because they worship differently than we do. But we want our children to see the value in the old way—the traditions, the community, the way we are set apart from the world. You do see the value, don't you?"

THIS CONVERSATION HAD taken place only a few weeks before, so Anna's usual brightness was diminished as they worked on the drapes.

Finally, she said, "You thought about the wedding?"

"Not yet."

"Well, if you don't want to go, don't hesitate to say so. I kind of invited you on a whim. It's fine if you say no."

"I'll think about it."

She longed to tell him about the conversation with her parents, but thought better of it.

When the last drape was removed, the colorful light from the trees illuminated the room, bringing into sharp relief the curling seams of the old, yellowing wallpaper, the chipped and stained varnish on the woodwork. The mauve colored carpet was graying in well-worn areas, the old windows peeling paint, caulking broken in pieces, lying on windowsills like mummified bugs.

They stood side by side, the pile of pink drapes at their feet, viewing the room in the harsh, unmerciful sunshine reflecting off the golden trees.

"Wow," Anna said softly. "This place would take thousands of dollars to make presentable."

"I was thinking it's a lot like people. Take away the cloak of appearances and see what they look like in the light of reality."

"That's quite a speech," she said wryly.

He looked down at her, "You don't agree?"

"I do. But it gives me the blues when you talk like that."

Puzzled, he asked why.

"Because you don't like the Amish."

This sentence was like a wisp of fog, nothing solid to hold onto, until he allowed himself to think she might care about him being English for the reason he would never dare hope. He turned away from her, walked over to the window, and stared unseeingly at the rustling yellow leaves below.

Wanting to ask why she cared, but lacking the courage, he unlocked the window and pushed it open, sending a spray of caulking to the worn carpeting.

"Let's open all of these," he said.

The air flowing in was pungent with the smell of autumn, dry brown grass, decaying leaves, and a distant smell of woodsmoke. Anna breathed deeply, then said she better get to work, which excused him right then and there.

He wasn't ready to leave, the absence of her too final without asking the question.

"Why do you care if I like the Amish or not?"

She shrugged, avoided his eyes, then said loudly and much too quickly, "I don't know. That's a stupid question."

She turned her back and lifted a chair, then set it in another spot, before grabbing the dustcloth.

Her lack of composure created an unbidden surge of boldness. He walked over and sat on the chair, took her hand, and held it firmly, in spite of the struggle to free herself.

"Maybe you do know, Anna."

"Stop it. Let me go. You don't know, either. Go now. I have to get to work. Oh, and by the way, forget the wedding. I didn't mean it."

He turned and went down the stairs, whistling soft and low, then burst through the door to the porch and leaped down the stairs. He started up the mower and bagged leaves, felt a part of the sun-dappled golden light, the scudding white clouds, and the wind. He had never felt like this a day in his life. He could barely stay on the mower, but felt as if he needed wings to fly, to swoop and turn and somersault on the clouds.

She did care what he thought of the Amish, and there could only be one reason for that.

In the mirror that evening, he was surprised by the reflection. A deeply tanned face, eyes looking more proportional due to the way his face had thinned. He'd lost almost ninety pounds. He still had a large nose, but it was well-built, and the mouth not terribly unattractive. He noticed the thick brown hair, cut short, and decided the closely shaved beard was definitely an asset.

At the gym the next morning, he worked the weights, felt humbled at bulging biceps, thought perhaps life was finally being kinder toward him. He felt as if he'd been kicked around, damaged, but was slowly lifting himself from the muck.

Yes, he had been lower than he'd thought possible, but perhaps, perhaps there was more to his life than defeat.

Chapter 20

Anna finished the fall cleaning, avoided him at every turn, until the very last week of October he cornered her in the downstairs guest room.

Her blue eyes flashed, and she started moving away.

"Anna."

"What?" But she kept walking.

"That wedding. I've thought about it."

"Why? I told you to forget it. I invited someone else."

"Oh."

"Look. I . . ." She turned. "You didn't want to go, so don't act as if you did."

"Well, you got all huffy and didn't even give me a chance to explain."

In the hallway, Lila stood behind the doorway, crooked a finger at her husband, who hobbled over and bent forward. Like synchronized swimmers, they listened gleefully, their hearing aids working to full capacity as the heated exchange continued. After a few minutes of suspense, they tiptoed away, shaking with laughter at their own folly, then wisely nodded their heads, agreed together about this being more than an argument. It sounded suspiciously like a real lover's quarrel. They talked for a long time in hushed tones, sometimes nodding seriously, and giggling like schoolchildren the next.

They came up with a clever plan.

For Thanksgiving this year, they would create an unforgettable meal right here in the lovely old dining room. They'd get Nancy to take down the china and the Waterford crystal, invite the help and their families, and anyone else they felt like. There would be turkey, shrimp, scalloped oysters, baked apples with cinnamon and nutmeg.

When heavy footsteps pounded down the hallway and out the back door, they drew back with raised eyebrows and winked broadly.

Amos was furious, but defeated more than anything. He shouldn't have allowed himself to hope. She'd gone and invited Marcus Stoltzfus. Who cared? Amish girls were about as trustworthy as March weather, so that was that.

He moped around the garage, scolded Fred and then apologized, before sitting on the couch with his hands jammed into his pockets.

Anna went to the wedding dressed in a beautiful shade of blue with a white cape and apron, sat beside her designated fellow all day in an uncomfortable folding chair, listened to the traditional wedding sermon, and thought there was simply no way Amos would ever become a part of these beloved people, this simply timeless way of life, ever again.

But what was it about him? She wished she could shake him off like dust on her shoes. She examined the young man in front of her, seated facing her with the bride and groom beside them, another couple on the other side. The *nâva-sitza*, an esteemed position, and one Anna had been proud to receive.

And here she was, thinking about Amos.

Her young man was actually quite good looking, in a thin, spidery way, with pale limbs and large, thin hands, dark hair and eyes. But she found herself thinking of the size and strength of Amos. Plus, she detected a faint odor of garlic all day, and she supposed he might have weak sinuses with an overprotective mother keeping him supplied with herbal garlic capsules.

The day dragged on, with everyone commenting how nice Anna and her "chappy" looked, but her mother detected a faint unhappiness and guessed the reason why.

The month of November stretched before her like a long endless road. Housecleaning at the Brown residence was over till spring, so she would not see Amos, and she made a solemn vow to never ever call or text him. If he wanted to talk to her, he could make the first move.

And Amos tossed his phone across the room in frustration, then picked it up and glared at it.

He finally relented and went to church with Scott, was greeted warmly, amazed at the luxurious interior, was moved by the band playing and songs of praise, listened closely to the rousing message from the pulpit, and thought he'd finally come home.

Yes, this was what he wanted. Here was love and acceptance, and he would understand the plan of salvation in time. In the English language.

So much easier, he thought.

He went out for lunch after church with Scott, his wife, and two well-behaved children. They discussed the sermon and he felt the stirring in his soul, then drove home and settled down for a good long Sunday afternoon nap. He turned on his right side, then his left. He punched his pillow and lay on his back. He checked his phone. Nothing.

Fred whined at the door, so he let him out, went absentmindedly to the refrigerator and found nothing of interest, then chuckled to himself. Not so long ago this uncomfortable feeling would have him gobbling ice cream and cookies and burgers. Anything.

He dozed fitfully, then sat up with his chin in his hands, his elbows propped on his knees. Fred barked at the door, so he let him in, grimaced as he shook himself, spraying dirt and moisture.

He looked at his phone. Should he? Should he send one message? Just a "Hi. How are you?" She wouldn't answer, would not get back to him. He decided against it.

He realized how restless he was, then put Fred in the truck and went for a drive.

He told himself it was over, he would forget about her in time. He had no intention of being Amish, couldn't imagine her in English clothes, so what was the sense in any of it?

He contemplated moving to another state as he drove. It would be easier to be somewhere else, without any memories of Anna. But he could not do that to Joseph and Lila. They had done so much for him, and he owed them his life.

"I don't know, I just don't know," he said aloud.

He thought of flipping a coin. Heads, call Anna. Tails, forget Anna. But knew he couldn't accept either one.

That night, he found himself wide awake the minute Fred yelped from his bed by the door. Before listening for the sliding, shuffling noise he burst out of his room, slammed through the door and onto the back patio, to find the hooded figure humped over the curbside garbage tote. In a flash, the figure straightened, wheeled, and took flight with Amos pounding after him, Fred barking hysterically as he ran beside him.

A moment's indecision, and Amos made a flying leap, grabbing the intruder's knees, both of them falling to the macadam with a sickening thud of flesh.

The intruder screamed and kicked, but was clamped into two hundred fifty pounds of honed muscle. Panting, Amos hung on.

"Fred, no. Calm down. It's okay."

He rolled the intruder on his back, peered into his face by the light of a half-moon, alarmed to see the smooth, dark skin of a youth. A very young boy.

"Get off me. Ow!" he yelled, whipping his arms, thrashing.

"Tell me who you are and what you're doing in my dumpster," Amos ground out.

"No. Get off. Ow! You're hurting my back."

Amos grabbed a handful of sweatshirt, leaped to his feet, hauled him up, and shoved him in the direction of the gatehouse.

"Who are you?"

"I ain't saying."

"Who are your parents?"

"I don't have any."

"Sure you do."

"Look, man, would I lie to you? All I need is some food. I'm hungry. Like, really hungry. You don't throw out too much."

Amos hesitated for only a moment.

"If you have a knife or a gun, I'm calling the law, okay?"

"I don't."

"Fred, get down. Come on." He lead him to his house, still holding onto his sweatshirt.

Inside, he turned the lights on, then stared at the thin youth, dark-skinned like aged honey, straight long black hair, enormous brown eyes out of a sharply contoured face.

"What's your story?"

There was no reply, so he told him to sit, watching as he eased into a kitchen chair, never leaving him out of his sight as he heated a can of chicken and vegetable soup. He didn't keep bread around anymore, but he found an old sleeve of saltines and set it on the table with some sliced turkey and cheddar cheese. He set it on the table and then returned to stir the soup.

"Help yourself."

He watched as the ravenous youth tore into the cheese, stuffed wads of turkey into his mouth, silently, desperately. Amos had never seen a starving person, had not known the feral intensity of getting food into a mouth. The soup was lukewarm, but he dumped it into a bowl and served it, realizing the boy would burn himself if he gulped it down hot.

He lifted the bowl and drank big gulps, then chewed the chicken and vegetables.

"Thanks, man." He rose to his feet. "I'll get on down the road now."

"Wait. Wait a minute. You didn't tell me anything."

"Name's Jamal. From everywhere. You know, here and there."

"But why do you creep around eating from garbage cans at night?"

"If I wanted you to know, I'd tell you."

"Come on. Sit. Tell me about yourself."

A wild look, a turning away as if to flee, but Amos placed himself directly in front of the door.

"You'll rat on me."

"I might, but I doubt it. You strike me as just a kid, not a hardened criminal. Tell me and I'll give you some food to take with you."

Reluctantly, the boy sat back down. He kept his eyes averted as he started to talk. He said he'd been in the foster system, had gone from one placement to another.

"I don't know how many different homes. I wasn't an easy kid to handle. I don't like people telling me what to do. When the last couple said I couldn't stay, I ran instead of taking my chances with another family. Some of 'em are weird, mean. My mom overdosed—got a bad batch of something. Grandma died when I was seven. So that's it. That's my story. Can I have the food now?"

"How long have you been hiding?"

"Ran away two years ago."

"Where do you stay?"

"Anywhere."

"Meaning?"

"Here and there. I can't get a job. No ID, no social security, nothing."

"How old are you?"

He sighed, rolled his eyes, and tossed his hood away from his face. "You know, I don't exactly know. It's not like anyone's throwing me birthday parties. I'm guessing fifteen, maybe sixteen."

Amos watched him closely, allowing suspicion to take over for a moment. Suddenly, he wanted him to leave, wanted the luxury of being alone, responsible only for himself. But he pushed aside the feeling.

"And where will you go tonight, when you leave here?"

"Anywhere."

"You have no specific place? No tent or shelter?"

Jamal rolled his eyes but stayed silent.

"Well?"

"You'll rat on me."

"Why? Unless you're hiding on this property, it's not my problem."

"I have a place. Stole the tent from a yard sale. Stole the sleeping bag from the Amish store."

He gave Amos a piercing look. "You'll keep quiet?"

"I will."

In the end, Amos asked him stay and sleep on the couch, and he did. He wondered if Joseph and Lila would mind, but decided they'd do the same. He told Jamal he had to use the shower and gave him clothes to put on that were much too big. He hoped desperately he didn't have lice or fleas.

In the dark of early morning, Amos awoke with a start, sitting straight up in his bed, bewildered. What was it? Then he remembered. Jamal.

Throwing back the covers, he leaped out of bed, but the boy was gone. There was a neat pile of clothing, a blanket folded with the pillow on top, but no sign of him. A wrenching loss tore through Amos then, almost like a panic. Where had he gone? What would become of him?

His first thought was getting in his truck and searching for him. But he hadn't gotten any specific information from the boy, beyond the fact that he'd stolen a tent.

In his state of anxiety, he lifted the clothes, refolded them, put them in the clothes hamper, paced. At breakfast, he decided to tell Joseph, who listened quietly, his bathrobe falling open to reveal protruding collar bones, his thin hand on his coffee cup trembling. Lila joined them, a hand clutching, worrying her heavy bathrobe, her feet pushed into plush slippers.

"That is very troubling," Joseph said finally.

"But comforting to know your intruder was just a boy," Lila added.

Amos nodded, "It's just hard, not knowing what will become of him."

"Well, he knows where you are, Amos, so he won't starve."

Joseph sipped his coffee, watched him over the rim of his cup. He could tell the anxiety was real, the caring genuine in a way he had not thought possible with one so young.

"If it would make you feel better, we could make some calls, ask the police to keep an eye out for him?" he suggested.

Amos shrugged, disconsolate. "I don't want to get him in trouble. He trusted me with his story."

The invitations were sent, the groceries bought, and the day before Thanksgiving Nancy was in the kitchen cooking and baking. With Jace still in jail, she was glad not to be home for the holiday this year. It would feel strange. Lila had invited Nancy's family to join them, and she looked forward to impressing them with the fancy dishes, expensive ingredients, and multi-course meal.

Lila's cheeks bloomed with a rosy color, and Joseph barely needed his cane as he supervised the opening of the massive oak table, instructing Amos unnecessarily. A beautiful table, that was what Lila wanted, so Amos was sent to gather twigs and thin branches, winterberry, pine, and acorns. He drove the tractor out, parked, and turned the motor off while he gathered the items. The plot of woods was hushed, crisp, the scent of decaying leaves and moist soil everywhere. Leaves rustled as squirrels dodged frantically, their broad, bushy tails spread behind them. Blue jays squawked at him from bare branches, and he lifted his face to watch the brilliance of their plumage.

He would always love this wooded area, adjacent to the orchard, but it brought memories of Skye Larkin with it. He cringed, thinking of his appearance back then. She had been nice to him, looking beyond the damaged skin and unwieldy size, and then mocked him so cruelly with her new boyfriend. He wondered if they were still together.

He looked forward to being with Joseph and Lila for Thanksgiving, along with Nancy, a few of the home-care nurses who came periodically, and someone who had helped repair the roof and done other handyman projects here and there when they were outside of Amos's abilities. Joseph and Lila had been a vit vague about the guest list, but that was OK. He was just grateful to have a place to enjoy Thanksgiving without the stress of his own family.

He felt sure Anna would not be present. She only came to work for a short period in the spring and fall, and besides, she'd spend Thanksgiving with her family. He had no wish to be in her company anyway. She was too feisty, too opinionated, got all bent out of shape about nothing.

Always, in the back of his mind, he was afraid of winding up with someone like his own mother—critical, controlling, never satisfied. It was wrong, thinking that sort of thing. She was his mother after all and had cared for him in her own absent-minded way, giving the love she was capable of, even if it was measured in small drops.

He hadn't visited home for too long and this bothered him, even though he dreaded the thought of going. Cathy would contact him in a flurry of messages, begging for money, then remain silent for months. He'd sent a hundred, then two hundred a couple of times, but when the demands became more frequent, he said no. "No, Cathy. I work for my paycheck and you need to do the same. I'm sorry." She had not spoken to him since.

He worried often about Lavina, knew he should check on her, but found himself unsure of how to help her. She was obviously not in a good place, and maybe he could help by reasoning with her. But who would care what he thought? Bitterness rose within him, but as he drove the tractor to the door, he mentally shook it off, not wanting to ruin the festive mood inside. He lifted bushel baskets of the table decorations through the back door and looked up to find Lila hovering, the excitement crackling from her old eyes.

"Beautiful!" she crowed.

Amos grinned at her, set the decorations on the floor, put his hands on his hips, and told her beauty was certainly in the eye of the beholder.

On Thanksgiving Day, Amos woke up with his mind in furious overdrive, filled with old hurts from his family, jealousy, and mistrust about Anna. He realized he was in no state of mind to attend a party with a smattering of acquaintances seated stiffly around a table decked out in fall décor and antique dishes. Too many people, too aware of himself and his sloppy social skills, his inability to use the right fork, say the proper words at the right time. It was tiring, mentally draining, this process of being converted to the ways of the high-classed when all he was was a too-large, too-awkward Amish boy with no confidence.

He swung his feet over the side of his bed, blinked to clear his eyesight, caught sight of himself in the mirror and quickly looked away. Who would ever want to wake up with that face on the pillow beside her?

More and more, he thought of being married to someone. He did not always want to be alone, but the thought of trusting someone was staggering. He knew he wanted what Joseph and Lila had, that closeness you could feel in the very atmosphere. Or Scott and his wife, with the looks they exchanged, the smiles and lighthearted bantering, touching to confirm their ongoing love.

His own parents loved each other, he was sure of it, in spite of his mother's constant complaints, the discontent like an aura around her. His father was patient with her to a fault, letting her run all over himself and the rest of the family. Was it really love that produced that kind of patience, or simply weakness?

And—the big question—how did one go about finding a perfect partner? Or was the perfect one only a myth, and actually a marriage always fell short of expectations?

He lifted the top of his Keurig, inserted a K-Cup, set his favorite mug underneath, and pressed the button. While the coffee dripped, he reached down to stroke Fred as he pushed his nose against his leg.

"Hey, buddy. You want out?"

The sky was gray, weeping a mist of oncoming rain, the chill hitting his bare legs like a slap.

Closing the door, he turned on the news, then reached for his coffee, absorbing the fact he did not want to go to this Thanksgiving dinner. He wondered what his family was doing. Maybe going to Doddy Beiler's.

He spent the entire morning doing nothing except staring at the newscaster on CBS, comprehending very little, his mind racing, darting from one childhood scene to another, from the gym to Skye Larkin, to Anna and the wedding he did not attend. He drank cup after cup of black coffee, got the shakes, and decided to go for a run. Fred whined and begged, but Amos knew he would only be a hindrance.

Hitting his stride, he began to feel better, more settled and in control of his thoughts. The cold mist on his face was invigorating, the wet road glistening between brown roadside growth, branches merging after most of the colorful foliage had fallen. He breathed deeply, felt the power in his legs, his arms pumping as he ran.

A runner appeared from the opposite side of the road, dressed in brilliant shades of green and yellow. The gap between them closed quickly. He met her eyes beneath the bill of her cap, and a jolt of recognition went through him.

He stopped, but she never faltered in her stride. Turning, he called out, "Hey."

She slowed, suspicious. It was clear she had no idea who he was.

"Skye!"

Breathing hard, she clenched and unclenched her fists, clearly puzzled. She bent her back, stretched the calf of her legs.

"It's me. Amos. Amos Beiler."

Incredulous now, she said, "What? You can't be serious."

She walked toward him, her green eyes alight with welcome, the bill cap removed, the sun-streaked hair caught into a thick ponytail.

"I'm serious," he said, grinning.

"Oh, my goodness. What have you done to yourself?" she asked, opening her arms as she advanced.

Amos found himself enveloped in a hug of genuine happiness. These hugs for anyone and everyone among the English was still startling to him, though he didn't stop her. His arms went around her loosely and soon dropped to his sides.

"Amos, look at you!"

Her hands ran down the length of his arms, gripped his shoulders, her face wreathed in smiles of admiration.

"Okay, tell me what you did. Keto diet? Personal trainer?"

Amos laughed outright. "No, not exactly. Just, you know, became addicted to the gym, learned how to eat right. Or better. Still not exactly perfect."

"Seriously, the transformation is incredible. It's like your features have aligned themselves in your face, and your body is unbelievable."

Amos felt the heat rise in his face, embarrassed now. English people. He'd never get used to it. The unabashed praise, the free way of handing out love and encouragement, presenting compliments as easily as breathing, and receiving them with a happy "Thanks!"

In the Amish world, it was not like that. There was a certain holding back, compliments not easily given or taken, flavored with a sense of discomfort, waved away.

Was it humility, repression, fear of revealed pride? He didn't know, but now he floundered, avoided her eyes, mumbling his thanks.

"I am not just handing out an empty compliment, you know," she continued. "I didn't even recognize you."

"Really?"

"Absolutely."

"So, how have you been?"

"Good, actually. School is going really well. I have some good classes, get along great with my roommate."

"Good. Glad to hear it."

"And you?"

"Pretty much the same. Keeping the grounds, going to the gym, that kind of thing."

She tilted her head, her eyes piercing.

"Still no girlfriend?"

He shook his head.

"You know, you're not the teenage boy I met. You've grown up."

"I know."

There was a space of silence, the mist settling like millions of invisible drops between them, the fields and fencerows flanking them on either side, a crow flapping wildly with a songbird in hot pursuit. They both stepped aside to allow a pickup truck to roar past.

"Imagine us meeting up like this. You're going to the Thanksgiving dinner at Joseph and Lila's, I'm assuming?"

"Yeah. Can't get out of it," he said wryly. "Are you?"

"Yes! It'll be great. My parents are going. You haven't seen them in forever."

And I haven't missed them, either, he thought bitterly, the sight of her mother turning him away as raw as the day it happened.

Out loud, he said, "Mm."

"What's that supposed to mean?"

"Nothing."

She stepped closer, reached up to touch his face.

"Oh, you wait till they catch sight of you now, Amos. They'll be singing a whole other tune. I'll see you later, then!"

He ran hard, his feet hitting the pavement with no restraint, a ball of anger in his chest. So now, since his appearance had changed, he'd be greeted with respect, would he? Nothing but vanity. Sheer vanity.

Chapter 21

He wasn't in a good frame of mind, but he would give his life for Joseph and Lila, so he threw on a navy blue shirt and black dress pants. He wasn't in the mood to care about his appearance one way or another, but he didn't want to disappoint the two of them. He'd just grit his teeth and get through this.

But he was met at the door of the big house with so much love, so much genuine caring, he couldn't help but receive graciously what the old couple presented. Guests were seated on surrounding sofas and chairs in the golden light of the antique chandeliers, the house glowing with gratitude and goodwill, Joseph and Lila like two elderly saints in light clothing.

Nancy Farmer and her cousin Bertha were cooking up a storm in the kitchen, decadent smells wafting through the house, causing Amos's stomach to rumble in anticipation.

The doorbell pealed and Lila returned with Anna's hand tucked under her arm.

Amos felt himself go cold, suddenly desperate to flee.

She was so small, so round and perfect, her brown dress fitting the decor, her heart-shaped covering and thick luxurious hair endearing. Was it his past, his upbringing, that brought this rush of admiration?

He watched, unable to tear his eyes away as she circulated, shaking hands, laughing easily, hugging Joseph just the way English people did.

Every emotion he had efficiently banished returned in force, along with the realization of how much he wanted her.

He needed her in his life but had to guard this secret of his with all of his strength. To let her know how he felt would only bring the hovering defeat hanging on the horizon, so he kept his hands behind his back and nodded curtly, never meeting her eyes.

She moved on quickly.

The grand arrival of Skye Larkin and her parents was a sight to behold, Amos thought wryly. They were, without a doubt, the best-looking people in the room, dressed in the way only the wealthy can achieve, the perfectly tailored trousers, the silk blouse, Skye's sweater, the muted colors enhanced by glinting jewelry, expensive watches.

They were as kind and gracious, as well spoken, as Lila and Joseph, but Amos couldn't forget what Nancy had once said about Skye's parents. He thought he detected the smooth underlying ambition in their over-the-top concern for Joseph's hip, their praise of Lila's table decorations.

They wanted this place.

They were used to getting what they wanted, their wealth opening doors at their command. He could see already that they would accomplish what they set out to do.

Amos willed the old couple to live forever but knew this was not possible. Someday, he would have to leave, this he knew, but till then, he would take pleasure in being the keeper of this fine old homestead.

He was seated beside Skye, with Anna directly across from him, candles flickering in brass holders, cloth napkins laid across fine old China, silverware polished to extravagant sheen. He noticed the three forks beside his plate with a sinking feeling. How was he to know which one to use when?

Joseph asked everyone to join hands, which was uncomfortable for Amos, with Skye's hand on his left, and the electrician's wife's hand on his right, but he bowed his head, closed his eyes, and listened to Joseph as he spoke the prayer of gratitude clearly, each word spoken slowly.

"Heavenly Father, we're gathered here with grateful hearts, for the love and caring of dear friends seated around the table you have provided. We acknowledge this day as one set aside by the forefathers of this great nation, of which we are humbly appreciative. Not by our own works, but by your grace and everlasting mercy do we receive this. Thank you, dear Lord and Savior, for the food, for health, for friendship, for blessing beyond measure. In thy Name we pray. Amen."

Resounding amens were repeated around the table, except for Amos, who felt miserably unable to pronounce the word. He felt foolish, not a part of Joseph's prayer at all. The only praying he had ever experienced as a child was in silence, except for the hurried four lines of the German children's prayer he had rushed through, never quite sure what it was supposed to mean.

He'd asked Cathy once, who laughed at him and told him he had to figure it out for himself. Why had he never been taught what the German words meant? He often wondered if his family was the only one lacking in spiritual guidance.

He found himself being observed and quickly brought himself back to the present. Anna's eyes were questioning, so he looked away and brought his glass of tea to his mouth, avoiding her.

A chorus of appreciation rose as Nancy served the turkey, a beautiful golden brown on a huge platter, surrounded by a heavy ring of parsley, sugared grapes, orange slices, and halved apples.

Beside him, Skye clapped her hands, applauding, and the others joined her. She touched Amos, bent her head toward him, and whispered that she was starving after that run. Her mouth turned into a delicate pout when he did not respond.

A mixed lettuce salad with goat cheese and pomegranate seeds was passed around, and Amos observed that it was to go on the smaller of the two plates in front of him. But which fork? He glanced at Skye, saw that she had picked up the smallest fork farthest from the plate. This whole meal would be endless, a tightrope walk of tension. He wanted to be anywhere in the world except here, with Anna across from him, Skye beside him.

He took a deep breath to steady himself, then took a bite.

"You like goat cheese?" Skye asked.

"I do."

She turned to smile at him, her green eyes enhanced with darkened lashes, her face made up flawlessly. She was, indeed, a beautiful girl, and Amos was only a man, finding himself drawn into her attraction.

She bent her head, whispered.

He had to bend his to hear what she was saying.

"You're looking great, Amos. Seriously."

He swallowed, mumbled his thanks, then looked up to find Anna looking straight into his eyes. Hers were the blue surrounding a night sky, dark, intense. With what? Bewildered, he kept holding her dark gaze.

What? What is it? Really?

He realized she was silently questioning who Skye was to him. He knew it, without a doubt. A great swell of unnamed feeling coursed through his veins. With all his might, he tried to tell her with his eyes: *Anna. Anna. It's okay, my Anna. Someday, it will be okay, although I don't know how or why or where. You're mine, in my heart, you are mine.*

He felt Skye's face against his arm.

She held on to his upper arm, then sat upright. He looked over, smiled politely.

"It's just so good to see you again, Amos."

"You as well."

"Thank you."

Once the salad plates were cleared, there were mounds of buttery mashed potatoes and thick golden gravy, a stuffing so good he could have eaten the whole pan. With the knowledge that Anna cared still, he found his appetite strengthening. He enjoyed the asparagus with a spicy glaze, candied sweet potatoes, baked butternut squash, all of it so good he helped himself to seconds of everything, his glass filled repeatedly with fresh tea.

Conversation flowed freely, with Joseph being the perfect host, constantly praised by the Larkins, whose faces had become a bit flushed as they tried to please the old couple. The electrician's wife, whose name was Natalie, asked about his occupation and they easily began an interesting conversation about caring for shrubs and trees, until Skye took his attention with a murmured conversation about his plans for the weekend.

"I am going to see my parents and sisters. I'm concerned about my sister Lavina."

"What about Friday night?"

He hesitated, and Anna took the opportunity to speak from across the table.

"Amos, I believe that's the Friday night we planned to visit with my sister and her family, right?"

He could hardly believe the words, but as smooth and seamless as if he'd practiced all week, Amos nodded his head, said of course he hadn't forgotten.

Skye drew back.

"Are you two seeing each other?"

"Oh no, just friends from way back," he said casually.

Anna touched her covering. "Amish, you know?" She smiled impishly.

Skye turned to the proffered pumpkin pie, smiled graciously, and, much to her credit, let it go. Amos felt an appreciation of her good manners, and allowed she was very well brought up, more than he could say about the triumphant Anna bristling with nerve, serving up that half-truth as if she was doing it every day. And yet, he had gone along with it, and frankly, he had loved it.

She gave him a look, half mystery and half understanding, which only heightened his sense of well-being, this strange and unexpected happiness like shafts of sunlight emerging from broken clouds.

In the course of the afternoon, Skye's mother approached him, fairly purring like a well-groomed house cat, proceeded to grill him about his appearance, telling him outright he had turned into a handsome prince.

"Oh, I wouldn't say that," Amos demurred.

"Oh, but you truly have transformed."

Her long sleek nails plucked at the fabric of his sleeve.

"You heard about Skye and Paul, right?"

"I don't believe I have."

"They parted ways."

"I'm sorry to hear it."

"Well, it wasn't meant to be. But. I mean, you can come over anytime. I believe you two have a shared interest in dogs, right?"

"We do, in fact."

She stepped closer, her many bracelets tinkling as she placed a slender hand on his arm.

"Well, good. And you may be aware of the fact we have an interest in this place, so perhaps you could stay on after the purchase. As a groundskeeper, of course."

"Hm," he answered vaguely, his heart rate increasing.

"You do an excellent job. I have never seen it look better. Absolutely fantastic. Fascinating."

A tap on his arm. He turned to find Anna's face upturned, her blue eyes intent with purpose.

"May I speak to you for a minute?"

"Certainly. If I may be excused."

Mrs. Larkin nodded briefly, turned away.

Anna walked quickly, leading him to the library, where she stood by the opened door till he passed through, then turned to close it behind her. She leaned against it as she found his eyes on hers.

"What?" he asked, clearly puzzled.

"I'm going to come right out and say it. I know you don't want me and I'm not crazy about you either, but you need to understand something."

She paused, her chest heaving, clearly agitated.

"You can be so blind," she said quickly.

"What are you talking about?"

"You come from the Amish, even if you aren't living like it right now. That girl, whoever she is, seems to be very interested in you. All

I'm going to say is, don't do anything rash. Don't make a decision you'll regret later in life, okay?"

"I am not planning on doing that at all."

"Look, I know you're thinking I have no business talking to you like this. And I don't, really. I'm sure she's a nice girl, but you have very different backgrounds and oh . . . well, whatever. I don't know. This is crazy. I'm so . . ."

She flapped her small brown hands helplessly and turned her back, hesitating for only a second, before opening the door. Or trying to, desperately wrenching the doorknob which seemed to be stuck, in the way old doorknobs in old houses will.

A few steps and his hand was on hers, gently removing it, holding it like a struggling songbird.

"Anna, look at me."

She refused, shaking her head from side to side, her lower lip caught in her teeth, a glistening trail of tears on one tanned cheek.

"I don't care about Skye Larkin. I did at one time. But I didn't really know her, and once I did, I lost interest. I know what—who—I want now. But I have a lot to straighten out before I can commit to a relationship."

There was a length of silence, then she tugged slightly, and he let go of her hand.

"So, what about Friday night? If we meet my sister and her family, it won't be a lie. Otherwise, I'll have to make a confession."

"Why would I meet your sister?"

"We could just say hi, then have dinner somewhere. Or just coffee, or maybe ice cream. You know, whatever."

"I just told you how it is, Anna."

"Well, really, since when is an introduction and a trip to the ice cream place a relationship?"

He laughed, a rare sound coming from him. It was a laugh of true joy, something he had never experienced quite like this, and it changed his whole countenance.

"All right. My treat. I'll take you to a special place, and I'll meet your sister."

"Okay. Great."

She smiled, and he smiled with her. Between them, there was a whisper of what could be, even as so much remained unresolved.

He went home to see Lavina, ashamed of himself for neglecting her because of his fear, hiding behind his own cowardice.

His mother met him at the door, her eyes swollen with fluid, her dress straining at the row of press buttons down her chest. Her bib apron was too tight, the straps across her back uncomfortably snug.

"Amos, my oh. I hardly know who you are. What are you doing that you're so thin? Are you on drugs? I read an article about people addicted to injecting stuff in their veins, and they get awful skinny. Their teeth go bad. Let me see your teeth. Why, Amos, what's wrong with that? I just want to look at your teeth. You're hiding the truth. See, that's what happens when you stop going to the Amish church. God is lost."

Amos closed his eyes against the barrage.

"Mom, no, stop. I don't do drugs. I don't, believe me. And God is not only in the Amish church. He is everywhere."

"How do you know? See, that's how it goes with you young people who leave. You're already misled. You think you know more than your parents and we remain steadfast."

"Steadfast to what?"

"Well, to being Amish. Our way of life."

"And that is what will save you in the end?"

"*Ach,* be quiet now. You're already mixing me up."

"I don't mean to, Mom. Let's just switch the subject, shall we? I didn't come to argue. Is Lavina home?"

She gave him a long cold stare, then crossed her arms over her chest, a pitiful attempt at self-preservation.

"What do you want with Lavina?"

"She wasn't doing well when she was at my house."

"Why was she there?"

"Wanted to see me, I guess."

"You're not a good influence on her."

"Where is she?"

"In her room. She . . . well, you'll see."

She made her way heavily down the hallway and knocked on the door of her daughter's room.

Amos looked around at the interior of his parents' home, the stifling amount of cheap home décor on every wall, the artificial plants set in corners, string lights, battery lamps, floor lamps, rugs and cushions and knick-knacks. Magazines, books, baskets of cotton throws and crocheted afghans.

His mother reappeared with his sister a few steps behind, her head lowered.

He stepped forward. "Lavina."

She was frightening. So thin she seemed lost in her dress, a skeleton in folds of loose fabric. Her skin was pale as milk, splotched with a red rash, her eyes dull and listless.

"We can't get her to eat."

Amos was shocked into silence. His eyes saw the apparition that was his sister, but his mind refused to accept it.

"Don't be dramatic, Mom. I eat sometimes." Her voice was hoarse, breaking up into fragments like broken glass.

"Hardly. We can't do anything with her. We took her to the chiropractor a few times, but it costs too much. Those supplements aren't cheap."

"I flush them down the toilet."

"Lavina, you're going to make me cry. Do you want to see me go to bed and cry like I did last time?"

"Go right ahead."

Amos held up a hand. "Mom, please. Lavina, stop."

He spoke softly to Lavina, which brought instant tears, a soft mewling cry that went straight to his heart. Then she returned to her room.

He pleaded with his mother to take her to a counselor, but she said he had no right to advise her, being the rebellious son. He waited until his father came home from work and tried to talk sense into him. His father broke down, saying he had no idea what to do, that Lydia would never agree to take her to a counselor or psychologist.

Amos went back to Lavina's room, his mother trailing at his heels. He sat gently on the edge of the bed where she lay.

"Lavina, please come back with me. Winter is my slow time, and we can hang out together. Would you like to stay with me for a while?"

Her heavy-lidded eyes were bloodshot, rimmed with red, her hair greasy and unkempt. She shrugged her thin shoulders, the neckline of her dress sliding to the right, exposing bone and pale skin.

"I can, if you want me to."

"Amos, you can't take her away. We'll take care of her." His mother's voice came from the doorway, commanding.

"Mom, I don't want to hurt you, or disobey more than I already have. Believe me. But Lavina's health, if not her life, is in danger. Maybe a change of scenery will make a difference. I will not just leave her here."

His mother wavered, then relented. "Don't let English people talk to her. People that would mislead her to another church."

He said nothing to this. He would promise nothing. His sister obviously needed help badly, and how or where that help came from was yet to be decided.

Gently, patiently, he helped her pack, alarmed at her lack of clear thinking, the lack of caring about one single thing.

She had no money since she wasn't working, but she supposed she didn't need any.

Her mother came with a gray Walmart bag rattling with plastic supplement bottles, and one of liquid magnesium, to be taken at bedtime. He nodded, agreed to try to get her to take everything, thanked his parents for allowing Lavina to stay with him, then listened again to their sincere warnings about English people who would make her leave the Amish. He could honestly tell them he would do his best, and meant every word, then drove home with Lavina's thin form draped in a corner of the seat, her dull eyes unseeing and uncaring.

As he drove up to his small carriage house, he felt a new purpose for his life, a fresh sense of living for someone other than himself. He knew he had a complicated trail before him, the steep climb probably more than he could take on some days, but he was willing to try.

He recognized the love he had for his parents in spite of their flaws. Surely something in his mother's past contributed to her unfailing grope for fulfillment, that desperate, misguided search for true contentment.

As he lifted the heavy luggage from the back of the truck, a shaft of evening sun broke through scudding navy blue clouds, creating the golden hour just before twilight. It enveloped him in its light, him and Lavina, his beloved cottage, Fred, and the truck. The voice of Scott's minister sounded in his mind: "His Name shall be Emanuel, meaning God with us."

He stopped, blinked, nodded his head, then opened the door of his truck and helped Lavina down.

She stood, watched Fred's advance, his whole hind end wagging with his tail, welcoming her, and she reached down and tentatively stroked his head, ruffled his ears.

"Home sweet home, Lavina," he said softly.

She nodded, then did an unexpected thing. She slipped a thin, cold hand into the crook of his arm, said, "Lead the way, bro," and smiled.

He would try to lead the way. He didn't always know where he was going or which path was right, but he figured if God was truly with them, things would turn out OK in the end.

THE END

About the Author

Linda Byler was raised in an Amish family and is an active member of the Amish church today. Growing up, Linda loved to read and write. In fact, she still does. Linda is well known within the Amish community as a columnist for a weekly Amish newspaper. She writes all her novels by hand in notebooks.

Linda is the author of several series of novels, all set among the Amish communities of North America: Lizzie Searches for Love, Sadie's Montana, Lancaster Burning, Hester's Hunt for Home, the Dakota Series, The Long Road Home, New Directions, Stepping Stones, Seekers, and the Buggy Spoke Series for younger readers. Linda has also written several Christmas romances set among the Amish: *Mary's Christmas Goodbye*, *The Christmas Visitor*, *The Little Amish Matchmaker*, *Becky Meets Her Match*, *A Dog for Christmas*, *A Horse for Elsie*, *The More the Merrier*, *A Christmas Engagement*, *Love Conquers All*, and *Christmas in Wisconsin*. Linda has coauthored *Lizzie's Amish Cookbook: Favorite Recipes from Three Generations of Amish Cooks!*, *Amish Christmas Cookbook*, and *Amish Soups & Casseroles*.

Other Books by Linda Byler

Lizzie Searches for Love Series

BOOK ONE

BOOK TWO

BOOK THREE

TRILOGY

COOKBOOK

Sadie's Montana Series

BOOK ONE

BOOK TWO

BOOK THREE

TRILOGY

Lancaster Burning Series

BOOK ONE

BOOK TWO

BOOK THREE

TRILOGY

Hester's Hunt for Home Series

BOOK ONE

Which Way Home?
HESTER'S HUNT FOR HOME • BOOK 2
LINDA BYLER
A romance set in colonial America by the bestselling Amish author

BOOK TWO

BOOK THREE

TRILOGY

The Dakota Series

BOOK ONE

BOOK TWO

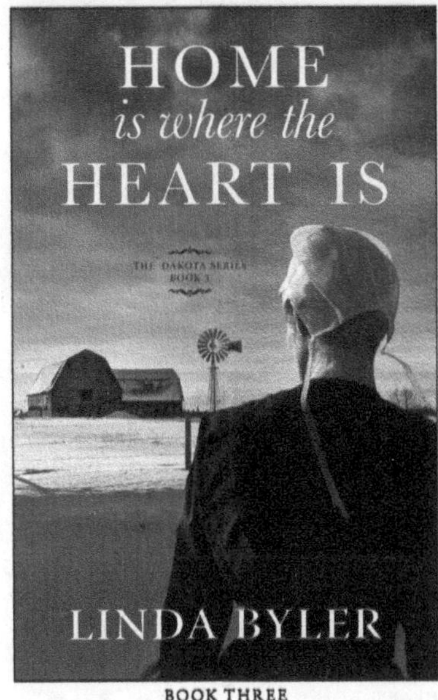

BOOK THREE

TRILOGY

Long Road Home Series

BOOK ONE

BOOK TWO

BOOK THREE

New Directions Series

BOOK ONE

BOOK TWO

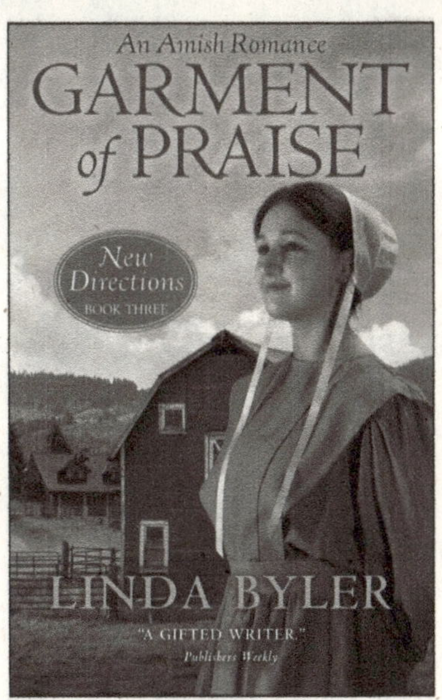

BOOK THREE

Stepping Stones Series

BOOK ONE

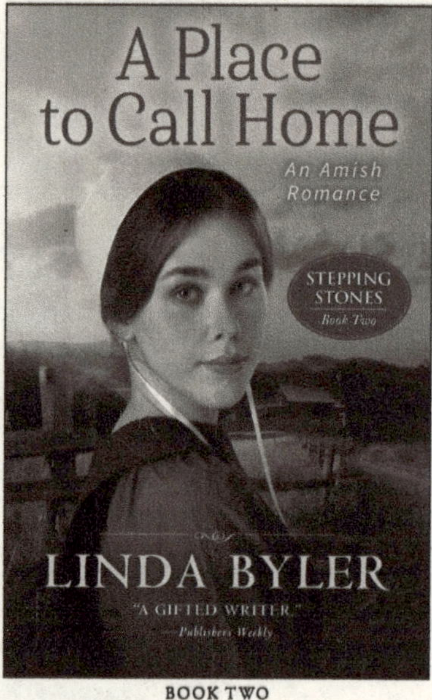

BOOK TWO

BOOK THREE

Buggy Spoke Series for Young Readers

BOOK ONE

BOOK TWO

BOOK THREE

Christmas Novellas

THE CHRISTMAS VISITOR

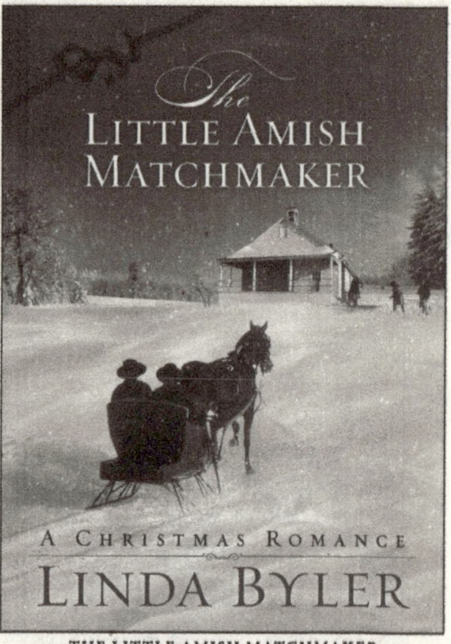

THE LITTLE AMISH MATCHMAKER

MARY'S CHRISTMAS GOODBYE

BECKY MEETS HER MATCH

A DOG FOR CHRISTMAS

A HORSE FOR ELSIE

THE MORE THE MERRIER

A CHRISTMAS ENGAGEMENT

CHRISTMAS EVERY DAY

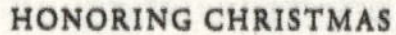

HONORING CHRISTMAS

LOVE CONQUERS ALL

CHRISTMAS IN WISCONSIN

Christmas Collections

AMISH CHRISTMAS ROMANCE COLLECTION

AMISH ROMANCE AT CHRISTMASTIME

Standalone Novels

THE HEALING

A SECOND CHANCE

HOPE DEFERRED

LOVE IN UNLIKELY PLACES